THE UNLIKELY HUNTER

by Lee Mark Sawatzky

 FriesenPress

Suite 300 - 990 Fort St
Victoria, BC, V8V 3K2
Canada

www.friesenpress.com

Copyright © 2019 by Lee Mark Sawatzky
First Edition — 2019

ISBN
978-1-5255-0467-9 (Hardcover)
978-1-5255-0468-6 (Paperback)
978-1-5255-0469-3 (eBook)

1. FICTION, LITERARY

Distributed to the trade by The Ingram Book Company

PART ONE

·

A SMALL TOWN

OUR WAY OF LIFE

DEATH COMES UNADORNED IN THE wild. Whether it arrives in spring's melt when a fast-moving stream seizes a child standing too near, or in winter when heartless cold turns flesh to ice. There is no fanfare when an animal's hoof fatally crushes flesh and cracks bone, no admirable sacrifice when the freed weight of a toppling tree is felt but for an instant before all goes dark. Ancient diseases forever tracking our kind show no emotion when they catch up to one of us.

* * * * *

Ed was breathing hard as he half-walked, half-ran through the small northern town of Bull Moose Run. He was on his way to Charlie and Sarah Duke's house on the last street before the Native reserve. Ed had coffee with Charlie on Wednesdays. Today, no matter how fast he went or how many times he looked down at his watch, he was going to be later than he'd ever been. He would have phoned ahead, but the lines were down on the south side of town.

Although Charlie and Ed shared certain bedrock values, their friendship benefitted as much from their different backgrounds. Charlie was a retired trapper with a lifelong connection to the land; Ed, who was less than half Charlie's age, was a man of the cloth whose family had come to Canada before the First World War to avoid religious persecution. Whereas Charlie had never learned to drive, Ed had grown up relying on cars and wasn't put off with the thought of travelling hundreds of miles in a day. And while Charlie thought in terms of days and seasons, Ed was obsessed with the dictates of the twenty-four-hour clock.

Charlie's great-grandfather on his mother's side had moved west from Quebec, where his family had lived for several generations, to work for the Hudson's Bay Company. Charlie was the product of stolen time shared by Charlie's mother, Angelique Duke, the only child of a widowed, alcoholic father who also worked for HBC, and a mystery man. Angelique, who was not much more than a school girl when Charlie was born, had died before his first birthday. Charlie had been raised by Angelique's best friend, Cindy Rivard, a member of the Moose Lake Band.

Cindy Rivard's house was four doors down, through unfenced backyards left in their natural states, from the house where the band's first Native manager, Randy Williams and his wife Esther lived with their three children. Charlie was the same age as Sarah, the oldest of the Williams' children. They had grown up together, sharing in the wide-eyed exuberance of children unaware there was any other way to live, coming to understand that people on the reserve were treated differently from people in town, and going through a time as high school sweethearts when they thought almost exclusively about each other. Sarah was one of only a handful of students from the reserve who attended college in Centre City after graduating from high school. She and Charlie were married not long after she moved back to Bull Moose Run to begin work in the band office.

Charlie and Ed met at the Dukes' house because Charlie had a hard time getting around after losing the use of his legs in a logging accident when he was forty-eight years old. The two men invariably started off by laughing freely at the dozen or so things men find funny no matter how many times they hear them. When the conversation deepened, it was Charlie who usually had the most to say about the dynamism of nature and the importance of family. At some point Ed could be expected to bring up the role God played in those parts of life that weren't readily explainable. A university-educated observer might have characterized what the minister had to say as colonial proselytizing, but Charlie would have disagreed. The old trapper had been raised to acknowledge the Creator, and his obeisance had only deepened in these, his final years.

Charlie had never been formally adopted by Cindy and didn't have a status card. That meant that Sarah and he had to live off the reserve. Their unpainted wood house, a seasoned dark brown, rambled through three distinct sections as a result of two additions built several years apart. The interior of the house was dominated by animal skins that helped keep the floor warm in winter: a black bear rug, two wolf rugs, and a huge grizzly rug on the living room floor, which had a taxidermy head full of white plastic teeth and a rough, red plastic tongue, much of the paint on which had chipped away. Like most trapper's houses, the house was smoky through and through from the wood stove, the fireplace, and the fish smoker in the backyard. In any nooks where there wasn't actual rising, shifting, or settling smoke, there was the lingering pungency of tanned moccasins and buckskin jackets, as well as the migrating smells of the smoked salmon and moose jerky kept in the storeroom.

The focal point of the Dukes' backyard was Sarah's garden, whose annual production put the lie to the limitations of growing vegetables in the thin, rocky northern soil. Deep into the fall, Sarah continued to harvest the kale, leeks, chicory, and Jerusalem artichokes she covered overnight to protect from frost. On the west side of the garden there was a small woodshed, and on the east, a bleached fish drying rack. Close to the back door of the house, for easy access, was the newfangled fish smoker Charlie had purchased through the Simpsons-Sears catalogue store.

Ed and Anne Maki lived at the other end of town in a parsonage bought by the church to lessen the financial pressures on its ministerial couples. From the outside, the parsonage looked like the rest of the low-cost, cookie cutter houses in a subdivision raced together in anticipation of the influx of miners and their families who'd come to town because of the new copper mine. Inside, the parsonage was unique in that there weren't any ashtrays on couch arms or boxes of empty beer bottles in the utility room. Also, two bookcases and a piano substituted for the standard black and white television in the living room.

Normally Ed visited Charlie just before noon when the retired trapper was at his best. Today, Ed was as late as he was getting to the Dukes' because his quarterly meeting with Roland, the district superintendent from Centre City, had gone on so long. Instead of the normal half hour or so, Roland had read from a list of questions for nearly two hours, the questions ranging from church attendance and finances all the way to the order of worship. Ed had found himself becoming increasingly frustrated and finally asked Roland what he was after. The district superintendent hadn't provided much of an answer.

It had been almost noon before Roland closed his notepad. Given the hour, Ed had felt obligated to offer lunch to his overseer. To his surprise, Roland had accepted. Despite the short notice, Anne had managed to prepare an enjoyable meal of soup and sandwiches, with frozen date loaf thawed out in the oven for dessert. Roland had almost finished eating when he'd excused himself to get something from his car, returning with the latest edition of the denomination's national newsletter.

— I don't know if you've received this month's issue yet, but you should really read the article by Tom Smith. I think he's onto something when he talks about ways to make the church more relevant to this generation.

Roland's comment could have started another skirmish in the doctrinal wars, but Ed had simply nodded.

Mainstream ministers like Roland had long since abandoned key theologies, including the need for personal redemption. Although they considered the Bible to be an historically significant record, they smiled knowingly when discussing miracles. They also discounted many of the rules and regulations in the ancient book. Some of the ministers were even willing to discuss whether the concept of God came about because of the need to explain right and wrong, the general unwillingness to accept that death was the end, and people's inborn desire that someone should be in control.

Ed (whom Roland had more than once called an out and out nutter), Ann, and the minority of Bible-believing pastoral couples saw things entirely differently. Not only did they believe in a God who loved them and with whom they could communicate, they relied on the Bible as a guide to day to day living and as a written history of the world from the beginning of time on into the otherwise unknowable future.

A few years earlier, Ed had received a letter from Roland's predecessor, citing him for preaching sermons suggestive of Pentecostalism. Ed had found the letter more bizarre than threatening, since while he had

never fully understood the full range of Pentecostal spiritual emphases, he had always admired the vibrancy of Pentecostal churches and
the general goodness of the people attending them. In response to
the censure, Ed had begun a sermon series about the unreliability of
church leadership as contrasted to the never-changing message of the
Bible. The series had been well received by everyone. That is, everyone
except the Wixwots, who resigned from the church before the series
was finished. Mr. Wixwot, a teacher, and Mrs. Wixwot, an X-ray tech-
nician at the town's recently constructed hospital, were among the
least rule-bound members of the congregation. While Ed admitted
the well-educated couple's wine cellar wasn't necessarily determina-
tive of their spiritual commitment, it had always given him pause.

* * * * *

It had been almost 2:00 p.m. before Roland finally left. Anne and Ed
had walked the district superintendent to the driveway and done their
best to continue to smile as he backed his car out to the street. Anne
spoke through her smile:
— Well, that was unexpected.

With that, she had gone into the house and begun clearing the
dining room table. She soon called to ask Ed, who had followed her
to the house but stayed in the boot room, if he was still planning to
go to the Dukes; and, if so, whether he wanted to be dropped off. Ed
answered, saying that, yes he was going but that he would walk. The
door closed behind him before Anne could respond.

Ed's rushed trip to the Dukes' was measured out by mainly older,
unfinished houses, tarred telephone poles, and open ditches. He
looked up now and again at the scarring on Begbie Hill where trees
were being cut down to make way for a local ski hill. *I hope they know
what they're doing. I doubt many ski hills have to deal with 45 below
weather.* The roads were quiet because kids were in school, with the
only sounds being those of the odd vehicle and, intermittently, dogs
barking. Ed undid the buttons on his coat when he started to sweat.

Ed sensed something was wrong when he arrived in front of the
Dukes' house. Hoping it was only the gloom of the cloudy day, he
entered the yard and walked up to the front door. While waiting for
someone to answer his knock, he noticed the curtains were closed.

He knocked a second time, and, not hearing any movement within, tried the door handle, having on an earlier visit found Sarah away and Charlie napping in the front room. The door was unlocked. He called out, "Charlie? Sarah?" as he stepped hesitantly into the house.

Although there was no one in the boot room, a flickering light was visible from the fireplace in the living room. Ed called out Charlie and Sarah's names again as he walked down the hall. By the time he entered the living room, Charlie, who was in the reclining chair by the fireplace, had picked up his .308 rifle from the floor and was holding it squirrel-still to his shoulder. It was pointed straight at the middle of Ed's chest.

Ed knew if Charlie pulled the trigger it would be a heart shot and his life would be over. The old trapper's hands were steady, but the smell of booze was in the room. Alcohol always meant that there were new rules in play in Bull Moose Run. Ed could see an empty whisky bottle lying near Charlie's chair, and another large bottle, containing a skim of liquor, behind the footstool. Several beer bottles lay on the bear rug.

— Charlie, it's me, Ed. Charlie, it's okay. It's me … Ed.

Charlie didn't say anything, but he didn't lower the gun. Ed stood rooted to the floor. There was a barely audible crackle from the fading embers in the fireplace.

— It's me, Charlie … Ed. Where's Sarah, Charlie?

Charlie slowly lowered the gun. Ed heard a sound from the back of the house.

— Charlie, I'm going to walk up to you. Is that okay?

Charlie didn't say anything as Ed approached him and lifted the rifle out of his hands. Ed continued on to the back the house holding the rifle. Sarah, her face expressionless, was sitting on the edge of the bed in her and Charlie's bedroom. Ed stood the rifle up against the wall beside the closet after engaging the safety.

— Are you okay?

— Yes.

— How long has Charlie been drinking?

— All night. Julien, his real mom's cousin, came over late last night and got Charlie out of bed.

— I've never seen Charlie like this before, Sarah.

— Charlie usually tells Julien he can't stay, but he let him stay last night. Julien's sleeping in Sam and Jody's room. He just found out his son, Eric, was killed at the lead mine near Fort Van. He and Charlie had both told Eric not to take a job at the mine.

— I thought Sam and Jody were coming this week.

— Next week.

Ed had turned to go back to the living room when Sarah added:

— He feels safer when he has his gun.

ED AND ANNE

FALL BEGINS IN THE NORTH with a display of colourful leaves as if the region is getting ready for a party. The weather, though, begins to worsen when the first leaves tumble tragicomically to the ground. It takes but a short while before early September's mist becomes a persistent rain; and then, when everyone is about ready to accept that nothing outside will ever be dry again, people awaken to frost— weather once merely untoward having turned dangerous.

Even though the pure white of the first heavy snowfall has the power to transform, for a time at least, the dirtiest streets, garbage-strewn yards, and sagging rooflines into the fresh and new, all that has really happened is winter's deep freeze has arrived. In a matter of weeks, a suffocating layer of ice and snow will cover most of the country.

* * * * *

Frank and Judy Wells had invited several families, including Darcy Dintsche, a young bachelor who had recently moved to town to work for the Forest Service, for a potluck lunch after the Sunday morning service. All of the food was homemade since pride of contribution and limited household budgets meant none of the guests considered bringing store-bought items. Judy's soft and chewy, quick-rising buns were a big hit as usual; Betty had used homemade mayonnaise in her potato salad; and Tanis had started cooking her moose meat stroganoff the previous evening to tenderize the meat. All of the pies had been made by somebody's mother, except the apple pie in a red porcelain plate, which had been provided by Mr. Francisco, the local baker who led the church choir.

Other than Jimmy Hodgson, who had speech and hearing problems, and Anita Nelson, who wasn't growing as fast as she should, the boys and girls stuffed around the kitchen table and the camping table temporarily set up for the overflow were in good health and reverberated with the excitement of youth. Although most of the adults in the dining room were stricter with their own children than they needed to be, they were all energized whenever a child, whether one of their own or someone else's, poked his or her head around the doorway to ask a question, seek consolation, or make sure that mom and dad were still there.

None of the jokes in the dining room were allowed to fall flat since shared dinners were celebrations. Predictably, Candace Rundell, a voluble realtor whose personality was the exact opposite of that of her staid school custodian husband, had the most to say and said it best. Her big story was about a wide-eyed European determined to buy part of the last frontier. The prospective purchaser, a German inspired by Karl May's westerns, had—believe it or not, said Candace—chosen Bull Moose Run as his destination based on what he had learned from the surface of a factory-dimpled desktop globe. Everyone took this statement, along with everything else Candace said, with a grain of salt, since she regularly chose the interesting over the accurate.

With her usual verve, Candace mimicked the German's ambition to buy a "twractck off vilderness." The table broke out in wild, knowing laughter when she described the foreigner's reaction to "all ziss craazy bugs."

— We hired Ralph Tway to take us by riverboat down Moose River and from there up Moberly Creek to acreage on Red Lake that is only accessible by water. I asked Ralph to cut the engine before we landed so we could look at the property from the lake. There was an audible hum when the engine was turned off. At first I thought it was just the ringing in my ears, but then I realized it was the sound of the bugs in the bush. Heinrich heard the noise too. He asked me what it was, and I said it was just the bugs. His eyes went as big as hockey pucks and he demanded, in German mind you, that we take him back to town right away. Ralph and I don't speak German, but we got the message.

— Are you serious? You could actually hear the mosquitoes and blackflies?

— And horseflies, no-see-ums, and whatever else was out there. I'm telling you, it was a bug metropolis; to be fair, Heinrich already looked like he had smallpox because of all his bites.

After dinner, the children went down to the games room in the basement and the adults moved to the living room.

— Me and my apprentice, Seth, were putting a new roof on a house that was purchased by a newcomer named Parm Singh up near the power station. Just before we came off the roof for lunch, one of the boozed up Norwegian brothers who live in that trashed mobile home out front of Hollyfield pond came stumbling into the yard. Sven, it was either Sven or his older brother, was drunk as usual, and he was carrying a two-bitted axe. He started yelling at us up on the roof, wanting to know where the such and such immigrant was 'cause he wanted to kill him. I wouldn't have believed what was going on if it wasn't good ol' Moose. The best I could figure was Sven was mad that he had been let go at the mill during the slowdown, and Parm, who has only been in Canada for a few years and can hardly speak any English, was still working—I guess Sven forgot he hasn't been in the country for that long himself. Thankfully, Parm wasn't home and Sven eventually left. Seth and me, though, waited up on the roof for a while in case he came back.

The guests went silent when someone brought up the recent murder on the reserve. The challenges faced by Indigenous people on and off the reserve had been around since long before any of them had moved to Bull Moose Run. The government's original plan of educating and assimilating Natives seemed obvious—it was, after all, what people in charge had always done—but times had changed and the plan wasn't working.

Candace asked Frank if any youth from the two local reserves were in the high school graduation class.

— Actually, two young men from Likem Reserve are expected to graduate this year, and it wouldn't surprise me if Clayton Donald, who's from the Moose Lake Reserve, is named the valedictorian. On top of being a great physics student, he's memorized most of what Robert Service wrote.

While walking around the room to offer more coffee, Judy Wells commented on the nuclear tests in Alaska. Tanis, an elementary school teacher, said she'd read that if a war broke out between the US and the Soviet Union, hundreds of nuclear warheads would be flying directly overhead. The room went silent as they all imagined world-ending armaments rocketing across their innocent skies.

— My brother, Lewis, works on the DEW line near Cold Lake. It stands for something early warning.

— Distant.

— Ya, that's it, Distant Early Warning.

— Didn't Lewis come fishing with us up to Seymour Lake?

— That was Lewis.

— Funny guy. Everything that guy said was funny.

— Ahh, you just caught him on a good weekend. No, you're right, I'll admit it. He's made me laugh my whole life.

Anyway, Jacquie and I visited with Lewis and his wife, Susan in Edmonton last spring. Lewis said there's something like 300 guys working at Cold Lake—radar technicians, electricians (Lewis is an electrician), army personnel, and tons of support people. It's kind of weird that a town could pop up all on its own like Cold Lake did, where guys are sitting around waiting for the Russians to come. I asked Lewis how many places there were like Cold Lake in Canada. I think he said there's five other places.

— Have they seen anything on their radar yet?

— Not from what Lewis says.

— They must see Santa Claus on Christmas Eve.

Most of the guests either smiled or laughed.

— That's got to be weird, sitting watching a TV monitor year after year, and seeing nothing. At least when you're on fire lookout for the Forest Service you get to see smoke now and again. Ain't that right, Darcy?

Darcy nodded.

Mostly, though, those gathered talked about the changes happening to society.

— The word I keep hearing now is "partying", and they're not talking about a birthday party. Young people acting out because of hormones won't ever change, but when you take away the rules and add in booze or drugs ...

16

— Exactly. "Free Love" sounds good until you realize what they're really talking about. No one considers how it's going to affect peoples' actual lives, parenting, loyalties, intimacies, for years to come.

— I guess if you don't believe in God, you might as well do what you want.

— Al Clayton told me there was another all-night party at the Parant's residence last weekend. Now there's a group of individuals—the step-dad, the mom, and all three teenagers—who've done more damage to the community than anyone knows. Al says he had to call the police twice Saturday night.

— I don't want to be gross ...

Tom Nelson made sure there were no children around before continuing with a lowered voice.

... but I was driving by the baseball field behind the Parant's late Saturday. I literally could not believe it ...

Even with the worst parts of the story removed, the listeners winced as they listened, wondering if they needed to hear at all, let alone in mixed company, about the actions of the couple who were undoubtedly drunk.

Even Darcy, who was the youngest in the room by at least ten years, was aware that societal mores were in flux. However, unlike the rest, he tended to think freedom was a good thing. Finally out on his own, he was reveling in the fact his parents weren't watching his every move. Not only could he listen to the music he wanted (and not worry about leaving risqué album covers around), he didn't have to hide the magazines he bought, and he could keep beer in the fridge. The last two weekends he'd driven to Footing to catch a movie, one R-rated.

By early afternoon, the dishes had been washed and put away, the children rounded up, and the thanks and goodbyes exchanged. Although the personalities hadn't meshed perfectly and things said that shouldn't have been, or at least could have been said better, the guests left with the abiding sense that Bull Moose Run was a good place to live: their friends saw life by and large the same way they did; families were basically safe—no one overlooked the role the local R.C.M.P. detachment played in keeping a lid on things; there were jobs in the mill for anyone who wanted to work; and, most importantly as Ed had reminded them during the morning service, God was still in charge.

* * * * *

The Makis started their ministry during the thrilling time when humans landed on the moon, an event that made everything seem possible and even likely. The consensus of the scientific community was that the universe had begun on its own with a big bang; billions of years later, a chemical stew had formed that led by pure chance/scientific equation to the simplest of life forms; and these life forms had, in additional huge chunks of time, evolved into dinosaurs and eventually into other animals—homo sapiens being one of the newer branches on the family tree.

Ed, Anne and the people attending their church rejected these sanctioned positions. They refused to accept that humanity was "an unintended byproduct of a random process"; and that the only things in the universe were visible matter and whatever unthinking forces like gravity were out there. Although the longtime parishioner, Sadie Gladstone, who taught home economics in the town's high school, was the only person in the congregation with even a limited understanding of what words like "singularity" and "inflation" meant, it didn't take a university degree to figure out that whatever existed at the start of the universe had to come from somewhere. To say nothing of the livability of the planet, the unparalleled abilities of humankind, and the sense of purpose that came with faith.

* * * * *

It was a full month before Ed went back to see Charlie. Arriving at the Dukes' front gate, he heard the sound of wood being chopped in the back. He walked around the house to find Charlie, soaked with sweat on the sunny day, working in the partly open woodshed. Charlie's canes were propped against the outside wall and he was using the exposed studs in the woodshed for support.

Charlie smiled and said a quick hello before getting back to work. Ed began stacking the chopped wood and bringing fresh blocks to Charlie. Although old trapper's legs were almost useless, his arms were still strong. It was an hour before he wiped his brow a final time and twisted away. It was Ed's turn. Ed didn't have Charlie's natural strength, but he was younger and was onto the next row when Charlie signaled they were done.

The two men began their slow return to the house. It had always amazed Ed that Charlie was able to move at all using only his arms and his stiffened legs. Wanting to avoid bringing up the gun incident, Ed asked about Charlie's three boys. Charlie began his answer by saying between deep breaths that Stoney and Nesky had bought another rental property and were going to be rich someday.

Ed had always admired the close relationship between the Dukes and their adult sons. The oldest boy, Charlie Jr., who was Charlie's spitting image and had his father's height from before the spinal injury, made sure to drop by his parents' house every week, even in the winter when he was busy running the family trap line (which he'd recently had to extend to maintain production). The middle boy, Sam, his wife, Jody, and their two school-aged children had their own house west of town, but moved back in with Charlie and Sarah whenever Sam took on mill work to supplement his guide and outfitter income. The youngest boy, Stoney, who ran a fishing boat on the coast, made a point of coming back to Bull Moose Run every spring, usually accompanied by his wife, Nesky and their little girl, Jessica.

Ed followed Charlie through the back door into the kitchen where Sarah was standing by the stove. When Charlie pretended to grab for one of the fresh baked buns on the counter Sarah slapped playfully at his hand before saying something in Carrier. Ed went to sit down at the little kitchen table, but Charlie gestured with one of his canes that he wanted Ed to follow him to the back of the house. The men made their way through the living room and past the bedrooms to the single stair in front of the storeroom. Charlie opened the door to the room's miscellany of hunting, trapping, and fishing equipment, dry goods, canned goods, fruit and vegetables in jars. A trap door off to the side led to the root cellar.

— Hey, Ed, I'm going to give you my .308. I don't have any more use for that gun.
— What are you talking about, Charlie? How long have you owned your gun?
— I got it in Centre City 'fore I got hurt.

— How many moose have you shot with it?

— Lots. I never got a scope for that gun, but it shoots so straight I never needed one. I 'member I was on my trap line, and a skunk bear was getting to my traps before me. I was crazy mad at him for biting up all my furs. Suddenly, I spotted that devil making his way up a ridge in the snow. It was a long way, maybe 200 yards. I sighted him in and shot. Wham, he shook like he had been slapped and fell back. It was a good shot too. Right in the head. I got the same for that skin I would have if I had trapped that bugger.

— Are you sure you want to give me the gun, Charlie? Why not give it to one of your boys? At least let me pay you what it's worth.

— The boys got their own guns. I'm goin' to give that gun to you.

*　*　*　*　*

Ed and Anne had three children, Tory and the twins, Gwen and Emily. Tory was named after a distant relative of Anne's who'd written a book about mathematics; Gwen was named after Ed's grandmother; and Emily was a name that Ed and Anne liked.

If possible, the children meant even more to Anne than they otherwise might have because she was an only child and both her parents were deceased. Anne's father, John Markstrom, was a middle-aged missionary doctor working in Nigeria when he'd met his bride to be, Lindsay, a newly arrived nurse. Anne had been born and raised on the mission field, and, despite being as pale as her Scottish cousins, she had always thought of herself as Nigerian. She'd gone to nursing school in Canada with the plan of returning to work in her parents' medical clinic. Her plans, though, had forever changed when she met Ed.

After a courtship so circumspect as to be almost sacred, Ed and Anne had set their wedding date to coincide with the upcoming furlough of Anne's parents. However, three weeks before John, who was nearly 60 at that point, and Lindsay were to leave on the long journey to attend their daughter's wedding—the month long trip involving travelling by ship to England, boarding a much bigger ship to cross the Atlantic and carrying on by train through eight of Canada's ten provinces—they were killed during a raid on their village by a neighbouring tribe. An elderly director at the mission's headquarters in Toronto, who'd known both of Anne's parents before they'd met each other, was given the task of phoning Anne to break the news.

The only think Anne could think of doing when the fateful call ended was to return to Nigeria right away, to do something ... anything. Before she could act, though, she received a letter from the clinic's administrator, Mr. Akbaje, extending his condolences and informing her that the clinic would not be reopening. Enclosed in the envelope along with Mr. Akbaje's letter was a sympathy card from Anne's childhood friends, Oby and Virgie. The three girls had gotten into untold amounts of mainly forgivable trouble growing up. One of Anne's favourite childhood memories was of a sleepover when, while staring up at the darkened ceiling, the three girls had agreed that Oby was going to be a scientist, Virgie, a teacher, and Anne, a nurse. On another occasion the girls had promised each other that they would choose character over good looks when it came time to pick a husband. Whenever Anne remembered her youthful promise she was grateful that she hadn't had to make that choice with Ed.

For years afterward Anne resisted thinking about her parents' lives in Africa because of the imagined horrors of their deaths. Only later, when she was raising her own children, did she allow herself to think about the hardships her parents would have faced living in Nigeria. Whereas Anne had been born into the heat and humidity of a sub-Saharan country, her mother's oft-repeated comment was: "This heat is like having a fever that never ends." There was also the constant threat of snakes and insects. Anne had never forgotten the look on her father's face when he was hooked up to a car battery in an attempt to minimize the pain from a scorpion sting. Most debilitating of all was malaria. Although both of her parents had been regularly bedridden with high temperatures, weakness, and disorientation from recurring bouts of malarial infection, by the time Anne was born there were antimalarial drugs and DDT to combat the mosquito population.

In addition to their own health issues, Anne's parents had faced the difficulties of dealing with a steady stream of extreme medical problems, most of an age-old variety but some caused directly or indirectly by modern conveniences like propane and motor vehicles. Try as the Markstroms had to protect their daughter from the terrible sights, sounds and smells associated with their work, it was inevitable that Anne would witness a certain amount of the suffering. Among Anne's most bedeviling memories was of an old man who had arrived at the medical compound wrapped from head to feet in a blanket despite the heat. Frustrated by his inability to communicate with Anne's mother because they spoke different dialects, the man had abruptly opened the blanket to show her mother, and inadvertently Anne, a hernia extending almost all the way to the ground.

*   *   *   *   *

It was the first day of school. Tory was beside himself with excitement as he put on the new pair of jeans his mother had left folded on the chair in his room. From that day forward the pant's robin's egg blue would be his favourite colour. When he went to the kitchen he barely noticed that his mother had made him a special breakfast of a fried egg and toast.

Tory pulled back when his mother tried to slick his hair down with water because he didn't like her messing with his hair at any time, especially not on a day when he didn't want any delays. At last they were out the back door and on their way by foot on the most important journey yet of his young life.

The streets were busy with parents and children, most of whom Tory had seen around. They finally made it to the school property, walking past the buses and, then, the two metal tetherball poles waiting for tetherballs that were secured in the dusty earth near the school entrance. Tory excitedly led his mother up the concrete steps to the school's heavy, wire glass doors. When they went inside, he subconsciously stored away the smells of cleaners and waxes. He would come to realize in time that all public buildings smelled the same.

A week later, Tory asked his mother when he would be able to walk to school on his own. She smiled and told him that she had made arrangements for him to go to school with the neighbour boy, Warren, starting the next week.

On Monday, the two boys set off on their own. For a week and a half they came straight home after school as promised. However, one afternoon in their second week of independence Tory convinced Warren it would be okay if they swung through the monkey bars before leaving the school yard. Their time in the playground went by in a flash, and Warren anxiously said they had to get going when he noticed the last of the yellow buses was pulling out.

Several rough-looking boys from higher grades were standing across the road from the school's main gate.

— Hey, kid, what do you have in your pack?

The boy was talking to Tory and not paying any attention to Warren, who, although two years older than Tory, was unassuming and small for his age. Tory was afraid to answer. The boy started to walk towards him.

— I said, what do you have in your pack?

One of the other boys started to say something, but Tory didn't wait to hear what it was and sprinted away. The chase was on. Soon Tory was beyond the symbolic protection of the school's iron link fence off to his right.

Tory ran as fast as he could, his feet slapping the pavement in time with his beating heart. He was a good runner, but it was a long way home. He knew he would be able to run faster if he didn't have a pack (which held a single book), but he didn't consider dropping it. He kept running even when he was out of breath. Finally, he was at the start of the parsonage driveway. In a few more strides he was at the front door. One of the boys shouted something as Tory yanked the door open and burst inside. He didn't think about Warren until after he'd caught his breath.

*　*　*　*　*

Ed's footsteps were light on the walk home after a day in his study. Although the snow from the first real snowfall had melted off the newly paved roads in town, it was still cold enough for him to justify wearing the tanned and beaded deer hide jacket that Sarah Duke's younger sister, Rose had made—the jacket and the matching mukluks being the only articles of clothing Ed was proud to own. It had been a good day with a minimum of interrupting phone calls, none of which had been too trying. He was grateful the controversy about letting the A.A. group use the church on Tuesday evenings was quieting down. *I've got to remember to tell Howie to ask the guys to use the outside ashtray.*

Entering the driveway, he saw that Anne had backed the car out of the garage so Tory could set up his hockey net. Greeting his son with a smile as broad as his mood, Ed grabbed one of the hockey sticks leaning against the garage wall to take a shot himself. He didn't make great contact on his first attempt because the bottom half of the stick was worn away.

— Hey, Tory, you want to go for a ride?

— Sure, where to?

— You'll see.

Ed went in the house to get the car keys. When he came back outside, father and son got into the old family car and headed towards Moose Lake. Ed turned right at the end of Beach Avenue and parked in front of a house that Tory didn't recognize. Ed led the way up the driveway and to the front door. An older man answered the knock.

— I hope I've got the right house. Mr. Chisholm?

— Yes. You must be Reverend Maki?

— Yes, and this is my son, Tory.

— Hi, Tory. The snowmobile is around the back. Give me a minute while I get my boots on.

Tory was confused. *A snowmobile? Mom and dad never said anything about buying a snowmobile. Aren't snowmobiles expensive?*

Mr. Chisholm came outside and led them to a shed behind the house. A blue snowmobile, its back end propped up by a wooden box, was parked under a makeshift cover extending beyond the shed roof. The snowmobile, which had two lights on its blunt front end, looked like a bulldog. Tory didn't recognize the name on the side of the snowmobile.

After telling Ed the snowmobile was owned by his oldest son who was working down south, Mr. Chisholm began to move the snowmobile away from the shed by alternately swinging its back and front over a foot or so at a time. Seeing how heavy the snowmobile was, Ed offered to take over. Freed up, Mr. Chisholm went into the shed and came back out with a red jerry can with the word "mixed" written on the side. As he was putting gas in the snowmobile he warned Ed and Tory there was going to be a lot of exhaust because they'd put oil in the cylinders.

It took several pulls of the starter rope before the two-stroke engine caught. "Brackaty, brack, brack." The oily smell of the blue-grey smoke was added to Tory's permanent memories. Paying no regard to the noise or the smoke, Mr. Chisholm got the wooden box from beside the shed and replaced it under the rack at the rear of the snowmobile allowing the track to spin freely when he pushed down on the throttle. Mr. Chisholm let the engine run for a few minutes. Finally turning it off, he lifted the cowling so Ed could have a look.

— I have to say it's in really good shape for a machine that's four years old. The ad in the paper said $500. Would you take $425?

— No sense going back and forth. Tell you what, you can have it for $450.

Ed couldn't believe he'd gotten such a good deal, and assumed it was because he'd followed Lars' advice to start with a really low offer. *Granted it's still a lot of money to spend on something that isn't much more than a toy.*

Buying a snowmobile had been Anne's idea. She'd brought the topic up one morning over coffee, saying that giving their son a gift he would never forget might help instill the trait of generosity, and it might also distance Tory from the influence of the rough kids in the neighbourhood. Ed had only argued so long since he knew that once Anne had made a decision it was almost impossible to change her mind.

Ed's initial resistance to buying a snowmobile, or anything expensive that matter, stemmed in part from his fear for the very lives of people who had too much. From his experience it was the people who had the most, whether it be the most money, the best looks, the greatest talent, who thought the most about themselves (and the least about God and others). *The moment people feel self-sufficient they lose sight of God. No wonder God chooses the poor.* He'd never forgotten his own father telling him that during the Great Depression it was the families in the marginal farming areas in the Prairies that were the most generous to the men riding the rails.

* * * * *

Tory was all a-jangle with excitement and barely noticed his mom had made his favourite dinner, barbecued pork chops.

— Tory, would you like a second helping?

— Yes, please. Dad, how much snow does there have to be before you can use a snowmobile?

— It depends on the ground. In a flat field like behind the school, you might only need six or eight inches.

— How about the power line?

— That ground's pretty rough with a lot of fallen trees. You might need a couple of feet there.

— When do you think the lake will freeze over?

* * * * *

Anne and Ed were doing yard work on the last warm Saturday in the fall. Not five minutes after Ed had managed to fall a small poplar tree 90 degrees away from where he'd intended, crushing part of the carport gutter in the process, their neighbour, Lars, who'd missed the fiasco, called across the fence.

— Ed, would you happen to have a red flag I could put on the load I'm taking to the garbage dump?

— I don't think so. Although I should have a bundle of them since everything I do should be red-flagged because it's either a bad idea or outright dangerous.

RICHARD REDMOND

THE OPTIMISM ENGENDERED BY A northern spring—a season that can be expected to have at least one false start—gives way to foreboding when melting ice and snow flood the roads. Even logging, the roughest and toughest industry there is, comes to a halt during the month or so they call breakup.

Photographs taken in July suggest the boreal forest can be as bucolic as Arcadia. However, anyone who has lived in the north knows that summer isn't made up of a long string of warm days perfect for outdoor activities. Rather, it's the time of year when non-stop heat dries everything out, including a defenseless forest; and masses of biting, stinging, blood-sucking insects and ectoparasites chase all but the bravest indoors. Not far into this, the so-called best season, northerners dream of fall when it won't be so unbearably hot and the bugs will be gone.

* * * * *

If Ed was a peg with four edges, the church's treasurer, Jonathan Morrey, a plumber who sold plumbing and heating supplies on the side, had eight. Ed was all about getting to know everyone he met, and not far into conversations with strangers was made privy to long hidden secrets. In contrast, Jonathan, whose smile could convert seamlessly into a smirk, wasn't that interested in people, except for potential customers and a couple of old acquaintances.

Not surprisingly the two men put different emphases on telling the truth. Although Ed granted himself some latitude when complementing people who needed encouragement, he regularly lost sleep worrying about having said something that wasn't strictly true. Jonathan didn't share Ed's preoccupation with honesty, especially when it came to business. As far as Jonathan was concerned, "The wheels of commerce sometimes need a little oil." He had no problem with exaggerating the quality of items he sold when prospective buyers considered his a high quote; and he was quick to assure the town's young building inspector that his plumbing work had been done to code even when that wasn't the case. Earlier in the year when Jonathan had handed his company's financial records over to his accountant he'd said with what might have been described as a greasy smile:

— Mind you, there were a few pluses and minuses that didn't quite make it to the books.

No one doubted that Jonathan provided for his family, or that the community benefitted from his skill as a plumber. It was just that the man could be so off-putting. Ed did his best to adopt an attitude of grace whenever he was confronted by a particularly stark conflict between Jonathan's professed faith and something egregious the plumber had said or done. He had found the going a little easier after Jonathan's longsuffering wife told him about her husband's difficult upbringing.

For his part, while Jonathan admitted that Ed spent a lot of time with people who should probably be written off, he doubted the minister would be quite so patient if he had to scratch out a living in the rough and tumble world of business where you didn't get paid until the job was done and sometimes didn't get paid at all. The other thing that had always bugged Jonathan was the way ministers got full time wages since everyone knew they worked at most three days a week, and less than that when there was a guest speaker.

Jonathan and Ed knew each other well enough not to talk too long. Recently, though, they'd found themselves on opposite sides of the debate over when construction of the new church should start. Ed sided with those who wanted to get going right away since there often wasn't a seat to be had on Sunday mornings; Jonathan and the rest wanted to wait until the entire budgeted amount was in the coffers. Ed had kept a low profile in the contest until he found out that the church's general contractor, Bill Fielding, a longtime member of the congregation with five young children, was having financial difficulty. Feeling obligated to push the matter forward, Ed chose as his next sermon topic the importance of trusting in God, using as his text the return of exiles from Babylon and the construction of the Second Temple.

Jonathan phoned Ed at home during Sunday lunch to tell him the sermon had been out of line. When Jonathan repeated the charge at the board meeting during the week, no one spoke up in his defense, not even Bill Fielding.

* * * * *

Ed heard footsteps on the cement walkway leading up to his study. He waited for a knock before getting up from his chair and opening the door to the cold of the late afternoon. He was happy to see Andy Bromville. He welcomed his longtime friend in with an exaggerated sweep of his hand. Andy, the town clerk, was the highest ranking nonelected person at town hall. Of far greater importance, he was a loving husband to his Korean wife, Sky, an involved father with his three teenage daughters, and one of the leaders in the church.

— Good afternoon. To what do I owe the honour of a visit this close to supper?
— I wanted you to be the first to know that I've accepted a job offer from the City of Calona. I'll be Director, Finance, which is basically second in command. I start work on March 1st. I had said I would let my name stand for another term on the church board, but of course I won't be able to now.
— Wow. That's big news. I'm going to—we're all going to—miss you and your family. It sounds like a good career move, though.
— I never thought I would get a job this good, at least not this soon. The girls are going to have to make new friends, but it will be a lot easier for them to carry on with their educations if we live closer to a university.

The two men talked comfortably for a while. Just when it looked like the conversation was coming to an end, Andy suddenly became serious.

— I have never talked about this with anyone else, but I'll tell you in confidence. A little over a year ago, Emily and Rosie were surrounded and groped—thank God it wasn't rape—by a gang of kids when they were walking home one night from a friend's house. It took a few days before Sky and I found out about it, but that's another story. The best I can figure is the girls were attacked because they don't quite fit in, either with the Native kids or the white kids.

— I don't know what to say. How are they doing?

— We think they're doing okay, but how do you measure the long-term impact of that kind of assault? A lady in the town's property tax department once told me nothing good ever came out of Bull Moose Run. I remember thinking at the time that she was one of those people who can find a problem with anything. After the attack on the girls, I began to think she might be right.

Sky and I have had tons of sleepless nights wondering what we could have done, or should have done. Why did we let the girls go out that night? Maybe I should have turned down the job offer from Bull Moose Run all those years ago, or maybe we should have built a house out of town, which was our original plan. Every time I see a group of teenagers on the street, I wonder if any of them were involved in the attack and I find myself becoming out-of-control angry.

The two men talked a while longer.

— I want you to know how blessed I have been by our little church. I've said it before and I'll say it again, I don't know how many times I felt done-in by Sunday morning and entertained the idea of staying home. But because I wanted to be a good example to the girls I usually went. I was always glad I did. Your sermons have a way of getting me thinking, you say things in a way I haven't thought about them before. And I like that you add in history. Then there's the way you're such a prayer guy. How do you put it, "Live your life punctuated by prayer"? Well, you really do. The other thing is I wanted to say is I'm always inspired by how you care for people, even the hopeless cases. For that and for a whole bunch more, thanks. Oh, and I should also say … and it's something that Sky is of course going to tell Anne herself … how much her and the girls have appreciated Anne's friendship. If Sky has told me once she's told me twenty times that Anne treated her like a sister from day one.

— Anne is special. Now, don't forget, though, there's a lot that Anne and I have to thank you and Sky for. Your family has been an important part of our church from the day you moved to town. I've always valued how you live and your leadership. I don't know if I ever told you that Mayor Desauliers said you were the best hire the town ever made. He said it isn't only your job skills, it's the way you treat others and what you stand for. According to the mayor you helped set the tone for the entire municipal office.

Andy was about to leave when Ed stopped him.

— Would you mind if I said a prayer for the girls, and for you and Sky?

* * * * *

Richard and Jean Redmond pastored a thriving young church in North Falls, which was forty miles due east of Bull Moose Run. In what was becoming a regular event, Richard had gotten out of bed in the middle of the night to go to the washroom. When he climbed back into bed as quietly as he could he was surprised to hear Jean ask him in a clear voice if everything was okay. He reflexively said yes, everything was fine. He spoke after a period of nighttime silence.

— Did you ever want to do something grand, to really take a chance and leap past your own expectations and the expectations of the people around you? I mean, wouldn't that be what they call the miracle of life?

— You'd better pray about that, because you can't do it on your own.

* * * * *

As far as Ed was concerned, Richard Redmond was one of the few guys who had it all. Friendly and interesting to talk to, Richard could preach a sermon without notes; and his voice was good enough to lead worship. He was also a good athlete: unexpectedly strong, with great hand to eye coordination, and deceptively fast—fast to turn, fast in a sprint, fast over a mile. On top of all that, Richard, who was a shade under five feet ten inches in height and Milanese slender, was good looking in a way that Ed assumed women found attractive. Once when Ed and Anne were talking about Richard, Anne had conceded that "Yes, some women might find Richard attractive."

Richard had been a near unanimous choice as student body president during his and Ed's last year in theology school. After graduation,

Richard could have continued on to graduate studies with a view to becoming a professor, or he could have joined the staff at the large church he and Jean had been attending. Surprising everyone, the couple had accepted a call to a non-denominational church plant in North Falls—years later, Richard told Ed that it was Jean who had pushed the most for the move north. Two months after the Redmonds made their announcement, Ed and Anne received their one and only invitation to candidate from the Bull Moose Run church.

In what seemed like no time at all Richard and Ed had gone from energetic young pastors with an ambition to fix every moral and spiritual ill to middle-aged clergy reconciled to the fact that life would forever mill out unsolvable problems. They lost another part of their earthbound optimism every time they walked a member of their congregation through money issues, comforted someone suffering from serious health concerns, or were asked to speak at the funeral of a child. Dealing with straight forward marriage breakdowns further depleted the ministers' reservoirs of goodwill, but more damaging yet was hearing about acts of physical abuse within marriages. Richard continued to be affected from being first on the scene after a murder-suicide of common law spouses who'd each lived troubled lives before moving in together.

Despite being committed to loving everyone (including their enemies!), Richard and Ed had to continually push back at the grubbier parts of their own humanity. This included suppressing their natural competitiveness, trying not to rely on stereotypes (not to say that the line between recognizing ethnicity or race and being prejudiced was always easy to identify), doing their best to hide frustration when dealing with needy people, and, of course, trying to fend off ever-present thoughts of other women. Even the friendship between the two men wasn't fully protected from their flawed makeups. There was an identifiable edge every time Richard accused Ed of being as obstinate as his German mother, who'd gotten into a heated argument with Richard about the gifts of the Spirit the only time they'd met. And Ed knew he took too much pleasure from reminding Richard about the time a logger had called the North Falls pastor a "girly-boy."

Early on in their careers, Richard and Ed didn't hesitate to drive eighty miles round trip on the gravel road between their towns to get another opinion about a serious matter, talk through something they regretted having said or done, or simply to be in the company of someone who would understood what they were going through. Although the road was eventually paved, the two ministers got together fewer and fewer times with each passing year. It had been almost six months since Richard and Ed had seen each other in person when they carpooled to the induction of a new minister in the tiny mill town of New Phoenix. It was like old times on the trip back.

— It's too bad we can't package up our experience and hand it over to young Jordan like a toolkit.

— I'm sure if we took the time to prepare a list of, say, the top 50 things we've learned, the very next day he'd find himself in a situation neither of us has been in.

They got onto the criminal prosecution of the treasurer in the White River church that had been the talk of the induction.

— You have to admit, it's a bit weird. If there are double fines for speeding in a construction zone, shouldn't there be an extra penalty for stealing from a church?

— Ya, right. Though, maybe it's easier to steal from a church because you know the money is supposed to go to someone deserving, and as far as you're concerned, you're that person.

— I read about how an alderman in Centre City made a bunch of money selling land near the site of the new community college. When you read about stuff like that, you realize no one's doing things entirely straight, don't you? How did one of my parishioners put it? "If you're not cheating, you're not winning."

* * * * *

When Ed told Anne about the upcoming trip to New Phoenix, he'd reminded her that she and Jean, who were good friends in their own right, were due a day out.

Anne took the cue, and early on a Saturday exactly one month after the husbands' trip, the wives drove to Centre City to go shopping. They arrived before the new mall opened and they had to wait in Anne's car, with the engine running to stay warm, until 9:00 a.m.

On their way to the children's clothing section in the eerily empty department store they walked past a strategically placed display of ladies' winter coats. Although they pressed each other to buy the new coats they both "badly needed", only Anne bought one, Jean deciding her dark blue coat had another year in it.

The women stopped for a late lunch at the bistro in the grocery store before picking up dairy products and frozen foods on their way out of the city.

— I don't know why I have to keep relearning that if I believe, you know really believe, that God is with me, I can be joyful even when things are going sideways. I, we all have it so good anyway. And there's always a better way to look at things. There is a family in our church that has two severely handicapped children. Not one handicapped child, but two! I'm sure I've told you about them. A while back, the wife, whose name is Bette with an e, said with more conviction than you can imagine that she and her husband were better people because of the difficulties their children had to live with.

They were getting ready to leave when Jean lowered her voice.

— I'd rather you didn't tell Ed, but I'm worried about Richard. He doesn't seem as happy as he used to be. Sometimes I think it's just because we're getting older and the pleasure of simple things is diminishing; other times I put it down to how busy we are. I keep worrying, though, that it's more than that.

Anne said she hadn't noticed anything the last time the couples were together. Jean agreed the change wasn't always obvious.

— Do you remember when we went to the funeral for Richard's father, Dean, in the spring?

— Yep.

— Well, Dean was quite a successful insurance salesman. He was also a bit of a Lothario. Richard's mother was Dean's second wife, and who knows how many other women there'd been in between. Their marriage only lasted a few years. Dean was in his forties when Richard was born, and Richard had very little contact with his father while he was growing up. Though, to give Dean some credit, at least he got Richard new hockey equipment every year. I only met Dean and his third wife the few times we took the boys to see their grandfather.

There was a slide show at the end of the service. Most of the pictures were either of Dean alone or together with his third wife, which I guess made sense but was still kind of weird … like part of his life didn't count. I only saw Richard in one slide, but he said he was off to the side in one of the group pictures.

I found it surprisingly emotional: there was Dean when he was young, when he was older but still healthy, and then after he got sick and had lost so much weight. I kept thinking how much he looked like Richard, especially the nose and the prominent forehead. There was one slide where Dean had a beard that looked just like the one Richard grew after we got married.

Richard says his dad was a workaholic, and that when he wasn't working he was golfing. Keeping busy was part of what made Dean successful, but it also makes sense that a guy like that—who had hurt so many people—would want to keep as busy as he did. If he would have ever slowed down and let himself think, he'd probably have gone loco.

— Imagine not being able to look forward to quiet moments. I hope I never have to live that way.

— One of the last slides was of Dean leaning against a cabin wall and smiling; it was shortly before he died. You couldn't help but think it wasn't a real smile. I'm worried that Richard has started to smile like that sometimes.

DARWIN WILLIAMS

THE INTRODUCTION OF THE PULP and paper industry in the 1960s brought about a dramatic increase in the demand for wood. With woodchips suddenly valuable, the size of trees mattered less and clear cutting became an accepted logging practice.

At the outset, professional foresters compared clear cutting with harvesting grain crops, albeit with longer growth cycles. In order to ensure sustainability, logging companies were required to replant logged areas with the previously dominant tree species and to tend to the seedlings until they were taller than the surrounding plants, which was when they were considered "Free to Grow."

*   *   *   *   *

Ed woke up before the buzzer went off. Anne had been up with Emily during the night, and he made sure to turn the alarm off before easing out of bed and quietly gathering up his clothes in the dark. Closing the bedroom door behind him, he tiptoed to the kitchen and turned on the light. Although he'd gone through his two rucksacks the night before, he checked once more to make sure he had packed his extra shells, which at $4.99 a box hadn't been an inconsequential purchase.

The Makis relied on moose and deer meat to live on Ed's salary. Moose meat was gamey and chewy when it was from an old bull, but the hamburger tasted almost normal when you cut it fifty-fifty with beef. As always, Ed had started road hunting the first day of the hunting season, disregarding the restrictions about shooting near the road when he was far enough from town. So far all he'd seen was a cow with two calves. He was starting to worry about being shut out when Stanley Bow offered to fly him up to a lake he had never heard of to go hunting. As good as the offer was, Ed had to wait to accept until Tom, the local probation officer, confirmed he would be able to take the Wednesday prayer meeting.

Stan and his wife, Lorna, lived near the Likem Indian Reserve on Tasim Lake, which was 125 miles northwest of Bull Moose Run. Stan was a pioneer type who, while mostly easy going, was known to have a bit of a temper. Lorna, who was a few years older than Stan, was a thin, fidgety minister's daughter from a small town in the Midwest United States. Equal parts academic and farm girl, she wasn't easily knocked off stride. Ed hadn't been surprised when Stan told him that Lorna had attended an Ivy League school on a full ride scholarship. Stan had met Lorna when he'd attended her home church in Wisconsin while on a motorcycle trip across the US, and the couple was married a year later. After the birth of their daughter they had moved north so Lorna could begin translating the Bible into the Carrier language.

One of the few assets Stan brought into the marriage was an antiquated floatplane. On the Makis' most recent visit up to Likem to see the Bows, Stan had taken Ed down to the dock to show him a repair he'd made to one of the plane's floats. Ed's first thought on seeing the patched-up fuselage up close was that the plane should have been retired a long time ago. Yet, because Stan had flown the plane so many years without crashing and because he had the special protections afforded missionaries, Ed wasn't concerned about their upcoming flight.

Ed heard the "scrunch" of frozen grass as he crossed the parsonage lawn in the dark with the first load of gear to put in the family sedan. Opening the driver's side door, there seemed to be an extra-long delay before the car's dim interior light went on. He put his thermos partway down the bench seat, and leaned farther in to prop his gun in the passenger foot well. *Wouldn't it be great to shoot a moose on my way to Likem? I'd have the whole week free.* He felt a little guilty about taking the car for so long and was glad he'd gotten Anne to arrange a ride to the grocery store with her friend, Lynn Holmes. One of Anne's weaknesses was not asking for help, and Ed had visions of her carrying heavy paper bags home from the store on a cold, wet day while he was away.

Once the car was loaded, Ed slipped back into the house to say goodbye. Anne was fast asleep, and rather than wake her he kissed her lightly on the forehead. Returning to the car, he was about to put his key in the ignition when he remembered … *first things first.* He closed his eyes and bowed his head to pray for his family and the church; then for Jonathan and Roland, two of the thorns in his flesh; and finally for safety and success on the hunting trip. He was almost done when he thought about Richard. Choosing his words carefully, he added a plea for the Redmond family and the other woman, whose name had slipped his mind.

The car started right away. *Good ol' Detroit steel.* They'd put almost 100,000 miles on the Chevy since Anne and he had purchased it, used, in Centre City. Although the tappets seemed a little noisier he hoped it was just the quiet of the morning. After checking the gas gauge, he shifted into reverse. *The clunk from the transmission sounds louder too.*

The trouble Ed had been having sleeping lately had worked to his advantage and he was ahead of schedule. The only vehicle on the road, he was soon past the town's last streetlight at the bottom of Swenson's Hill. On his way up the hill, his headlights shone first on the turnoff to the Jackson's place and, when he was near to the top of the hill, on the electrical substation. The path to the drunkard's cabin known as Camp 36—which was the minimum number of hours it took to make moonshine—started off behind the substation. Lars and he had once walked in to the rundown cabin to see what it looked like. They'd been a little nervous and had purposely made a lot of noise along the way to avoid getting shot at. It turned out there was no one at the cabin. When they were about to leave Lars had suggested half-seriously that they do the town a favour and put a torch to the unholy works.

Ed drove across the short, un-walled wooden bridge over Trickle Creek at the end of the pavement. A couple of years earlier he'd driven Tory up to try out his new casting rod at the big pool past the bridge. On their way by foot to the pool they'd come upon the two oldest Newton boys in a clearing near the creek senselessly killing frogs—as hard as it was to believe—by throwing them at a tree. He'd thought at the time how only experimenting youths or someone pure evil would ever do such a thing. He was glad that the boys seemed to be doing okay based on what Frank Wells had said.

Ed made sure to keep his car to the far right on corners because the road up to Likem was a main logging road. Sure enough, not far past the Downey Road turnoff, he met, mid-corner, a fully loaded truck with a pup trailer. He would have had more warning, but the lights of the two vehicles, weakened by the emerging daylight, had overlapped on the trees at the outside of the bend. The morning frost meant there was very little dust as the vehicles charged past each other. In order to be on the return leg this early, the trucker would have had to have left home by 3:00 a.m. Ed knew all too well from his counseling work the havoc hours like that wreaked on a marriage.

The signal from the AM country music station out of Centre City was still strong and Ed turned up the volume at the start of a Johnny Cash song. His mind soon wandered and he began to divide his attention between avoiding potholes and looking for moose on the side of the road. By the time he got to Mile 57 it was light enough to see a spiral of smoke rising from the Williams' chimney. Knowing what he did about Darwin Williams, the smoke was likely from last night's embers rather than an early morning fire. Two late model pickup trucks parked in front of the house were proof that crime had continued to pay even after the Likem Reserve had voted to go dry. *You just know the old bootlegger is involved with this marijuana thing like everyone says.*

* * * * *

One of Ed's more memorable home visitations had been to the Williams' residence two years earlier. He'd made the long trip up to Mile 57 after feeling guilty about setting a three-mile limit for out-of-town home visits. For some reason, he'd been led to bring a hardcover Bible from the church's little supply room along with him instead of the usual bundle of tracts. The road seemed long on the way up, and he'd had to keep reminding himself that in God's upside down economy, it didn't matter how much gas at $0.23 a gallon he used. It was getting dark when he'd pulled into the Williams' driveway and parked behind several other vehicles.

A large dog of mixed breed ran up and stood barking beside his car door. Ed liked dogs and got out of the car without fear, talking all the while to calm the angry animal. With the growling dog, that was growing less certain of itself, at his heels Ed made his way to the house. Northern clay and wet gravel clumped to his boots, and he stopped to scrape the worst of the dirt off his boots at the bottom of the wobbly stairs before climbing up to the rough and tumble porch. He knocked on the door and waited a while. Darwin Williams himself finally yanked the door open. The bootlegger looked bigger than ever.

— What do you want?

— Hello. My name's Ed Maki. I'm a minister in Bull Moose Run. I'm visiting homes in and around Bull Moose Run, and I was wondering if you and your wife would care to hear about some of the things our church is doing?

Darwin said he wasn't interested and closed the door before Ed could say anything more. It took Ed a second to process what might have been his fastest rejection ever. *I guess I didn't expect that out here, in the middle of nowhere.* The laughter that followed inside made it clear there was someone else in the house. On his way back to his car, Ed saw two boys come out of a large shed at the back of the property. The taller boy called the dog over.

Ed didn't remember the Bible until he got back to his car. After a moment's hesitation, he grabbed the blessed book and headed back to the house. The laughter was still carrying on, and he was pretty sure the four letter words he heard were being used to describe him and the church. He slipped the Bible out of sight on the boot rack on the porch, hoping that someone other than Darwin would find it. The dog came back to the driveway while Ed was backing up. It chased the Chevy down the gravel road a ways before giving up.

* * * * *

Several months after Darwin Williams slammed the door in Ed's face, the church had received an offer of smoke-damaged furniture from a furnished suite in a low rent apartment building. A retired couple from the church had gone to check out the furniture and came back with the surprising report that it was in reasonably good shape.

The Care Committee pressed the usual volunteers who owned trucks into picking up the furniture; and on the following weekend Ed rode over to the apartment building with Mark Ellison. He did his best to engage Mark in conversation, but as could have been predicted the lathe operator didn't have much to say. Ed considered the irony of the name, "The Sunshine Hills Apartments" as they drove up the frost-damaged asphalt driveway leading to the apartments. Built fifteen years earlier to take advantage of a short-lived federal rental program, the featureless, rectangular building, and two others like it on the street, were already among the more unsightly structures in town.

Mark parked his pickup in front of a rotting picnic table that sat sideways on a ragged patch of lawn. He and Ed got out of the truck and stood at the edge of the lawn waiting for the second pickup. A man who looked to be in his early forties with long, oily hair and wearing a stained t-shirt that didn't quite cover his rounded, hairy stomach came around the front of the apartment building. The man had the smile of someone who hadn't always done the right thing but was proud to be doing it this time.

— Good morning, Pastor.

— Good morning … Bruce, right? This is Mark. We're waiting for one more pickup that should be here any moment.

Bruce nodded at Mark and turned back to talk with Ed.

— When the insurance company said we'd get new furniture, I asked the owner if we could give the damaged stuff to the church. Both my girls attended summer camp, you know.

When Gene and Ted finally showed up Bruce led the church volunteers to a storage shed out back. The last lower floor apartment had fresh siding, as well as new windows and a new door.

— This is where the fire started. The tenant, ol' Sue, is quite a smoker. She must have missed the ash tray. The fire chief said we saved the building by getting on the fire so fast with the garden hose. At least they put Gyproc on the walls and the ceiling.

To Ed's amazement, the furniture in the shed looked almost new. Even without help from Bruce, who said his back was acting up, the men had the furniture loaded in no time. They were about to leave when Bruce remembered there was another chair he wanted to give to the church. Ed told Gene and Ted not to wait since there was lots of room for the chair in Mark's pickup.

Mark and Ed followed Bruce up the loose stairs to the second floor, exterior walkway. The walkway's plywood floor was spongy and uncertain, and Ed held onto the rail as he made his way along. Bruce opened the door to the last upper floor apartment.

— The firemen couldn't believe the fire didn't make it up here.

The grimy, worn-out room, which looked like it hadn't been lived in for a while, smelled of beer, cigarettes, and mildew. There were several boxes in the middle of the floor, and a worn out wingback chair off to the side that should have been thrown away years ago. Ed tried to sound gracious as he asked Bruce if he was sure he didn't want to keep the chair; but Bruce was adamant, saying he wanted to do his bit. After testing the chair's weight, Mark said he could carry it by himself.

Ed took the lead on the way back down the walkway. A door to one of the other apartments was now open. Glancing in, Ed could see all the way through to the bedroom in the back where a large, naked man was fast asleep atop mussed blankets. Ed knew instantly that it was Darwin Williams. Tina, an aging party girl of no known occupation, was standing beside the bed with her coat on, rifling through Darwin's wallet.

*　*　*　*　*

The shadows were beginning to shorten when Ed arrived at the Bows' turnoff some five miles before the Likem Reserve. The narrow dirt driveway wound its way through a hundred yards or so of mixed trees before widening in front of the Bows' house and oversized garage. The house, which had started life as a cabin, and had been added to before being dressed up with pale green asbestos shingles, looked unnaturally bright in the early morning sunshine. From where he was parked, Ed could see the blue of Tasim Lake.

The Bows' two dogs, an old golden retriever and an even older standard poodle, got up stiffly from the front steps where they were sunning themselves and hobbled over to greet the visitor. Ed opened his car door and waited to pat the eager dogs before climbing out. Both animals, who had managed to slough years off their lives, pressed him with sidewinding, puppy dog cheer all the way to the house.

Stan, who was dressed in overalls and wearing a baseball cap, came outside and stood on the porch. He greeted Ed with energy from their upcoming adventure.

— Welcome to Bow manor.

— I hope I'm not too early.

— No problem, we've been up for an hour. The kids have already eaten.

Stan's smile waned.

— I've run into a little problem with the plane, it's not running as smoothly as I'd like. I'm hoping it's just a spark plug. Why don't you go in and say hi to Lorna while I figure things out. She's in the study at the back, so don't bother knocking.

Ed took off his shoes off before entering the house, which smelled lived in but clean.

— It's Ed Maki. Stan told me not to knock.

A woman's voice answered,

— Come on in. I'm at the end of the hall.

Ed crossed the kitchen floor whose cracked old linoleum was lifting at its seams and entered the short hallway. The Bows' two children were playing in the first room off to his left. The girl, who had a pink hair band and looked as pretty as every little girl does, was sitting at a student's desk near the window. Her younger brother, whose hair had sprung free after being wetted down, looked up happily from the worn out, braided wool rug where he was playing with a toy truck.

— We're gon' to town with Mommy.

The girl turned to look at Ed before looking at her brother.

— Mommy said if you were good she would take us to town.

Ed asked the girl about the picture she was drawing before continuing on down the hall.

The jammed up bookcase at the end of the hall was fair warning of the riot of books and paperwork in Lorna's tiny study.

— Good morning. Captain Stan wasn't lying when he said your family got up early.

— And good morning to you. Morning is the best time of the day, isn't it? The kids got up on their own because they knew Daddy was going away.

— Ya, it was nice of Stan to offer. Every year I worry I won't get a moose. Hopefully going farther north will improve our chances. Is it going to be hard on you and the kids for Stan to be away?

— We'll be fine. It might even be good for Jessie.

— He said you're headed to town.

Lorna laughed.

— He tells people that whether or not we're going to town. He just happens to be right this time. The kids and I are planning to go into the Moose and stay at the Swartz's for two nights. We're hoping to leave tomorrow.

— You look busy. How is the translation work going?

— I'm always making progress, even though it sometimes doesn't feel that way. I was thinking this morning how it's been a few weeks since I've had to tweak the alphabet. Maybe I've finally got it right, or as right as I'm going to get it. One of the difficulties with writing down an oral language is that what you think you hear is often different from what's being said. I'd be sunk if the elders weren't as patient with me as they are.

— How far along on the Bible are you?

— I've completed most of Matthew, and a little over a hundred stand-alone verses.

Lorna stopped to check on the children as they made their way to the kitchen. Jessie clung to his mother's leg until she asked him to show Mr. Maki his new fire truck.

Ed declined Lorna's offer of coffee when they got to the kitchen, saying he was already jittery from drinking a full thermos. While they were talking they heard the floatplane's engine start and stop several times.

— Esther's in grade one, but she is doing grade three math. She just loves to learn. It would be hard on us to have to drive her into Likem every day, but the main reason we're homeschooling is so we can integrate the Bible into her studies. And, to be fair, I'm more committed to her education than I could expect from a teacher with a classroom of kids. I was homeschooled until grade ten. When I finally got to regular school, I was so far ahead they didn't know what to do with me.

— I read somewhere that the Romans taught their own children because they viewed education as too important a task to be left to slaves.

Lorna mentioned a missionary family near North Falls that was also homeschooling their children. Since she didn't ask about the Redmonds, Ed decided not to say anything.

Ed watched through the small kitchen window as Stan walked up the path from the lake and came towards the house. After noisily kicking his boots off on the porch, he opened the door and joined

Lorna and Ed in the tiny kitchen. There was a red and white stripe at the top of the gray sock pulled over his right pant leg.

— I cleaned the spark plugs, but it's still running rough. Maybe it's the carburetor, but I don't think so. I'm thinking of driving into Likem to ask Bud Prince if he'll come and take a look. He's the best mechanic around. He'll have been at work for a couple of hours by now.

* * * * *

Ed wouldn't have known how to get started on describing the Redmonds' situation to the Bows. Six months earlier, on an otherwise uneventful day, Ed had gotten a phone call in his office from Tony Tynesdale, a member of the North Falls Church.

— The board met with Richard Redmond last night. He's admitted to having an affair. When we asked him if there was a minister in the area he would feel comfortable talking to he gave us your name.

Hearing the news was like being hit on the head with a steel pipe. It was all Ed could do to stay engaged for the rest of the conversation. He was closer to Richard than he was to his real brothers; and now his minister-brother had done something unforgiveable, at least in human terms.

While Ed knew that under the right circumstances there are no limits to what people are capable of, Richard having an affair was beyond anything he could have imagined. It flat out didn't make sense given the precepts of Richard's faith, especially the sanctity of marriage; how perfectly matched Richard and Jean were (*or at least that's what everyone thought*); and the runaway success of the Redmonds' church in North Falls, which in a few years had gone from several families grateful to have the use of a public school classroom to a congregation of 300 plus people gathering every Sunday morning in a newly constructed building.

Ed dialed the Redmonds' home phone number as soon as he was off the call. Jean answered. In a voice flecked with both heartbreak and anger, she confirmed that Richard had been involved in a sexual relationship with a single mother.

— I don't know what to do.

Ed told her he'd come right over. Not until he was locking his office door did he think about asking Anne to go with him. *Thank goodness I've got the car today.* He was halfway home when he realized he was driving too fast and had to slow down.

His mind buzzing, he parked in the parsonage driveway and walked across the lawn to the back door. Anne, who had flour on her hands from making bread, stuck her head around the corner to the boot room to ask him why he was home so early. He waited until he was sure the twins were out of earshot before reporting in a hushed tone on the phone calls. Anne's face went white.

— Jean asked me not to say anything, but a while ago she said she was worried about Richard.

Anne tried to call Lynn Holmes to ask her if she could look after the twins on short notice, but the party line was in use. Ed felt he couldn't wait any longer and set off to North Falls on his own.

Jean had said the other woman, Marny, was in charge of scheduling ice time at the North Falls Arena. The hockey connection was the only thing that fit. Richard had been a star hockey player until he'd broken his ankle in his second year of Junior A and he still played in a men's league. The last time Richard and Ed talked Richard had said he had been asked to replace Coach Drake, the storied coach of the North Falls Triple A bantam team. Richard had smiled, adding it hadn't hurt his chances that his boy Luke, who was the captain of a pee wee team, would be playing bantam next year.

Jean was standing outside the main entrance to the North Falls Church when Ed arrived. His first thought was she looked a lot older. After they hugged in silence, Ed explained that he'd wanted to bring Anne, but they hadn't been able to get someone to look after the twins on short notice. Jean said that was just as well since she'd arranged to take the boys for dinner to the house of one of the single ladies from church.

Jean and Ed stood talking in the quiet of the empty parking lot, trying but unable to get a handhold on the unscalable disaster. When the conversation slowed Jean suggested that Ed should go and see Richard.

— He stopped by the house a few minutes after you called. When I told him you were driving over, he said to tell you he was going out to Ahuttla Beach Park.

Ed had been to Ahuttla Beach Park with Anne and the kids before, but he wasn't sure whether to take the first or the second road after the railroad tracks. He chose correctly and was soon at the park entrance. Richard's dull grey Impala convertible, with its fading paint, failed suspension, and taped-up plastic rear window was the only car in the gravel parking lot. Ed parked beside the Impala and walked down the leaf-covered path to the public beach. Richard was sitting on the top of a picnic table, its brown paint almost entirely flaked off, his feet on the bench seat, staring at Johnson Lake.

— Hey. Jean told me you were here.

After shaking hands, Ed sat alongside Richard on top of the picnic table. The two men spoke in short sentences as they looked out at the dark, restless water. When Richard said that he hadn't meant to hurt anyone and knew it could never be fixed, Ed tried to come up with something encouraging to say but inwardly agreed with Richard's analysis.

*   *   *   *   *

Shocking and consequential news finds hidden paths of travel just like water coming off a roof. Although the details of Richard's actions were always relayed in confidence, it wasn't long before everyone, including the Redmond boys, knew that Richard Redmond had been caught fooling around and that his wife was leaving him.

The affair affected everyone Jean and Richard knew, and even people they didn't. Those closest to the couple felt they had suffered their own personal reversals; acquaintances felt their inner gyro-scopes of right and wrong had taken a knock; and, depending on their backgrounds, complete strangers were either confirmed in their views about the hypocrisy of religious types or reminded of human-kind's frailties.

In the months that followed, Ed kept returning to the puzzle of why Richard had turned his back on the surprisingly short list of what people should and shouldn't do. He couldn't help thinking the influence of Richard's self-centered father had played a role; and there was also the possibility that the values instilled in Richard when he was a youth had resurfaced. Another explanation was that Richard's many successes had proven a hothouse for the contagion of pride.

Regardless, Richard knew what lay ahead. The two ministers had talked numerous times about the imbalance between the brief pleasures afforded by affairs and the lifetime of splintered loyalties and corrosive regrets that follow.

The North Falls Church had continued to pay Richard's salary for three months after his termination. Around the time the extended payments came to an end Richard agreed to meet a second time with Ed, this time in Ed's study in Bull Moose Run. After talking awkwardly for a few minutes, Ed said they should open with prayer. When he was finished, he kept his head bowed in case Richard wanted to add something, but Richard stayed silent.

It soon became obvious that Richard was only comfortable talking about practical matters, such as finding an apartment to rent, applying for employment, and the monotony of the mill job he had taken on in the meantime.

— I showed up with work boots, a hard hat and gloves and was asked to start right away.

Every now and then, though, Richard would let something consequential slip, referring at one point to the demands on pastors and, later on, to how cutting Jean's criticisms had become. He also went out of his way to list some of the hardships Marny had faced, including an abusive former spouse.

When Ed asked Richard about the chance of reconciliation with Jean, the former North Falls minister stood up and said he probably shouldn't have come. He turned around in the doorway with a strained look:

— You should know that Jean and I hadn't been physically close for some time.

BUD AND LAWRENCE

TREE BEETLES, WHICH ARE TYPICALLY native to specific trees, are integral to forest renewal. Not only do they speed up the death of weak and dying trees that are unable to pitch them out, they aid in the decomposition of dead trees. In the 1970s, for the first time in local history, mountain pine beetles began to attack healthy lodgepole pines. At the peak of the pine beetle population explosion that followed, swarms of beetles could be seen flying in clouds like locusts to new stands of timber.

* * * * *

Ed and Stan drove over in Ed's car to Bud's garage at the start of the Likem Indian Reserve. Out front of the garage there was an antiquated narrow gas pump with a red and white Texaco standard that Stan said still worked. Stan yelled out "Hello" as they approached the pickup truck up on the hoist in the single bay. A sturdy Native dressed in blackened overalls and wearing an oil-stained shop cap with a welcoming tilt came around from the front of the pickup. The man smiled when he recognized Stan.

Once introductions were out of the way Stan told Bud about Ed's and his upcoming hunting trip, eventually getting to the problem with the floatplane's engine.

— I'd be happy to come and have a look, but I'm not an airplane mechanic.

Bud followed Stan and Ed back to the Bows' in his pickup, which had a dark brown cab and a sienna box transplanted from a second truck. After parking in tandem in front of the Bows' garage, the men headed down to the dock. The plane's engine cover was already off and Bud asked Stan to start the engine. It caught after several slow turns of the propeller. The noise was so loud that Ed stepped back and covered his ears. Neither Bud nor Stan seemed bothered by the noise. Bud stared intently at the engine for a minute or two before signaling to Stan to shut it off. Bud waited until Stan was back on the dock.

— It could be the ignition wire on the bottom right cylinder.

Stan pointed at one of the wires on the engine.

— No, not that one. The next one up. Yes. Let's take that wire off and try it again.

Bud took the ignition wire off the spark plug, and Stan climbed back into the cockpit to start the engine a second time. It sounded exactly the same as before. After Stan turned the engine off, he opened the plane's door and addressed Bud.

— How did you do that?

— If you listen to the engine, you can hear things. It seemed like that cylinder wasn't firing. Do you have a spare ignition wire?

Stan clambered down to the dock before answering.

— I might. I've got a bunch of parts in boxes.

Bud made a good-natured crack about the age of the plane when Stan turned to go. Ed wondered how Stan would react to being made fun of, but the pilot's face showed only feigned disappointment.

Bud and Ed began to talk.

— Where did you get your training?

— My first job was cleaning cars at the Chev dealership in the Moose on weekends when I was in high school. Pretty soon I was changing oil and helping the mechanics. I was the first apprentice at the dealership. I worked there for almost ten years.

— I know a guy that works there, Tim Tran. I think he's the sales manager.

— Tim's a great guy. He knows everything about cars, except what's under the hood. He used to get me to check out the engines of cars that were being traded in.

— Stan says you own your garage. What's that like?

— It works out pretty well, because the band manager makes sure I get paid. It's way easier to run a business when you don't have to collect money.

— Did you always want to work for yourself?

— They say you get what you want, so I guess I wanted to own a garage in Likem. I didn't figure it out right away, though. When I was working in the Moose I was offered a stint with an economic development agency in Nigeria. My initial contract was to teach small engine repairs, but one thing led to another and by my last year I was wrenching U.N. vehicles and diplomatic limousines. I found that rewarding enough, but despite Africa being as great as it is I started to miss the north. I even missed the snow if you can believe it.

— Nigeria. What's the chance of that, eh? My wife was born in Nigeria.

Bud told some stories about Africa before they got to Stan and Ed's hunting trip.

— I've been trying to get up to see my uncle, Lawrence, on Chum Lake. Chum's not that far from Alces. I was thinking of asking Stan if I could finagle a flight with you guys.

— I can't see why that wouldn't work.

— That would be great. One of my cousins said uncle wasn't moving very well this summer. I was hoping to check on him and bring him some supplies before the snow comes. The only logging road anywhere near Chum Lake stops at the south end of the lake, but I've been afraid to try it. The bridges on the road were in rough shape a few years ago and I can't imagine how bad they are now. You can get to Chum by riverboat through the Naquat, that's the way my cousin went, but it's a long trip with no help if you run into trouble.

— I didn't know there was a community up at Chum Lake.

— There's just my uncle now.

— How'd he end up there?

— He was born there. His mom died young and his dad never left when everyone else moved to the reserve. Lawrence lived for a while at the Moose Lake Reserve before moving back to live alone at Chum Lake. Most of our family ended up in Likem.

They went up to see how Stan was doing. Walking up the steep path, Ed had the passing thought that if Lorna had been in charge of airplane parts, they'd already be airborne.

They found Stan rifling through a box of odds and ends outside the garage door. Looking up, he said he hadn't found the right box yet but hadn't given up hope.

A half an hour later, Stan stood up stiff from crouching for so long.
— I can't find that frickin' thing.

He apologized for keeping Bud so long and offered to pay him for his time. Bud answered with a twinkle in his eye.
— I'll just tack it on to your next bill for the Land Rover, which I expect back in my shop any day now.
— Sure. In the meantime, I'm still waiting for the other half of the bill for the brakes.
— It's in the mail, but you know how the service is up here.

Stan glared at Bud in a way that looked more pretend than real before turning towards Ed.
— It looks like we're going to have to put our trip off. If I can get an ignition wire sent up on the bus from the coast it could take a week or so, but it'll take a lot longer than that if I have to order it from the States.

Bud spoke up.
— Let me see that wire again.

Stan handed Bud the wire.
— You know, I might be able to splice this together with a new lead if I can find one long enough. I'll do my best since I'm hoping to catch a ride with you guys.

Remembering Bud's earlier request, Ed told Stan that Bud had asked about getting a ride up to Chum Lake. Bud spoke up before Stan could answer.
— Be careful. The wrong answer might affect the quality of my work.

* * * * *

Stan and Ed had just gotten back from a hike through the bush to see a forgotten memorial for a European explorer that was close to the Bows' residence when Bud arrived back in the yard. Getting out of the cab of his pickup, he proudly held out a bespoke ignition wire for inspection. The wire, once a dull grey its entire length, now converted part way along, after a wrap of black electrical tape, into bright orange.

The three men walked quickly back down to the dock. Stan started the plane's engine as soon as Bud connected the wire. From the look on Stan's face through the pilot side window the engine was now running like it was supposed to.

With much of the day gone, Stan suggested they delay leaving until morning. Bud said he was good with that since it would give him a chance to round up supplies for his uncle.

* * * * *

Lorna was thrilled Stan would be around for another night, and said she had more than enough leftovers for everyone. She asked Stan to relay a message to the Swartz's through his ham radio contact in Bull Moose Run that she'd be a day or so late.

— That reminds me … I should get Corporal Gussin's radio back to him. Ed, are you up to taking another trip into Likem? There's a fifty-fifty chance the corporal is in rotation. If he isn't, I'll just drop the radio off at the station.

— Sounds good.

A drive in the family's war surplus Land Rover was the perfect outing for Esther and Jessie, and both children were soon asleep despite the clouds of circulating dust in the vehicle's interior, the un-sprung bouncing and banging around, and significant engine and transmission noise. Ed made several attempts to converse with Stan, but the pilot was focused on not missing a shift and gave only one word answers. Ed began to imagine he was on an African safari with a crazy British guide.

Likem's R.C.M.P. station was down one of the reserve's unmarked gravel streets. Except for a small sign out front, the station looked the same as the ageing box houses on either side of it. Stan shook Esther and Jessie awake after parking. Esther got up in a flash and was keen to get out and walk, but Jessie was drowsy and had to be carried. A game of pickup softball was underway in the worn out ballpark across the street. One of the young outfielders yelled out, "Hey, Mr. Bow". Stan shifted Jessie in his arms and did his best to wave back.

Stan knocked on the station door and there was a muffled welcome, — Come on in.

A uniformed police officer in his fifties was sitting behind a desk near the door in a serious conversation with an elderly Native man. Ed thought the desk at the edge of what was formerly the living room couldn't have looked more out of place. The officer said hello before asking the four visitors if they would mind waiting in the kitchen.

Ed was at the back of the group and closed the door behind him when they got to the kitchen—the addition of a kitchen door being one of the few design changes to the house. After placing the borrowed radio on the kitchen table, Ed sat down next to Stan who was already seated, his son on his lap and his daughter leaning against him.

Corporal Gussin joined them a few minutes later.

— How's it goin', Stan?

— Good, and you?

— Only two days until I'm off, so definitely good.

Corporal Gussin addressed Stan's daughter.

— And what's your name?

— Esther.

— How old are you, Esther?

— Six and a half.

— Wow. I used to have a girl that looked just like you, but she's twenty-three now, and about this tall.

Corporal Gussin lifted his right hand up to his chest. Still smiling, he turned to Ed.

— I don't think we've met.

— Albert, this is Ed Maki. He's the pastor at the church on Fort Street in Bull Moose Run. Ed, this is Corporal Albert Gussin.

— Nice to meet you, Pastor.

— And you, Corporal.

Stan gestured at the ham radio.

— I finally got my own radio back from the repair shop. I had meant to bring yours back sooner. It worked great. I even got into a ragchew with a ham in Argentina, which is as far away as I've ever reached from Likem.

— I'm just glad I didn't toss the old girl out like I was going to.

— Not as glad as I was. I think I told you that I communicate with the mission headquarters by radio.

The two men talked ham radios for a while.

— Before I forget, have you heard if James Broadman is running for band council? We're still trying to figure out if we're going to need extra staff.

— I've heard there might be a bit more of a contest this year, but I haven't seen Jimmy around for several weeks. Someone said Jimmy was planning on taking some courses at the college in Centre City.

* * * * *

Lorna served reheated, slightly greasy goose, clumpy rice and cold beets, for dinner. Although Ed made sure to complement his hostess, he couldn't help but wonder what Anne was serving for dinner back home.

Feeling guilty about the allocation of household duties during the day, Stan pressured Lorna to stay at the table while he did the dishes.

— When we drove through the reserve this afternoon, I kept thinking how reserves are fundamentally wrong—Likem, Moose Lake, all of them. They're like holding pens with no jobs and nothing for people to do. No wonder there's so much drinking—although I guess Likem's been dry now for a while—the houses are in such disrepair, and people dress rag tag. It's amazing when someone like Bud manages to avoid the minefields.

Stan interjected from the kitchen.

— Bud avoided a lot of problems, but the rest of his family hasn't. One of Bud's brothers died when he was quite young, and another brother is an alcoholic. Bud hasn't seen his sister since she moved down south with her ne'er do well boyfriend a few years ago. Bud says it's bad news every time he hears about her.

Lorna spoke up.

— Did you know Bud used to work for the U.N.?

— He told me about his time in Africa.

— Hopefully he's part of a wave of things changing for the better. Like Likem's new elementary school. Everyone was thrilled when it opened.

— What grade does it go to?

— Grade seven. The high school kids still bus into Bull Moose Run every week.

...

— Stan and I talk a lot about how grateful we are to have been accepted by the Likem community. One of the things that's helped is Stan makes his plane available in emergencies. This summer he flew one of Bud's cousins who was having chest pains to Bull Moose Run. It turned out the poor man had suffered a minor heart attack. We've developed some real friendships, especially with the Castles. Mama Castle is one of the elders. She knows more about the Carrier language than anyone else around. I can't tell you how many times I've gone to her when I've reached a dead end and she's been able to help me out. Mama and her husband, Bob have even invited us to the neighbourhood potluck a few times.

Stan chimed in.

— The young man who waved at us from the baseball field was Donnie Castle. He's one of Mama's grandchildren.

— One of my favourite stories is when I had Esther with me once when I went to see Mama. Some of Mama's grandchildren came and asked Esther if she wanted to play cowboys and Indians with them. One of the boys said to her, "You can be on our side, because you guys are like us."

It wasn't long before Ed had to stifle a yawn. It was time to shut down.

— I have to say I'm struck by your commitment.

— It doesn't feel like a commitment. His burden really is light. If we don't finish the translation work—not that work like ours is ever finished—at least we did what we were called to do. Sort of like Thomas Gallaudet who set up the original school for the deaf in the US. Have you ever heard of him?

— I'm not sure.

— I know a fair amount about Gallaudet because I did a paper on him in undergrad. He started out as a traditional minister but his real calling was working with the deaf. A while ago I came across a biography about him in the Bull Moose Run library. I skimmed through the book and was disheartened to see the writer had glossed over Gallaudet's background and the fact the school's original curriculum was based on the Bible.

— It's like not acknowledging the words "Soli Deo Gloria" on Bach's church music.

— Exactly. There's a lot of divides, but the biggest is between people with and without faith. I remember sitting through a lecture at Harvard where the Prof went on and on about a particular poet, I've forgotten which one, who the Prof said wrote poems that were like secular prayers. No one who has ever witnessed the power of prayer would ever dream of making a comparison like that.

* * * * *

Ed slept on the braided rug in the Bows' living room. He got up once during the night to go to the bathroom but fell right back asleep. He woke up for good when Stan came down the hall and turned the light on in the kitchen. When he joined Stan a few minutes later, the hollowed-out silence of the early hour made sounds sharper and every word whispered across the Arborite kitchen table seem important. Not long after hearing doors opening and closing at the back of the house, Lorna, who was dressed for the day, came to get a coffee.

As soon as it was light enough Stan and Ed rinsed their cups and cereal bowls and went out into the dull chill of the morning. Stan stopped by the garage to get a rag to check the oil in the plane's engine. When they got down to the dock, Ed walked to the end of the grey but still strong planks and stared at the far side of the lake. Later, when he was nearer the start of the dock, he looked down into the clear water at the rocks on the bottom of the lake, which were almost identical in shape, colour and size. *Maybe it's just the pastor in me, but those rocks look like they've been individually placed.*

When Stan and Ed went back to the house they found Bud taking boxes out of his pickup. In short order the men had the plane loaded. Stan became more serious when he began to review his pre-flight checklist.

Bud offered Ed the co-pilot's seat when it was time to take off but Ed said he was happy sitting in the back. Before starting the engine Stan handed around taupe earmuffs whose plastic seals were cracked by age. The noise from the engine diminished by half the moment they lifted off the water. Momentarily stabilized by the ground effect, the plane continued to rise at an impressive rate. Bud and Ed craned their necks to take in as much of their ever-widening view as they could through the side windows. Bud pointed down and said something Ed couldn't make out. He smiled back, assuming that Bud was pointing at his garage.

It wasn't long before they were at cruising height. With the clouds high above them, they had a clear view of the landscape being scrolled out below. Ed was surprised he could distinguish between the different types of evergreen trees, which included pine, subalpine fir, mountain hemlock, and the predominant Engelmann spruce.

He soon took note of the chaotic, yet repeating patterns of the water features. There was standing water, plenty of smaller lakes, creeks, bustling, larger creeks, and a full-sized river that would merge with untold other water sources on its long journey to the ocean. Ed knew that more important to wildlife than the clear water were the drab marshes, swamps, bogs, and fen. Such was the bounty of water-based food found in the abundant wetlands, ducks and geese wintering a half a continent away chose to migrate north every spring. The plant-ridden ponds were also a primary store of food for moose during their abbreviated feeding season, one of the most iconic images from the north being that of a big bull, belly deep in water, eating pondweeds and lilies. Because of the connectedness of all things, the region's carnivores were equally reliant on the plentiful sloughs.

Ed had a better sense of where they were when their flight path took them between the Upper and Lower Mezron lakes. Although the two lakes had similar shapes, he knew that Upper Mezron, a dark blue, deep lake that was rumoured to be bottomless in spots, attracted sports fishermen from around the world; whereas the only fish in Lower Mezron, which was greenish and had a shallow, silty clay bottom, were northern pikeminnows, formerly called squawfish.

He wondered what insignificant spring somewhere below them represented the headwaters of the Mackenzie River, Canada's longest river with the second largest drainage basin in North America. The southern reach of the great river hadn't meant much to him until he'd caught an Arctic grayling with its large dorsal fin in Tinhorn Creek, a scant seventy-five miles north of Bull Moose Run.

An hour later, they were flying alongside a thinly treed, elevated area. According to the Department of Energy, Mines, and Resources map Ed was looking at, this bulge in the landscape was Mount Charmant. Not many weeks earlier, he had read an article in Bull Moose Run's weekly newspaper, *The Leader*, about a geological survey taking place on the mountain. He leaned towards the window to get a better view of the topography, trying to imagine where a mine might be located and how it would change the look of the area. *While it's a barren enough spot, it's got a type of beauty that would be lost. ... Plain and simple, you can't make the world more beautiful than it already is.*

When Chum Lake came into view Ed put the map down on the empty seat beside him and re-engaged in the flight. Stan completed a flyby to check the lake for partly submersed logs, prophetically known as deadheads, before circling back for the landing run. After its speedy final descent, the plane splashed down, "Vvooosh!", the heft of the water immediately slowing the plane to a near stop. The waves were bigger on Chum than they had been on Tasim.

Stan piloted the plane towards a small, rickety dock on the north side of the lake. After assessing the structure, he directed Bud down onto the pontoon to grab on. Bud was onto the second mooring line by the time Ed and Stan climbed down from the cockpit. A flock of geese flew overhead while the men were stretching out. The cacophonous racket made by the impossibly close skein sounded even louder because they had just taken their earmuffs off. Bud waited until the geese had passed before speaking.

— I was a little bit worried about how hard the landing was going to be given all the cracks in the front window.

— Okay. I wasn't going to say anything, but it's been a while since I've seen someone tie a granny knot on a mooring line.

Ed detected an edge to Stan's response.

They followed Bud, walking past an overturned fibreglass canoe at the water's edge and then up the rooted path to the cabin. When they got closer to the cabin, they saw how old it was and that it had sunk in the far corner. Bud knocked on the cabin's door and waited a moment before opening it. The cabin was empty. After checking to see if the stove was still warm, he came outside and began yelling "Hello" as he led the crew around back. Ed saw what was left of two other cabins through the trees as they made their way through the clear, regularly walked over yard.

After a while, there was a barely discernible voice from the woods. In a few minutes, a thin old man who was moving slowly emerged into the open. The man's hair was almost pure white, and his heavily lined skin the colour of brown that Europeans dream about when they lie in the Mediterranean sun. He had a shiny wooden staff in one hand and, in the other, a willow branch that skewered a medium-sized rainbow trout. Bud went up and stood in front of him.

— Hey, Uncle Lawrence, are you sure that fish is big enough to keep? Lawrence finally recognized Bud.

— Bud! Whatchy're doing up here? I heard dat plan flyin in an' I raced home fasssh' asssh I could.

— I got a ride up here with these fella's to make sure you were okay.

— No need worry 'bot me.

61

Bud took the willow branch with the fish and began to speak in Carrier. Stan could tell Lawrence and Bud were talking about family. Lawrence switched back to English.

— Who you got with you? Hey, you wit' te hat, is dat yur plane? Buddy boy ain't got no plane. Dat's the firsssh' plane on this lake since maybe five years. I'd like to shhee 'dat plane.

Lawrence was clearly someone who took joy from everything he was given, and today he had been given three visitors and the chance to see a floatplane. The men followed Lawrence as he made his way down to the dock at his painfully slow pace. Bud touched Ed's elbow to hold him back before speaking in a lowered voice:

— He needs a cane mostly because he can hardly see. We think he's got cataracts, but he won't go to a doctor.

Lawrence was excited to learn everything he could about the plane, even squinting up into the sparse cockpit when Stan opened the door. Lawrence didn't react at first when Stan began handing down boxes of supplies from the plane. After a while, though, a wry smile formed on his face.

— Whatch're bringing all this stuff wit' you for? I don't think I can use it. I got 'nuff moss tea and moose jerky.

Bud announced that he was going to rustle up brunch and invited Stan and Ed to stay. Although their original plan was to fly straight on to Alces Lake, they ended up accepting the invitation.

Bud took charge when they got to Lawrence's cabin: Ed was set to work cutting up some of the potatoes and onions that Bud had brought and Stan to getting firewood from the nearly empty woodbin before helping out in the kitchen. After reviving the fire in the stove, Bud divided the prepared vegetables into two cast iron pans and doused the contents with salt and pepper. When the potatoes were getting close, he added the trout, as well as the bacon that Stan had volunteered, to the larger pan. The last steps were cracking eggs into the smaller pan and propping bread slices against the stovepipe.

The men took their generous portions outside, positioning themselves to catch whatever glints of sunlight there were. Ed said a silent prayer before beginning to eat. Lawrence, who was missing a number of teeth, took twice as long as anyone else to finish the main course but kept eating until he'd finished a second slice of Lorna Bow's lemon cake. It took a while before Bud broached the subject of Lawrence's plans for the upcoming winter. The old woodsman danced around the question like an expert witness before answering.

— Yur right. Winter can be pretty hard when yur on yur own. But tat's okay when it's go'n be your lasssh' winter.

— What do you mean your last winter, Uncle?

— I lived a long time. Way longer'en both my brothers. I lived good too. I seen everytin' I want to see. I done everytin' I want to do.

— Why don't you come back with us. I'm sure Stan would fly you down to Likem.

— Happy to.

— Then you can move in with me, Kim, and the girls, or with one of the other cousins. Or go back to Moose Lake. If you're feeling good, you can come back next summer.

— Yur not hearin' me. Whatc'you mean live witc'you? This is where I live. Nex' year, I don' thin' your goin' fine me here. I'n gon be out there wit' my frien's. Ter's a strong pack of wolves now.

Nothing more was said on the topic.

Stan asked Lawrence if he had built the cabin by himself. Lawrence said he had, almost fifty years ago. Ed's comment about the view of the lake twigged Lawrence's memory.

— One time ter' was a cow moose and two lil'uns crossing the ice. T'ey was in a hurry 'cuz the wolves was getting' near. Ih' was getting spring and d'ice wasssh t'in. One calf he fell right t'rew. I wasssh stan'in right over there, watchin'. And dat cow moose she kep' makin a big noise, looking back where de calf wen' t'rew. He kep' trying to climb out, but he coud'n. And dat cow she stayed there all day, makin' dat noise. Den she came back de nex' 'ay, and den 'nother. Dat cow she kep' coming back. Five days af'er dat, I was snowshoeing and I see dat cow agin.

— Tell'em the wolverine story.

— It wasssh real col' that one win'er. An' I stayed inside almosssh' all da time, doin' some carvin'. T'en one week it wasssh col'er dan ever. I put blankets on de window and over the door, and I kep' dat sssh-tove red hot.

Ev'ry time I wen' out to the outhouse I come back as fasssh' as I can. So's I'm racing out there reel early wun' morning and I go to sit down, and wowee I feel somepin' unner me. And I jump right up, crasssh t'ru the door with my pants down. While I'm line' in de snow I look back, and dere's a ssshleepy ol' wolverine lookin' up from the outhouse hole. He mussa gone in der' to keep warm, cuz he's freezing too. I'sssh sssho scared I ran back to the cabin with my pants down. I mussa fallen ten times. Dat wolvervine kep' hwatchin' me fall down an' run an' fall down agin and agin.

The men couldn't stop laughing at the imagined sight of Lawrence, pants down, lying in the snow and looking back at the frozen wolverine who had hunkered down in the warmest place he could find. Ed voiced what everyone was thinking when he said it could have turned out a whole lot worse.

After a while Lawrence got up stiffly and said he was going to lie down. The three visitors talked quietly among themselves after the cabin door closed behind their host.

— Bud, are you going to be good here?

— Uncle's an independent old bugger, but I'm sure he'll appreciate the company. I'll talk to him again about coming south, but he seems to have his mind made up. If he says he's going to do something, then it's a pretty sure thing that's what he's going to do.

— What was that about this being his last winter and not finding him? And the wolf pack? I don't want to be weird about it, but does that mean he's going to give up and throw himself in the snow?

— One thing's certain, he doesn't want to die with people feeding him and keeping him clean. Dying quickly ain't a bad thing. You don't see a lot of sick and injured animals in the wild do you?

ALCES LAKE

SCIENTISTS BELIEVE THAT THE 70'S pine beetle epidemic was primarily caused by global warming. Not only had the province's pine trees been weakened by increasingly hot and dry summers—there were reports about people saving trees on their properties by diligently watering them—winters were no longer cold enough to freeze hibernating beetles. Another contributing factor was likely the reliance of the Forest Service on outdated silviculture methods, including blanket fire protection and replanting cut blocks with single tree species. There was also speculation that logging companies played a role because of a bias towards identifying pine trees, which reached "Free to Grow" status faster than other seedlings, as the previously dominant tree species in cut blocks.

* * * * *

Stan pulled Ed aside after they had finished eating and suggested they give Bud a hand that afternoon.

— I mean if it wasn't for Bud, we wouldn't be here. Anyway, I'd just as soon get to Alces early in the day.

Bud hadn't expected the offer; but after discussing what needed to be done around Lawrence's cabin said that if Stan wanted he could work on repairing the outhouse door, and that Ed, who had stressed his limited manual skills, could split wood for winter.

Lawrence eventually emerged from the cabin and sat at the front of the house listening to the banter and feeling the work rhythms.

In mid-afternoon Bud came down off the roof and said he was going to get started on an early dinner. Stan and Ed kept going until Bud gave them a ten-minute warning. After washing up down at the lake, they sat down to a meal of schnitzel, pickled red cabbage, potatoes, carrots and butter baked in tin foil, with what was left of Lorna's lemon cake for dessert.

Instead of passing Stan the salt when he asked for it, Bud handed him an unmarked herb bottle containing dried garlic.

— Try this. I grew the garlic, dried it and ground it myself.

— Where'd you learn so much about food?

— You pick a little bit up here and there. I even know how to make a few African dishes.

They were soon ribbing each other about the things that had gone wrong in the afternoon. Stan adopted just the right amount of irony to describe the "joy" of working on the outhouse. Ed started out waxing philosophical, even attempting to integrate some theology, about the meditative qualities of chopping wood. He had to give up, though, in the face of a flurry of jokes involving the number and length of his breaks. Funniest of all—so funny that Ed laughed until he began to cough—was Stan's description of when Bud raced down the ladder after sticking his hand in a wasp nest on the roof only to slip off the bottom rung.

— Hey, how was I supposed to know that wasps that can't fly can still sting?

Trying to engage his uncle in the conversation, Bud told Stan and Ed that Lawrence's real name was Dragonfly.

— I never t'out much 'bout dat name when I become Lawrence, and dat's da end of Dragonfly, exsshept for bu'aba and bu'ama.

One year I wasssh tracking a moose t'rough du woods. I wasssh movin' quiet. I could hear every little t'in' goin' on. Birds and squirrels. I wasssh waitin' for a moose to maybe come crashing back, cause it wasssh ruttin' time.

'Ten a dragonfly lans right dere on my shoulder. He's eatin' a wasp. I watch'em chew that wasp all the way down. Den he flies away. I never seen dat before, and I never seen dat agin' neither.

Lawrence said that while moose usually stayed clear of his cabin, they sometimes watered at a nearby pond. Bud asked him with a smile:

— Hey, how come you didn't tell us that before we spent all day working on your cabin?

— No'one asssh me.

Bud asked Lawrence how far away the meadow was and Lawrence answered in Carrier. Bud translated for Stan and Ed, saying it sounded like a twenty-minute walk. Since there was still some daylight, Stan and Ed said they might as well give it a go.

Stan and Ed were getting their guns from the floatplane when Bud yelled down at them.

— Make sure to grab your red mackinaws. You white guys should dress in red every time you go into the woods.

Although Stan and Ed did their best to duplicate Bud's noiseless movement through the forest, it seemed like every few feet one of them would step on a dry branch or get caught up in a bush. Intent on their footwork, they lost track of time and were surprised when they found themselves at the top of a ridge bordering a meadow that had several ponds. Bud pointed out a fallen tree for Stan to wait behind and led Ed to another natural blind farther on. Freed from his charges, the mechanic slipped out of sight into the largely leafless backdrop.

Looking down at the meadow, Ed thought about how human beings had gained too much of an advantage over big game animals, both in terms of the number of hunters and their firepower. Equally devastating was the way roads and towns had chopped up the wilderness. *It won't be long before there are only scrub animals left, just like in Europe.* He thought about the story a Czechoslovakian émigré had told him. Not long after World War II ended, wealthy hunters from Prague had paid boys from the émigré's village to act as bangers and scare the deer in the direction of a dell where the hunters were waiting. The ambush had proved so successful the local deer population had been basically wiped out.

As far as Ed could figure, there were several distinctly different types of hunter. There were Native hunters, like Lawrence and Charlie, for whom hunting remained an indivisible part of who they were. Then there were hunters like Ed's Scandinavian friend Olaf, who came from regions with strong hunting cultures. And, of course, there were men like Stan and himself who hunted mainly for food. Not to say that hunters were only men. He knew two women, Rebecca Young and Julia Nelson who had the hunting gene, or whatever it was that made people want to hunt. Interestingly, both women had daughters who also hunted.

Separate and apart from the other hunters were the men Ed thought of as the hunter killers. These hunters, who wanted only to dominate and kill, had no love for living things. The father of Tory's friend Victor was a classic example. A few months earlier, Ed had driven over to pick Tory up from Victor's house late on a Saturday afternoon. Victor's father, who had the nickname Blackie, had cornered Ed on the front porch and begun to talk nonstop. At some point his longsuffering wife asked him a question from the kitchen, and he had gruffly shot back that she would have to figure it out for herself. Not long after that repellant exchange Ed had said that Tory and he had better get going so they wouldn't be late for dinner. Blackie had waved off the minister's concern, and as much as dragged Ed down to see his hunting room in the basement.

Two falsely-proud, taxidermy deer heads were mounted on the wall opposite the doorway alongside several, stretched out skins. On the end wall to Ed's right, there were shelves with animal skulls; and on the wall to his left, there was a collection of photo's, some framed and others just taped to the wood paneling. Blackie pulled Ed by his arm over to a blown-up photograph of a pickup truck bed filled with dead geese.

— My buddy, Jonny, shot thirty-one and I got thirty-eight.

— That's a lot of geese to pluck.

— Jonny kept a few, but we threw most of them away because we didn't clean them in time. Not much of a loss since I don't like geese.

Ed's thoughts reverted to the present. He watched the ducks in the pond below his blind dip their heads under the ice-cold water. *You can't tell me animals and people are basically the same. Those ducks actually love the cold water.* His mind flitting between thoughts, he wondered how close he could get to the pond before he got stuck in the peaty ground. After a while he began looking around nearer his blind. The poplar tree trunks lying on the ground in the interstices of the maturing spruce trees reminded him of collapsed stone columns at a Roman ruin.

He began to think about the worrying signs of cockiness and deception in Louis, the neighbour boy who was a year older than Tory. From Ed's experience, those character traits, once acquired, were almost impossible to get rid of. Although Ed was sympathetic to Louis' need for friendship as the only child of a single mother, he also knew about the inordinate influence of a child's peers. He still shuddered thinking back to when Tory had innocently told him that Scott Timlin and his older brother sniffed gasoline. *No wonder parents move with the speed and intent of mother black bears when there's the slightest hint of trouble.*

As usual when assessing the dangers faced by young people, Dr. Erickson came to his mind. Ed remembered how thrilled he'd been when the personable Dr. Erickson was appointed as his thesis advisor. One afternoon when they were reviewing an early draft of Ed's paper, Dr. Erickson had confided to Ed that his oldest son had gotten in with the wrong crowd as a teenager and was now serving a life sentence for murder. Dr. Erickson said his wife's and his greatest solace came from the story of Adam and Eve, earth's first couple, who had made the worst decision in the history of humanity despite having been brought to life and watched over by God Himself.

The ducks quieted and the colours began to leach away, leaving only shades of light and dark. It wasn't long before Ed had a hard time making out individual trees across the meadow. Soon he could barely see the contours of nearby bushes. Moments after realizing that Bud was standing beside him, there was the sound of branches breaking on the other side of the meadow. Bud spoke softly.

— It's too much noise for a deer, so it's got to be a moose.

— Should we try the flashlight?

— No, it's too far.

It was quiet for a while, and then they heard the animal crashing through the underbrush farther off. After that, there were only the sounds the woods make at night.

* * * * *

Ed tried to remember the fast disappearing details of his dream. He had walked up to a rough looking man standing beside a car. Several big game animals were tied down on the car's hood, one of which, a buck deer, was still moving. The man, oblivious to the animal's suffering, was laughing sardonically about something unrelated. That was where the dream had abruptly ended.

It had been so hot in the cabin that Ed had lain outside his sleeping bag after returning from a nighttime water stop outside. From what he could make out from the patchy luminescence on the scratched face of his windup wristwatch it was almost 7:30. *I can't believe I slept so long.*

In the near dark, he wrestled his boots on, fumbled through his rucksack until he retrieved his well-used Bible, grabbed his flashlight off the table, and removed his coat from the pile by the door. Finally ready, he went outside.

Even using a flashlight he still managed to bang his knee on a block of wood on his way to the outhouse. There was more light by the time he got out and he didn't bother turning his flashlight on. Grateful for his coat in the heavy frost, he sat on the cold, split log bench in front of the cabin. He soon turned to look up at the open sky in the east and watched as the cupped sunlight began to spread.

Ed closed his eyes to pray. When he was finished, he watched a loon out on the glassy lake form a wake that was straighter than any draftsman could draw. *There is so much beauty to this place; even Stan's plane looks rejuvenated. … No one is more aware of the timelessness of his surroundings than Lawrence, that's for sure. Thankfully we're judged on our hearts and the words we have heard. Who knows, there may even be special promises for people living alone in the wilderness, like there are for the Jews.*

Out of nowhere, he suddenly became convicted about the sermon he'd preached about the construction of the new church. *Jonathan was right. It was dictation from a bully pulpit.* Instantly flushed warm with embarrassment, he prayed: *"God, please forgive me."* By which he mainly meant, *"Please make what I've done disappear as if it never happened."*

It was light enough now to read. He was about to open his Bible when he noticed a folded magazine sticking out from under the cabin wall. He leaned over and pulled out a weather-beaten entertainment weekly left behind by an earlier visitor. Feeling like a spy with the opportunity to walk unseen through the enemy's camp, *a chance to see what the people out there are doing,* he began flipping pages. Almost immediately he felt threatened for Tory and the girls. *They're headed into a world of godlessness. Of appearance, wants and ambition, as if each person is an end to themselves.*

Determined not to look too long at any of the alluring pictures, he flipped through the pages quickly until he got to the letters to the editor at the back of the magazine. The first letter asked readers to have "positive thoughts" about a gravely ill actress who, given the date on the magazine, might already be dead. Ed looked up and away without seeing. While the expression "positive thoughts" might be no more than a way to express care and concern, he'd always thought it signaled people's inner sense that there was a way to affect matters beyond their physical reach.

Ed had finished his morning Bible reading when Bud came outside carrying two cups of coffee in one hand and a can of evaporated milk in the other. Ed accepted one of the cups of coffee but declined the milk. He held the cup with both hands to warm his fingers.

— Something special about being outside in the woods in the early morning, isn't there?

— There sure is.

Ed took a sip of the black coffee whose intensity was bolstered by floating grounds. Bud looked down at the lake.

— I used to start thinking about hockey when the ponds started to freeze. Then the arena on the reserve got artificial ice and I started thinking about hockey at the start of September.

Ed had become distracted by his own thoughts and didn't respond.

— How about you? Did you ever play?

— Never organized hockey. My son does. But he doesn't have great hand to eye.

After sitting without talking for a bit, Ed added:

— I like everything about hockey except all the games on Sunday.

The two men got to talking about the day ahead.

— I was wondering, do you think Stan and I should stay and hunt around Chum Lake instead of flying on to Alces Lake? We could go back to that meadow, or wherever Lawrence tells us to go. I can't imagine the hunting is going to be that much better at Alces Lake.

— I asked Lawrence about that. He said he thinks you should go to Alces.

— Well, if that's what Lawrence says. I mean, if he doesn't know, who does? Did you talk to Stan about getting picked up?

— Ya. I'm supposed to be ready to leave at the end of the week.

Ed asked Bud about Lawrence making it through the upcoming winter.

— He's a resourceful old bugger, but there comes a time when you need help doing even simple things, like making a meal or getting out of bed. There's extra risks living up here too, like if you get injured, or forest fires. Lawrence said that one fire got all the way to the meadow we were hunting at.

— I didn't see any burnt trees.

— It's been too long for that. But you probably saw the husks of the old poplar trees lying among the spruce trees?

— Ya. I thought they looked like Roman columns.

— Those are fire poplars. They're the first trees to grow after a fire. They give shade to young conifers and die when they're no longer needed.

Ed walked down to the lakefront when Bud went back into the cabin. Standing at the water's edge, he looked across the lake at the tufts of white clouds. *They look like cotton balls.*

Stand and Ed were walking around the abandoned cabins when Bud came over and offered to make breakfast.

— Thanks, but no thanks. We should get going.

Bud helped them carry their gear down to the plane. The wind had come up and Ed asked Stan if he was worried about the chop on the lake. Stan said all that mattered was the waves couldn't be higher than the plane's floats, which they weren't. Bud untied the mooring lines when they were ready to leave.

The takeoff was surprisingly smooth, the lift from the oncoming wind making up for the resistance of the waves. With limited jostling, the plane rose to height. Again, the clouds were high enough to fly under. All distances are long in the north and, despite a flying speed of 120 knots, it seemed like they weren't making much headway. Listening to the engine's rhythmic thump, Ed began to think of the collection of moving metal parts like a reliable old friend.

The next thing Ed knew Stan was nudging him awake. He looked out the window and saw they were approaching a long, narrow lake. Stan must have been satisfied there was no debris on the lake because he didn't bother with a flyby and began his descent immediately. They were almost on the water when Ed spied a trapper's cabin in a small bay on the north side of the lake. Touching down, he thought about how hard water feels when you dive in at the wrong angle.

Stan spotted the young bull moose first. It was standing knee-deep in a grassy area a few hundred yards past the cabin. Instantly charged with adrenalin, Stan pointed excitedly to make sure Ed saw it too. Ed was enveloped by a like thrill when he realized what Stan was pointing at.

Making the snap decision that their best bet would be shooting across the narrow lake, Stan turned the plane towards the southern shore. Nearing the shoreline, he saw an open beach. He waited until they were in front of the beach before he turned the plane so it faced north and then lifted the pontoon rudders. The action of the wind and the waves pushed the plane backwards onto the sloped gravel. Stan waited for the floats to grind in a little before turning the engine off.

The men removed their earmuffs.

— That was slick.

— The wind has to be just right.

Ed looked to make sure the bull hadn't moved.

— I can't believe he's still there. Maybe he couldn't hear the plane because we were downwind. You'd think he'd have seen us though. If not, then moose have even worse eyesight than they say.

— The lake can't be more than 200 yards wide at this point. I was hoping you'd try a shot, since I don't trust my 30-30 beyond 150 yards, even without a wind.

— I've never shot anything from this far away. How much drop do you think I should allow for?

— I don't know. With your gun, maybe an inch or two.

Ed reached into the back seat to free up Charlie's tanned and beaded gun case. The .308's butt banged against the inside of the plane's front window as he was pulling it out of the case. He opened the door to give himself room to insert a clip of bullets.

Once the gun was loaded, with the safety on, he carefully stepped down onto the floatplane's pontoon but promptly lost his footing. Slipping into water that came nearly to his knees, he instinctively lifted the gun higher to protect it.

The two men stood together on the narrow beach staring across the lake at the moose. Despite the distance, and the covering noise of the wind, they spoke softly. Stan suggested that Ed use the blown-down spruce at the end of the beach as a gun rest. Ed nodded and took a dozen strides down the sloped beach before, going against

Stan's advice, he lifted his gun to shoot from a standing position. Although he knew the slightest movement would send the bullet wild on a circus shot, he couldn't wait. Positioning the gun's sights over the moose, he steadied himself before pulling the trigger. "Boom-Whomph-Crash!" The recoil rammed the gun into his shoulder and the raging sound, which was instantly layered over by fast-diminishing echoes from the nearby hills, rang in his ears. The moose continued to graze, unaffected.

Disappointed, but thrilled to get a second chance, Ed continued on to the spruce. He maneuvered around the tree's exposed roots to access a promising branch. The moose had shifted, and, after propping his gun on the branch, he had to wait for the moose to turn again and stand in profile. Taking a deep breath, he studiously pulled the gun tight against his shoulder and, moving slowly enough to notice the machined striations on the trigger, took a second shot.

The bull collapsed in two linked motions. Stan yelled.

— You got him! What a shot!

They ran back to the plane as giddy as children. Ed forced himself to go through the routine of taking the clip out of the gun and ejecting the bullet casing before stepping up onto the pontoon. He had made it safely to door before he remembered they had to push the plane into the water.

— Give me a minute.

Ed put the gun back into the leather case and then returned to the beach. Already wet, he volunteered to steady the plane in the water until Stan got the engine started.

When Stan finally signaled for him to get in they had been at Alces Lake for just shy of forty minutes.

Stan, who was wearing his earmuffs, shouted at Ed, who had forgotten to put his earmuffs on, as they taxied across the lake.

— I was sure you'd screwed it up by taking that first shot.

— Me too.

— I take back what I said about it being 200 yards. It must have been 250 yards. By the time we get to town, I won't argue if you say it was 300 yards!

Ed laughed like he'd heard everything Stan said, which he hadn't. Halfway to the other side, Stan suddenly pushed hard on Ed's shoulder.

— Look. He's up!

Ed didn't need Stan to tell him that the young bull was back on its feet because he'd seen it himself. Stan pulled the throttle out to slow the engine down before shouting again.

— You must have only nicked him. We can go back to the beach to take another shot. Or do you want to try shooting from the middle of the lake?

Ed shouted back.

— The beach.

Keeping his head turned, Ed kept his eyes on the bull until Stan beached the plane in the same spot he had previously, although this time the plane faced inland. Ed got his rifle out and, as if in parallax, climbed out of the cockpit, made his way down the pontoon and headed back to the spruce tree. Along the way he felt the marble-sized gravel grind underfoot, heard the water *schlussing* in his soaked boots, and noticed a partially crushed and rusted green tobacco can just off the beach he hadn't seen on his first trip to the spruce.

He finally remembered to put his clip of bullets in when he was setting up to take another shot. The bull was standing broadside when he was finally in position. After levering a shell into the chamber, he sighted in, allowing for a little less drop than the first time, and pulled the trigger. The bull went down again as the sound of the second shot rang around the lake.

— You got it!

— That's what we thought the last time.

They waited on the beach with muted excitement until they were reasonably confident the moose wouldn't get up a second time. Stan and Ed worked together to push the plane out into the lake, and turn it around. This time there was no whooping and hollering as they taxied across the lake.

Since the water was shallow and weedy in front of where the moose had gone down, Stan turned right, towards the cabin, looking for a place to land. There was a beach that worked around the first point.

Worried the moose might not be down for good, Stan and Ed took their guns with them as they hurriedly made their way through the trees on the point. They split up to cover as much ground as possible when they got to the meadow.

Ed saw the huge, lifeless bull lying in the tall grass first.

— I found it!

— Are you sure? Because I'm pretty sure I'm looking at it!

It didn't take them long to realize that Ed had shot two young Alaskan bulls that were now lying within twenty yards of each other. The second bull must have been hidden by the willows until after the first bull went down. Except for the nearly healed gash across the face of the bull closer to the lake, the moose could have been identical twins, right down to the bullet holes on their sides.

The moose should have been more scarred than they were given the many threats they would have faced during their short lives. During their first year, their mothers (or mother) would have been their main protectors from predators. From their second year onward they would have had to rely mainly on themselves, although moose sometimes group together in winter.

By three years of age the bulls would have participated in the rut. While quarter is usually given to retreating losers in these titanic, one-on-one challenges, the clash of palmate antlers during a fight often results in serious injuries—at least there are fewer bacteria to enter open wounds in the fall rutting season because of the colder temperatures.

If the two young bulls had lived on they would have had to eventually deal with the illnesses and diseases common to all mammals, as well as the ticks and other parasites unique to moose, most notably the meningeal worm that causes a degenerative condition known as "moose sickness." As it was, long before they had reached their primes the bulls had fallen prey to the most lethal threat of all, humans. Of far greater significance than their own deaths, the potential lineages of two members of the largest species of deer had been lost forever.

HOWLING WOLVES

THE HOWL OF A WOLF sounds a lot louder when you are alone in the wilderness.

* * * * *

Stan and Ed cut the jugular veins of the bulls before exerting the superhuman effort required to drag both carcasses a few feet to drier ground. After taking a moment to catch their breath they began to butcher the young bull closer to the plane.

— It's too bad we aren't near a tree so I could use my little block and tackle.

— I don't think we should be complaining about anything right now.

The process of lifting the heavy fur and cutting the thin, foamy fat between the skin and muscle was easy at first but became more difficult as the freed up skin began to accumulate. After skinning past the bull's spine, they started to butcher the exposed quarters. Midway through trimming the meat around where the bullet had entered Stan stopped to sharpen his hunting knife on a small grinding stone. Ed's short knife with a tightly wound leather handle held its edge longer.

They took their first trip with meat to the floatplane once they'd freed up the exposed quarters. The plane's cockpit seemed to have suddenly gotten a lot smaller and they had to fight to load the meat into the back seat.

— You forget how much meat there is on a moose.

— And we've got two to deal with. It's a bit like when the disciples got more fish than they could have ever hoped for.

— Right. Not that it's a real problem, but even if there was enough room for all the meat in the plane, which there isn't, the payload would be too big to take off.

They went back to the meadow without saying how they planned to get home.

After carefully removing the valuable strip loin and the tenderloin (which are up and away from contact injuries) they rolled the bull's carcass back onto the loosened skin to field dress the other side. Although they talked less and less as the day wore on, now and then one of them would say how blessed they were. It took two more trips to load the meat from the first moose into the plane—on their second trip to the plane they stopped long enough for Ed to put on dry socks. Although they left the moose's head and antlers behind, nothing was wasted, not even the liver or the heart.

They decided to have lunch before tackling the second moose. After washing up, Stan brought out their drying, day-old peanut butter and jam sandwiches that tasted far better than they should. Ed pierced the top of a large can of apple juice, and, after taking a swig, handed the apple juice to Stan.

— Any wolves or bears within ten miles will have smelled the blood by now.

— I know. I keep checking behind the bushes. It's funny that people can't smell blood like animals.

— But we sure can smell smoke.

— And gasoline. I've always wondered if fish have our sense of smell. If they do, their lives must be wrecked from all the gas and oil that that gets dumped in the water.

Still hungry, Ed sawed open a can of stew. He began to eat the stew cold after first offering the can to Stan.

— If the plane can only carry the two of us and the meat from one moose, then we're going to need to make two trips. You take the meat from the first moose and some from the second moose. I'll stay in the cabin overnight with the rest. You can come back and get me and what's left of the meat tomorrow.

They had settled on their only option.

It was well into the afternoon before they had finished dressing the second bull and couriering the meat by plane over to the trapper's cabin.

* * * * *

Ed watched from the narrow shore in front of the cabin as the over-burdened Cessna lifted off Alces Lake and disappeared behind the trees. He thought the plane had taken a long time to get airborne, but admitted to himself that he didn't know enough about planes to assess their flight characteristics; *and I'm too tired to think straight anyways.* He had the fleeting hope that Lorna hadn't left for Bull Moose Run yet and would be at home to help Stan carry the meat up from the dock. *Stan's not perfect but he's a real trier.* After saying a quick prayer for Stan's journey, he purposed his legs to take him back to up the cabin.

There were things to do before he could shut down, the first of which was to get some firewood. He limbed and chopped into lengths a fallen, dried-out spruce tree that was twice the size of a Christmas tree. The chopping further tightened the overworked muscles and tendons in his hands, and he had to clench and re-clench his fists several times in order to pick up the pieces of wood. Later, it was all he could do to light the propane lantern with unresponsive fingers.

Too tired to start a fire in the cabin's potbellied stove, he cut open a can of processed ham to eat unheated. He momentarily panicked when a stack of moose meat slid over behind him while he was standing, the half-finished can of ham in his hand, looking out the cabin's doorway,. *It's not that I mind being alone, it's that I might not be alone.* He knew bears were cautious, but he didn't know much about wolves. *Hopefully they're half as smart as crows and know to stay away from men and guns.*

The last thing Ed had to do was secure the cabin door. He pushed and pulled on the cabin's door when it was closed to check its strength. The top hinge was strong, but the bottom one was twisted and missing a screw. He worked the rudimentary door latch. *A man could easily knock the door down, to say nothing of a bear.* As a final precaution, he decided to pile his supplies, as well as a cupboard that had been knocked off the cabin's wall and now served as a woodbin, in front of the door. After making sure his .308 he'd put on the floor beside him was loaded and the safety off, he went to sleep fully dressed, his boots on, atop his sleeping bag.

* * * * *

He awoke to the sound of howling wolves. Grabbing his gun, he sat up. All was dark, although when he looked up through the cabin's little, broken window he could see stars in a small opening in the clouds. It took him a second to remember he was alone at Alces Lake and that the harsh smell was from the moose meat stacked up behind him. As his mind cleared, it didn't make sense to him that he could hear the wolves this well given how far the cabin was from the meadow.

He visualized members of the wolf pack fighting over innards, bones, tousled skin, and the two incongruously intact moose heads. *If there are only a few wolves, there should be more than enough wastage. But what if the pack is big like Lawrence said?*

As uncomfortable as he was sitting up on the floor without a back support, he didn't chance getting to his feet in case he missed hearing something.

The din finally diminished. *Maybe the wolves have had their fill. ... Or maybe they've run off, frightened by the smell of man.* He wondered if the wolves had run by the cabin on their way to the meadow. *Hopefully my animal qualities would have woken me up if they came near the cabin. Then again, people are a lot softer now.*

He had started to relax when he heard what might have been a falling branch. He strained to listen. Suddenly, he heard what he was sure was a low growl. Rifle in hand he leapt to his feet and began stomping on the cabin's floor in the dark, covering up whatever noises there were outside. After banging into the stove, he decided to light the lantern. Carefully putting his gun down, he groped with stiff fingers for the match box he'd left on the firewood in the woodbin. The first lit match led him to the lantern; and, after awkwardly pumping the gas container in the dark, he used a second match to light the mantle. Momentarily blinded, he turned away while his eyes adjusted to the gaudy illumination. All was quiet. He glanced at his wristwatch, which showed 3:16.

He did his best to keep listening while he rolled up his sleeping bag. After staying focused and hearing nothing for what seemed like a long time he knew he had to do something if he was going to stay awake. He was putting firewood in the stove when a snarl came from right outside the cabin door. Without thinking, he grabbed his gun and shot through the door.

Despite being partly stunned by the explosion, which was so much louder than he expected, he levered another shell in the gun, swept his supplies and the woodbin away from in front of the door, yanked the door open, and stepped outside into the dark night with his gun at his shoulder.

Even after stepping to the side to avoid blocking the light from the lantern inside the cabin, all he could see was the formless bank of trees beyond. Still not thinking straight, he took another shot, this time in the direction he thought a wolf might have run. He didn't go back inside until he realized he was shivering from the cold. He was met by the heavy smell of gun smoke. Only when he was bracing the door did he notice the intense ringing in his ears.

* * * * *

Ed's ears were still ringing when he woke up. His last thought from the night before was being determined to stay awake. *So much for that.* Collecting his energy, he stood up and stretched. Although all was quiet and he sensed he was alone, he took his gun with him when he went outside to the clotted pale dawn.

He used the firewood he'd chopped to start a bonfire. Once the fire was going good, he filled his dented campfire coffee pot with water from the plastic jug and carefully balanced it on the bent, blackened grill. The comfort of the fire soon melded with the early optimism of a new day; and he was smiling by the time he poured his first cup of black coffee.

He went looking for wolf prints after the morning mist dissipated. Although there weren't any near the cabin, there was a mass of prints on the path down to the lake.

After frying up some ham and eggs for breakfast, he had his devotions beside the fire. He read a Bible story about the time God imposed a confusion of languages on people living in a city who were sure they could do anything after they had started to build a tower.

THE BLUE CANOE

EVEN PEOPLE WHO REJECT THE claims of faith of others can't fully rid themselves of Karmic theories. Those with but a slender faith find themselves thinking back to when it seemed like they were helped by an unknown source; and those with more faith talk openly about when God protected them. Ironically, since faith is the belief in things unseen, the truly faithful are said to be able to watch as YHWH holds water back, moves mountains and even changes lives.

* * * * *

It was early on Saturday. The house was quiet and the streets empty when Ed left the parsonage on foot and headed downtown. Ralph Lidmore, the manager of the local grocery store who was one of Ed's long term projects, had called Ed midweek to suggest they meet for breakfast on the weekend. Ed had agreed right away, thinking that back of the call was the diagnosis of MS that Ralph's wife Edna had recently received. From Ed's experience, people who got news like started looking beyond the here and now.

The first person he encountered was an athletic looking young Native man headed in his direction across the bank's empty parking lot in the town's block-long business district. The young man noticed Ed looking at him and said, "Hey," before veering towards the pastor.
— Good morning.

Ed's confidence surprised the young man.

When they got near to each other, Ed realized how tall the young man was.

— So, where are you off to this early?

The young man, whose mind was clouded by something, hesitated before answering.

— A friend's house.

— Are you from around here?

— Philips Lake.

— I've been up there a couple of times. It's a beautiful spot.

* * * * *

Ed thought about the difficulty of growing up Native in a white man's world as he waited for Ralph at the little cafe. Closing his eyes he said a silent prayer: *"Please, God, your image within us is covered over so quickly. Be with that young man today. Help him to find some place safe to stay. Put the right person in his way to help him find you. I pray this in Jesus' name, amen."*

On his way home, Ed picked through what Ralph had said over breakfast, hoping to identify a call for help that he'd missed. However, as far as he could figure, it had been the same old, jokey Ralph throughout. The couple of times Edna's diagnosis had come up the store manager had shown a brave face, referring to his wife's great attitude. *Ralph let his guard down a little when he talked about my general optimism; but I dropped the ball, given Edna's condition:*

— I can only think it's the way I see the world, Ralph. That God is always there, alongside me. That's what I actually believe. Even when things go bad, it's not long before it dawns on me that I've probably been saved from something far worse. You can't believe how empowering it is to believe that no matter what happens the Creator of the Universe has the power to turn it to good, although it might be a different good than what you were hoping for.

Ralph had changed the subject, and they'd rounded out the morning talking about the upcoming federal election.

Ed took the path behind old man Smythe's property on his way home. He'd walked the path so many times he barely noticed the faltering fence and the disarray of junked vehicles beyond that had been accumulated by an angry, bitter man who lived alone. Ed was still thinking about his coffee with Ralph when he climbed over the fallen tree lying across the path: *Ralph's like most, he thinks he knows as much or more than anyone and that's the end of it.*

* * * * *

Another Saturday. Although Ed had been looking forward to the canoe trip over to St. Timothy's Church all week, he hadn't gotten enough sleep the night before and woke up fearful his day was going to prove a disappointment. As life would have it, Frank and Judy Wells had stopped by unannounced the previous evening and had stayed too long. Ed wouldn't have minded if the visit had been all friendship and frivolity, but that hadn't been the case.

Ed's mood worsened when he saw the bushes outside the kitchen window being pushed about by a wind that was strong enough to turn the leaves inside out. With so much riding on the day he tried to encourage himself: *Just because things don't go as planned that doesn't mean you give up.* The first thing he had to do was circle around and pick up Jay Graham's paddle. He'd planned to pick the paddle up earlier in the week, but had forgotten about it until he was putting the roof racks on the car Friday evening. Thankfully, Jay was home when he'd phoned over and had offered to leave the paddle outside by the garage door.

With the canoe loaded, he'd had to park the car overnight in the driveway. He scraped the frost off the front window and, after turning the defogger to high, set off. Even with the ice gone it was a while before the window was fully defogged and he had a clear view of the road ahead.

He was glad to see that none of the town's alcoholics had tried to sleep it off on the grass around the tourist information booth at the front of the recently restored fort. According to Staff Sargent Beedie's column in *The Leader*, there had been over 2,500 falling-down drunk arrests in town during the previous twelve months. It was a number that didn't make sense in a town as small as Bull Moose Run. Although Ed was focused on changing individual hearts, the column had gotten him thinking about broader social ills: *booze, drugs, and dysfunctional families. And for the Natives a community-wide loss of self-respect. ... If I didn't know better I'd say it was hopeless.*

The paddle was propped up against the wall beside the Grahams' garage door as promised and Ed was soon on the return trip through town. Driving past *The Leader's* faded yellow offices, he thought about Jody Duke's poem in the Saturday edition of the paper a few weeks earlier. He still wasn't sure which had been the bigger shock, seeing a poem in the editorial section of the paper or finding out the poem had been written by one of the Dukes. Sarah had told him that Jody was an avid reader, but he had no idea she was a writer, let alone a poet. While he knew Sam and Jody well enough to stop and talk when their paths crossed, he'd only seen the couple once since the gathering after Charlie's death.

Titled "Into The River", the free verse poem described the mercury poisoning of fish in the Lonzi River. The first section of the poem described the musings of the pulp mill's chairman:

"... I don't claim to know what it's all about. No one does.
My hope comes from effort, and chance I guess.
You do your best when you make choices.
I'm here for me, well, and my family.
We live in a nice house, and have seen the world.
All our kids went to university ..."

The poem's second section contained an excerpt from the would-be minutes of a meeting where the pulp mill managers weighed the options of letting the effluent from the pulp mill's paper-bleaching process continue to build up, or flushing it down the river. One of the managers gave voice to the joint decision, "There really is only one choice, isn't there?"

In the poem's third section, Jody assumed a clinical distance when describing the effects of poisoning on the band members in the Native village downstream from the mill: the initial onset of numbness leading to ataxia and then permanent paralysis. Ed had skipped the more horrific parts when he re-read the poem.

* * * * *

Ed turned in at the entrance to the public beach. The empty gravel parking lot was dotted with iced over puddles. Not many months earlier the parking lot had been jammed with cars and trucks, and the swimming area filled with people splashing about like they were at the South Seas.

After turning the car's engine off, he studied the choppy, gray lake that now looked so threatening. *Hopefully I don't tip the canoe over like I did at Bible camp.*

Opening the car door, he spotted a ripped beer bottle case containing several empties under a bare bush at the front of the car. Walking over to pick up the case he was confronted by streams in the wind of the sharp smell of beer. *Someone else's late night good times are taking a run at my early morning peace and quiet.* He found two broken bottles beside the case, one with beer still in it. After dumping the beer out, he put the larger pieces of glass in the case along with the empties and carried the lot over to the garbage barrel near the entrance. He stood the empties up beside the barrel so they could be returned.

Ed regretted bringing his light cotton gloves rather than the tanned, leather ones. *Oh well.* After removing the roof-rack tie-downs, he pulled on the upside down canoe until it was perched at the edge of the car's roof. Intending to carry the canoe above his head to the picnic area, he steeled himself before lifting it off the rack in a single motion. He had it almost balanced overhead when he stumbled on loose gravel. All he could think of as he fell was ensuring the canoe landed right side up; and, not bothering to protect himself, most of his weight was on his outstretched left hand when it hit the frozen ground.

Pain from his wrist shot through him. Jumping to his feet, he stripped off his torn left glove and watched the abrasions begin to bleed. He knew, though, that the real pain was from his wrist. Needing to do something, he walked down to the lake and carefully washed his hand in the icy water, holding his wrist under the water for as long as he could. He repeated the process several times before gingerly putting his gloves back on and going back to the parking lot. Relying on his right hand as much as possible, he lifted the canoe up to his waist and held it tight to his side before shuffling over to the picnic area. After catching his breath he dragged the canoe down to the lakefront.

He stood for a minute looking at the darkening skin on his wrist before going back to the car to get his rucksack and the paddle. The rucksack held his lunch, a pad of paper and two pens, as well as the Bible he'd bought to replace the one that he'd accidently left behind at Alces Lake. He was locking the car doors when he remembered the bulky old red lifejacket in the trunk. He'd begun to think of the lifejacket as his own since it was unclaimed a year and a half after the father and son fishing retreat.

St. Timothy's Church was a mile or so across the bay. Ed's plan was to combine a fitness workout with sermon preparation time by paddling across the bay and spending the afternoon in the calm ... *dare I say holiness* ... of the environs of the abandoned church. Although St. Timothy's hadn't been in regular use for decades, it continued to be maintained by the Roman Catholic Church and still hosted special events, including its own centennial anniversary the previous summer. To add to the pomp and circumstance of that occasion, the invited guests, including the local Member of Parliament, a taciturn former businessman who had been appointed Minister of Indian Affairs by dint of his longstanding party loyalty and the northern location of his riding, had set off in a three-boat flotilla from the same public beach.

According to fading oral history, a stubborn, old bishop had made the decision to build St. Timothy's at its inaccessible location against the opposition of his parishioners. Less than twenty years after it was built, with the bishop long since deceased and attendance at the church down to a few loyal families, the diocese had funded the construction of a new, larger church, in town. Despite having been largely abandoned, Ed thought St. Timothy, plainly visible as it was out at the end of Narrow Point, continued to have the important job of reminding Bull Moose Run's citizens that nothing they did was done in secret.

Ed trolled the canoe and its contents down the lake to the diving raft that had been pulled partway out of the water. In order to launch on the leeward side, he had to drag the canoe out of the water and across the sand in front of the raft. When he got the canoe back in the water he considered his options. Finally making his mind up, he crouched as low as he could and negotiated his way down the raft's sloped, icy boards, holding onto the canoe with his right hand. When he got to where the water was deep enough he grabbed the far side of the canoe to climb in. However, he had to let go because of the pain from having used his left hand to brace himself.

After letting the pain subside and repositioning himself, he made a second, successful attempt and slumped into the canoe. He shifted around in the canoe until his knees were on the lifejacket, all the while gingerly holding onto the raft with his left hand. When he was finally ready he picked up the paddle with his good right hand, and, waiting until he was between waves, carefully pushed off. In a handful of J strokes he was beyond the swimming area.

* * * * *

This was Ed's first chance to try out the fibreglass canoe he'd been given by Robbie Swidick. The first time the men had met was when Ed had stopped to see who was building the new house on Gray Road. Not wanting to risk getting stuck on the freshly cut driveway in to the house, he'd parked out on the road and walked in. In the middle of a cleared area, he'd found a clean-cut man about his own age pulling plywood forms off a recently poured foundation. It turned out that Robbie, an electrician by trade, had moved to town to work on the new school and had purchased the five-acre parcel to build a house for his family. Ed had made sure to invite Robbie and his family to church before the visit ended.

Although Robbie and his family never made it to a service, the two men remained friendly and often chatted when they ran into each other in town, usually at the town's lone building supply store. A little over a year ago, Robbie, clearly distraught, had phoned Ed at home at suppertime to ask if he could come over.

When Robbie arrived, Ed led the way out to the privacy of the parsonage's backyard. They weren't yet at the fence overlooking the greenbelt when Robbie blurted out that he had just found out that his fourteen-year-old son, Ford, had been sexually assaulted by a man who was boarding at their house. Robbie angrily explained the boarder, who had come north to work in the mill, had been introduced by a shirttail relative. After enquiring about Ford, Ed asked Robbie if he'd reported the assault to the police. Robbie said he hadn't, and that the boarder had left town before Robbie could confront him.

— I've never wanted to kill anyone before, but now it's all I can think about.

Seeing tears in the hardworking electrician's eyes, Ed reached over to put his hand on Robbie's shoulder as he listened.

— Julie and I feel helpless. We don't know what to do.

Ed suggested it might be helpful for Ford to talk to someone unconnected with the situation. Robbie agreed that had to be better than doing nothing.

After the Sunday morning service the next day, Ed drove to the Swidicks' house to visit the youth. Although his initial conversation with Ford was entirely one-way, a rapport of sorts was established over the course of several visits. What worked most in Ed's favour was that Ford had previously attended Friday Fun Night at the church and trusted the prematurely gray minister. For some reason Ed had never made the connection between Ford and his father.

Ed's weekly visits to see Ford came to an end before school started up in the fall. Halfway through September, on a day Ed had stayed late in his office, Robbie backed his pickup truck down the parsonage driveway and unloaded a brand new blue canoe onto the parsonage lawn. When Anne came outside to see what was going on, Robbie said the canoe was a gift for Ed.

* * * * *

Put the paddle in the water. Pull the paddle through the water. Lift the paddle. Flex his bad wrist and shift his knees. Then, do it all over again. Ed had known something was up when Frank and Judy showed up without phoning ahead. The Wells had seemed relaxed enough when they arrived, but Frank had become serious the moment Anne went to get a board game from the hall closet.

— If I were to give you any feedback on your preaching, it's that you need to be more upbeat.

Ed had fought to maintain his smile.

— Is there something I've said recently that struck you as negative?

— You keep talking about the end-times, like the world is falling apart and there's nothing we can do about it. I sometimes wonder if you want us to sit and wait for the next big flood. You know, doomsayers have been around a long time. They weren't helpful before and they're not helpful now. First it was fire from the sky and then the plague. In my lifetime it's been the bomb, which, by the way, still hasn't been dropped; pollution; which we seem to be dealing with; and overpopulation—have you ever driven through some of the states in the US? They need more not fewer people, and we've got even more room here in Canada.

Sure heaven is out there somewhere, but I don't think we're supposed to spend our lives moping about how bad things are and waiting for it all to come to an end. Give humanity some credit. Show a little trust. And quit talking about the U.N. like it's a nefarious world government. Course a world government wouldn't be a bad option for some things at least.

Frank had backed off as soon as Anne returned to the dining room.

Although Frank had been part of the original group from the church that had complained about Ed to the district office, the principal was now one of Ed's main supporters. Not that the two men saw things exactly the same. Frank's big cause was encouraging the young to continue on with their education; whereas Ed was intent on leading people to make commitments of faith.

As with all serious-minded people, from time to time Frank and Ed engaged in by and large civil debates about the things they saw differently. A few days after Mariner 9 had begun its orbit of Mars the two of them had gone back and forth over the benefits and drawbacks of scientific advances. As he paddled, Ed tried to remember if he'd said something during that exchange that might have infuriated Frank. *I was fairly worked up when I brought up the history of eugenics … but Frank seemed to have answers for most of what I said.*

One thing Frank is right about is that people will only listen to bad news for so long before they turn you off. Even news as important as the world is spiraling down (before being reclaimed by God, mind you). No wonder the prophets didn't have many friends. … Seriously, how many end-times sermons did I preach in the last year? There was just the one. … Although I guess my series on the writings of Apostle John would count. … But what am I supposed to do, skip the passages in the Bible about the coming apocalypse and the return of the Son of Man? … Humankind has had an incredible run; but like Joe said about the old pine tree at the back of the church property, "Nothing lasts forever." … Judgment isn't going to be unfair. It's not like there is a privileged group who are good enough to make it through; it's almost the exact opposite: those who know they're not good but have repented are going to be blessed. … How did that minister out of New York put it, if there wasn't judgment then it wouldn't matter how anyone lived. … Granted, I should talk more about God's love. … The problem, though, is as soon as you tell people how much they're loved they begin to think they don't have to change. ... We really are such a combination of good and bad. Take Richard ... or me ... or any of the Bible heroes.

Prophets were on Ed's mind. A few weeks earlier, while reading in Genesis, it had struck him in a new way that attending church wasn't one of the Ten Commandments. He'd told Anne about his revelation over supper, but she hadn't seemed impressed.

When he'd arrived at his study the following morning he'd opened the door to the persistent ringing of the telephone. Picking up the handset, he'd heard the sweet voice of elderly Mrs. Aver who began by apologizing for calling so early. She'd proceeded to ask Ed if he might be able to find the time to fit in a visit with her husband, James. This was an unexpected request since Ed had only spoken with Mr. Aver a few times—not long after the Makis had arrived in town, Mrs. Aver had explained to Ed that Mr. Aver chose not to attend church and that for the sake of their marriage she accepted his decision.

Mrs. Aver had continued on by saying James, a retired school librarian, had recently learned that his cancer was spreading far faster than originally expected and he was having trouble sleeping. She then said she was hopeful a visit from the pastor might help. Ed replied that he'd be happy to come by and only needed to know when. Mrs. Aver had hesitantly asked if he had any time that afternoon.

Whatever notions Ed had about the visit washed away the moment he got to the Avers' house and saw Mr. Aver lying on the couch with the thin look of death. Mrs. Aver only stayed with the men a minute or two before leaving for an extended period of time under the pretext of getting coffee and a snack. Mr. Aver turned serious as soon as his wife was gone and began to talk openly, volunteering that while he believed in a higher power and had always prayed he had been put off churches by the people who attended them. When Ed pressed him, Mr. Aver referred to a holier-than-thou couple who'd turned their backs on him after a business investment they'd introduced to him went bad.

— Once I figured out that there was nothing special about people who went to church, I decided to keep Sundays to myself.

As Ed listened to Mr. Aver, he got back on the mental go-around about how, on the one hand, holding a church responsible for the conduct of its members was like blaming hospitals for the sick and injured in its care; and, on the other hand, how those who attended church were its very face.

*   *   *   *   *

Ed had received an important lesson about churches when he'd been assigned as a theology student to preach at a tiny congregation in a poor part of the city. Not far into his very first sermon a couple in the front row had noisily walked out, complaining what a waste of time church had been. Try as Ed might, he hadn't been able to recover his equilibrium and he'd cut his sermon short, convinced that he would never be a public speaker.

The church's soon-to-retire minister who'd witnessed the goings on from a back pew had sat with Ed after the service to encourage him. The minister had begun by telling Ed about the time a drunk had wandered into the sanctuary while he was preaching and had stood in front of the pulpit accusing him of being the "Holy Ghost".

— He was so adamant I began to wonder if God was trying to tell me something.

Ed's low spirits notwithstanding, he'd found himself laughing along.

When the old minister finished telling this and one other self-deprecating story, he'd taken Ed out to a garden off to the side of the church's parking lot where he'd pointed out several deadly nightshades growing among the other plants.

— I don't think anyone else knows what kind of plants those are. I like them being there because they remind me that just as there are poisonous plants in the church's garden there are poisonous people inside the church. There were black widow spiders in the foundation of one of my early churches that served a similar purpose.

Ed couldn't count the times he'd thought back on what the old minister had to say; including this past summer when a visiting missionary had related to him that Protestant church officials in Kenya had been caught funneling money back to England to help ex-pats avoid the capital controls that had been instituted by the newly independent country.

*   *   *   *   *

Ed had wanted so badly to give dying Mr. Aver a message of hope, but, not knowing what to say he'd sat silent, his emotion building. It was then he remembered his epiphany about the Ten Commandments.

— Mr. Aver, whatever your sins are, not attending church isn't one of them. Church attendance isn't even one of the Ten Commandments. Your wife might have missed your companionship, but I know she was at peace with your decision. Maybe the only thing that's been lost was some of the younger people in church missed out on the chance to learn from you.

It was exactly what Mr. Aver needed to hear. When Ed reported on his visit to Anne she'd said matter-of-factly that he was a prophet.

* * * * *

Pull the paddle through the water, trying to keep his bad wrist stiff. Ed acknowledged to himself that Frank was right about it being impossible to judge people because of their unique building blocks and backgrounds. *Judgment is negative in both directions. When you judge someone you can't love them; and if someone knows they're being judged it's impossible for them to feel love.* He was trying to think of a way to fit these thoughts into his sermon when it hit him that his preparations wouldn't matter if the Holy Spirit took over on Sunday. *When that happens, and it seems to be happening more and more often, then I'm just along for the ride.*

A few minutes later he caught himself thinking about his recent salary increase: *isn't that just like mammon, vying for my attention out here in the middle of the lake.* He would never have gotten such a large raise if it hadn't been for Dr. Tait. The good doctor had only been in town for a year when he'd been voted onto the church board because of his standing in the community. To give the doctor his due, he'd sat and listened during the first few board meetings. However, according to Tom, Dr. Tait had taken the lead during the in-camera discussion about Ed's salary. When Ed was welcomed back to the meeting the chairman, Jim Swenson informed him that he would be getting a $300 a month raise retroactive to September. It was such a huge increase that Ed hadn't been able to think straight for the rest of the evening; and it was the first thing he told Anne when he got home.

— Jim told me after the meeting that, going forward, my salary is going to be tied to what school teachers make, because of our similar levels of education.

As usual, Anne had her own take.

— I don't think they should treat ministerial positions like other jobs. Part of being a minister is trusting in God. The more you have the less you need to trust.

Wisely, he'd suppressed the rejoinder that Abraham, the father of many, had so much wealth that he didn't even notice when he gave something away.

Ed was close enough to the rocky outcrop at the end of Narrow Point to make out the branches on the hardy, undersized trees. *Those trees have to be super tough to survive those conditions.* The rocky beachfront in front of the trees, which ran the length of the point, reminded him of lakefronts in Guysborough County, Nova Scotia where he'd grown up. He thought about how Anne and he had only been back to Nova Scotia once since Tory was born. *Maybe next summer.*

Except for some stiffening in his knees, he was feeling as good or better than when he'd started. He was almost at shore when he abruptly decided to turn left, bypassing the point, and paddle out to Poplar Island, which was another mile or so towards the middle of the lake. Analyzing his impromptu decision, he wasn't sure if he was motivated by the idea of having an even bigger adventure or if he just didn't want to get down to work.

He considered going back when he rounded Narrow Point and saw how big the waves were on the open lake. But like most men, he'd only gotten as far as he had because of constant striving, and he kept going. To maintain his speed, he had to dig his paddle deeper into the water, making sure to keep his left wrist stiff. He thought about putting on the life jacket that was pillowing his knees but was worried about what might happen if he stopped paddling.

He looked up now and again to see how close he was getting to the island. Sometimes he thought he was making good progress, other times not. He finally admitted to himself that paddling out to Poplar Island hadn't been his best idea. *What if I get stranded out there? The last thing I want to do is cause Anne to worry.* With that, he decided to turn back, no damage done. He lifted the paddle out of the water and plunged it deep into the water to act as a fulcrum. A searing jolt of pain from his wrist froze him, and before he could carry on a wave broadsided the canoe, flipping it over.

Ed was shocked by how cold the lake was. His more immediate problem, though, was water had gotten up his nose. By the time he had coughed the water out, the flared, blue bottom of the canoe was several yards away in the moving furrows. He continued to tread water while he fought to take off the soaked sweater that was tangling him up. The canoe was out of sight by the time he had the sweater off. He began to swim towards the outline of Bishop Mountain presiding over the north side of the lake. It wasn't long before he noticed he was losing feeling in his hands and feet.

The shoreline groaned.

* * * * *

Anne had opened the oven door and was about to put a pumpkin pie in when she heard a car pull into the driveway. Sensing something was wrong, she put the pie down on the counter by the phone and, leaving the oven door open, went to the front door. Sergeant Davies and a lady R.C.M.P. officer who Anne hadn't seen before were getting out of a police cruiser. Anne waited for them to come up the walkway.

— Mrs. Maki, your car is down at the beach. Does your family own a blue canoe?

* * * * *

There was standing room only at the funeral service held in the high school auditorium. Somehow Anne made it through the eulogy without crying, her quiet acceptance of Ed's death a further testimony to her faith. When she was finished, Tom, who led the service, invited Grace, the church's long retired pianist, to the front to play Ed's favourite hymn. Although Grace's touch was no longer certain, she rallied whenever she got to the ascending melody in the chorus. By the end of the song the church members mixed in with the crowd were audibly singing along.

Jonathan Morrey seconded the motion at the board meeting to continue paying Ed's salary until summer.

* * * * *

Anne went to pack up Ed's study on an afternoon when there weren't any scheduled activities at the church. It took her several tries before she found the right key on her late husband's overburdened keychain. The first thing she saw when she entered the room was Ed's tufted grey sweater splayed across the back of the old, rolling office chair. Overwhelmed by emotion, she had to lean against the doorway to regain her composure. When she was able, she walked across the room and sat down at the heavy wooden desk. Reaching for the desk lamp switch, she remembered Ed complaining about the lighting in his study.

Taped to the wall in front of the manual typewriter were both typed and handwritten flash cards, some with Bible verses and the rest with famous or inspiring quotations. There was a partly typed sheet in the typewriter. Anne lifted the typewriter's paper arm and held the curled sheet up so she could see it better. She imagined hearing Ed's voice as she read.

— Five hundred years ago, Martin Luther said that the most important things to consider as a congregation are the story of Jesus, the meaning of grace and the Ten Commandments. The reasons for Mr. Luther's choices are obvious. You need to believe in Jesus to be accepted by God; you need to learn about grace to begin to understand how much God loves you; and the Ten Commandments are foundational for day to day living.

Today, I'd like to talk about grace. One of the best examples of grace I know is in the novel, *Les Miserables*. For those of you who haven't read the novel or don't remember the plot, a policeman named Javert relentlessly pursues a man called Jean Valjean who breached his parole decades earlier but has gone on to become a kindhearted, leading citizen. The policeman's pursuit doesn't make sense, especially since Jean Valjean's original crime was the theft of a loaf of bread to feed his sister's children.

The transformation of Jean Valjean from a criminal into gentleman begins when he is shown grace by a caring old priest. Shortly after being released from prison, Jean Valjean steals silverware from a church but is immediately caught. However, when the arresting officer brings Jean Valjean back to the church to corroborate the theft, the old priest assures the officer he gave the silverware to the former convict as a gift.

I'm not sure if it holds up theologically, but I have often thought the do's and don'ts of the first half of the Bible are like Javert, always chasing us down; and the divine grace available through Jesus described in the second half of the Bible is like the life-changing forgiveness and generosity of the old priest.

That's where Ed had stopped typing.

* * * * *

Although Anne originally planned to reinstate her registration as a nurse and finish raising her children in Bull Moose Run, she eventually decided to move the family to Halifax, Nova Scotia to be near to Ed's two brothers and their families. Both of Ed's brothers and their wives had made the long trip west to attend his funeral; and Anne had formed a special bond with the older brother, Jens and his wife, Doris who'd stayed on for a week after the funeral to help out.

The last scheduled event before the family's move was Tory's graduation in June. A week prior to the ceremony, the town's Assistant Forest Ranger, Darcy Dintsche—Anne told Tory that Mr. Dintsche used to attend their church—offered Tory a summer job with the Forest Service's fire suppression crew. The mill Tory had been working at on weekends had been down since Christmas because of low lumber prices, and he accepted the offer right away.

Anne was devastated when Tory proudly told her he'd be staying in town for two extra months to work for the Forest Service. Seeing the pain on his mother's face, Tory assured her that he would join the rest of the family in the end of summer.

Almost half the church showed up to help Anne finish packing and load the rented moving truck Mark Ellison had volunteered to drive to Winnipeg where Jens Maki was taking over. When the moving truck was nearly loaded, Tory drove his younger sisters in his beaten up Beetle to the local burger joint for one last ice cream. The sisters, thrilled to be with their big brother, were excitedly talking in side by side blue streaks when Tory brought them back to the parsonage.

Anne felt the young man-strength in her son's shoulders when she hugged him goodbye.

*　*　*　*　*

It was a cold, wet summer, and the fire suppression crew that Tory was on spent most of its time helping out with the pine beetle eradication program. Once a beetle site was identified, the crew was sent out to cut down the trees; skin off enough bark to obtain bug samples; and then either cut and stack the wood to be burnt, or, if the area around the site was wet enough, burn the trees right away using gasoline to start the fire.

Tory was slotted in as the crew's chainsaw operator. He got a thrill from starting up the powerful and noisy saw, hearing the engine's "Crack-Pop-Bang", turning the force of the saw on unaware trees in a shower of fizzing sawdust, and watching the trees crash to the ground. He could never quite believe how quickly one little gas-powered saw could dramatically change a site that had looked the same for so long.

Despite the fire suppression crew's efforts the number of beetle sites doubled every few weeks during the summer. One day when Tory was travelling to a new site with Assistant Forest Ranger Dintsche, he asked if there was anything else that could be done.

— You're right, what we're doing is largely ineffective, since most of the beetles have flown off by the time we cut the trees down. But you have to remember the pine beetle problem is brand new. Until we know more, the best we can do is plot the sites and send reports to the scientists at the provincial office. A special lab has even been set up to analyze the bug samples in case there's something about the bug that has changed.

We had hoped the problem would go away on its own, but it doesn't look like that's going to happen.

PART TWO

·

THE BIG CITY

HUNTER

THOSE LIVING IN THE WEST are, as a group, better off financially and have more personal freedoms than anyone else in history. Governments provide basic education, health care and a minimum income, and most people get to choose where they live. Cell phones have a video phone option; cars with enough power to push back a line of Roman chariots can be purchased on credit; and trips abroad are available online, apparently soon even into space.

* * * * *

Torrance awoke from an enjoyable dream that like most dreams didn't have a proper beginning or ending. He was much younger in his dream, in his 20's, and he had just met a young woman about his age. It was love at first sight, and, if possible, more than love. His overriding sense during the dream was that his life going forward had been set, and it was going to be the best of all possible lives. When he told the young woman how meeting her had made him feel, she replied in her innocent yet knowing way that she felt the same way. They had stood talking effortlessly in her family's store that sold garden tools and equipment. After a while she took him to meet her father and her brother who were working in the shop behind the store. Torrance liked both men immediately.

* * * * *

A southpaw with a solid build and an friendly face, Torrance had moved to the big city thirty years earlier, and he had been happy enough living there ever since. He'd seen a fair sample of what life served up, both bad and good, and he could tell an entertaining story. The tension between his natural trust and small-town reserve, added to his overall likability. Whenever he found himself unsettled he did what was necessary to change his situation or his mind set.

Torrance's promotion to manager of sales for Hothouse Produce Ltd. hadn't surprised anyone. For Torrance, it was just one more piece of life's puzzle, which included adding to his RRSP's every year and buying a detached home.

Towards the end of summer, Martin Smith, Hothouse Produce's logistics manager, stopped by Torrance's office to ask him if he wanted to go moose hunting. Although Torrance's first thought was *"not on your life,"* he made sure to show interest. Torrance considered Martin a good guy, not least of which because he was one of the few Hothouse Produce managers not taking antidepressants. The two men had even spent some time together with their spouses outside of work. *But, hunting?* The last thing Torrance wanted to do was go into the woods to kill a defenseless animal. It wasn't that he was against hunting per se, or didn't eat meat like a lot of people he knew, it was just that there were only so many wild animals left. As far as he was concerned, hunting in whatever tracts of forest remained, often with ATV's no less, was no more sporting than shooting penned up animals in a zoo.

Growing up in a small northern town, Torrance had snared rabbits when he was in grade school and had graduated to shooting grouse and ducks. When he was fourteen his father had taken him on his first deer hunt. They'd set out in the family's old car down a logging road with ruts so deep only the most determined pickup drivers would have kept going. In spite of regularly scraping the undercarriage, his father had kept going until they reached the roughed up surface of the first landing in a cut block. They had at that point split up to walk both sides of the valley beyond. Just shy of an hour later, Torrance had spotted a three-point buck standing motionless among the trees. Thrilled to the point of not breathing, he'd slowly lifted his rifle, sighted in, and pulled the trigger. He'd been charged up with excitement the moment the buck fell forward; and he'd barely noticed being scratched by the unforgiving underbrush as he raced to claim his kill.

However, his excitement was riven with despair the moment he'd reached the lifeless deer and looked down at its unmoving eyes, lolled tongue, awkwardly tilted neck, and tawny, still warm skin, ripped open and bleeding from a bullet hole.

As Martin droned on about his proposal, Torrance, behind a mask of attentiveness, thought about how the hunting era was nearly over: killing wild animals didn't used to matter, but it did now. Although humans had once needed to hunt and fish to survive—Torrance had been fascinated to learn in a biology class that human teeth, stomach cells and intestinal tracts were suited to digesting both meat and plants—it was becoming clear, that humanity needed to focus on saving a few species for the next generation.

Torrance re-engaged in time to hear Martin say that he'd gone hunting every fall since his friend, Conrad, who worked as a salesman at a nearby heavy-duty equipment dealership, had invited him along on a hunting trip.

— This year we put a $2,500 nonrefundable deposit on a floatplane in January. The problem is Conrad just found out that he is supposed to be in Japan on business the same week the plane is booked.

In an effort to be transparent, Martin admitted that it had been several years since Conrad and he had gotten a moose, although they'd shot a deer two years earlier.

— But all that means is we're due. And anyway, getting a moose is a bonus. The best part is being in the woods with no one else around.

According to Martin, they would be hunting in one of the few places left where hunters didn't have to enter a Limited Entry Hunting draw. Martin went on to talk about how beautiful and untouched the area was.

— ... and that was the first time we saw the Northern Lights.

Martin was nearly finished when he said the floatplane was based in a town called Bull Moose Run, which was a couple of hours north of Centre City.

What Martin didn't know was that Torrance had grown up in Bull Moose Run. Hearing the town's name was like hearing his own name on the radio. Suddenly, the invitation wasn't about hunting, it was about going home.

Torrance had become increasingly aware of the importance of his early years. There was the basic information everyone learns early on, like stoves are hot, lemon pie is delicious, and some people are good and others are not. But that was only the start. He knew that whenever he was stirred by enchantment, love, anger, or fear, or was worried, happy (or sad), or in the undertow of guilt or jealousy, what he felt was, at least in part, a remembered emotion from his youth; that his mind routed through the past whenever he smelled mildewed clothes, fragrant flowers, thawing loam, and two-stroke engine exhaust; and that his fundamental appreciations of colour, shape, and style had been set long ago—the intensity of the excitement he felt whenever he spotted an early model Mustang continued to surprise him.

Torrance thought about the Pacific salmon run whenever he considered the importance of birthplace. After several years in the ocean, all five species of west coast salmon are compelled by something within to return and reproduce in the same non-descript rivers where they broke out of their eggs to become alevin. Mature salmon have to elude, whales, seals and sea lions, and make their way past fishnets and moneyed anglers in coastal waters, before they begin the freshwater portion of a journey that, in some cases, takes them hundreds of kilometers through water that is by turn, slow and deep, fast-moving and shallow, clear, murky, filled with debris, and often overheated. For the entire distance of their inland route they face the threat of legal and illegal fishermen, as well as Native Canadians exercising their food fishery rights. Those fish that manage to make it to their destination draw their last, gill-strained breaths within hours of spawning.

Recently, Torrance had read a magazine article that described how certain lake eels in eastern Canada, in the reverse of salmon, leave their fresh water homes and swim back to the sea to reproduce and die; and he had recorded a TV documentary about horseshoe crabs in aquariums who will only mate when sand from the very beaches where they themselves were hatched is placed in their aquariums.

Martin ended his sales pitch by saying he would appreciate if Torrance could get back to him by the weekend. With that, he headed down the hall.

* * * * *

The demands of the workplace took over as soon as Martin was gone. Torrance worked in Hothouse Produce's head office near the

Canada-United States border. The formerly family run business had in two short decades gone from a single greenhouse supplying produce to local grocery stores, to a midsized business with twenty-seven corporate greenhouses and mushroom barns with a sizable portfolio of independent grower agency contracts marketing into all of the western states and provinces. While it made sense that a Canadian food producer would be able to sell locally, it beggared belief, Torrance's included, that tomatoes, green peppers, cucumbers, and mushrooms grown in glass buildings regularly surrounded by snow, and trucked hundreds of miles could still compete with food grown out of doors in the warm and fertile U. S. of A.

Since commerce is a stream that flows in the direction of the country with lower costs, Hothouse Produce's sales across the line, which were made possible because of the relatively cheap Canadian dollar, would only ever form an eddy off to the side. Such was the importance of the currency exchange rate, Hothouse Produce's managers all started off their days reading the business section of the paper with the hope of finding news about lackluster economic indicators in Canada and expansion south of the border. That morning, the news had been bad across the board, what with resource prices and the American trade deficit both rising.

* * * * *

Times had changed. On the weekend Kelly and Torrance had walked up to one of the changes and looked in. They'd driven out to the eastern edge of the valley to see a new horse that one of Kelly's friends had purchased. It turned out the person selling the horse was the mother of one of Kelly's early friends, Jenna Cook, who Kelly had lost track of after high school.

— Mrs. Cook, I can't believe Jenna had four kids.

— I'm with you. Now, don't call me Mrs. Cook. I haven't been Cook for a long time. Just call me Lucy.

For some reason, Lucy, who was well past retirement age, was determined to take Kelly out to one of the barns. Torrance was talking to Lucy's live-in, Henry when Lucy and Kelly left, and it was a few minutes before he could break away to follow them. His first impression on entering the long, low barn was that it was amazingly clean and well organized. He expected to hear the women, but all he heard was a country music song quietly playing through several mounted speakers. When he got to the door at the far side of the barn he continued on outside. There were two commercial sized air conditioners, and a large water tank around the corner of the building. *That doesn't make any sense. Mind you, neither does the condition of the barn, the doors with electronic key pads, the heavy electrical wires, and the security cameras. You don't think … ?*

Kelly stuck her head around the corner.

— Tor, you've got to come and see this.

He followed her through a side door into a room with white plastic sheeting on the walls and ceiling that was as clean as an operating room. There were three fans mounted on the wall and on the floor a number of pots with what had to be marijuana seedlings in them.

— That's nothing, come in here.

Kelly led him into a second, much larger room with like sheeting on every surface. There were high tech lights mounted directly above a dozen or more rows of waist high trays filled with mature marijuana plants. Metal guide wires above the trays ensured the orderly growth of the plants. Torrance looked down at an equal number of plants about the same size that were in moveable carts between the fixed trays.

— Those are "extra's" since we don't have medical licenses to grow them. Here, let me show you how we change the level of CO_2.

On their trip home Kelly had explained that Lucy and Henry had gotten into the venture to supplement their pensions.

— They've almost paid off all of their equipment. Now they're looking for a way to deal with all the cash. At least they get to pay cash to all the people they hire to prune and harvest the plants. $25 bucks an hour, no tax.

— When she held up that garbage bag outside the infrared room, I wasn't sure if she was holding up a bag of marijuana buds or a bag of dollar bills. It all sounds so amazing, but we're talking about walking close to the line and then going over it. Did you see the look on Henry's face when Lucy said she'd taken us into the grow rooms? He must have said five times that they don't use the stuff personally, and that it wasn't his idea to start growing it. He expects the police to show up anytime.

— It's only going to be a problem until cannabis is legal in October. After that it will just be dealing with regulations.

— You know, with bags of the stuff sitting around wouldn't you start to worry about being robbed?

— Lucy says they're just small players and that there is a much bigger operation down the street.

— Cannabis ranches, who knew?

* * * * *

With Kelly's children, Debra and Neil, away at school activities, Torrance and Kelly had the rare opportunity to eat supper alone. After talking through Debra's obsession with getting a tattoo, Torrance brought up Martin's invitation.

— I didn't know you liked hunting.

— I haven't thought about hunting for years, but the neat thing about this trip is I'd get a chance to go back to Bull Moose Run.

— When was the last time you were there?

— I haven't been back since I was nineteen.

— You don't talk much about your time there.

— I guess that's true, but that doesn't mean it's not important. I mean, there's lots of things I ... we ... don't talk about. Do you remember when my buddy from high school, Dave, dropped by a couple of years ago? I dunno why, but seeing him meant a lot to me.

— But what about work? Should you be taking time off? How long would you be gone?

— Not that long, no more than a week: one long travel day up, or an easy going day and a half. We fly out of the Moose as soon as we get there; and have four days at the lake.

— Do you have to buy a bunch of stuff?

— I still have my dad's old gun, which I assume still works.

Kelly couldn't understand why anyone would want to return to their hometown. As far as she was concerned the past should be left behind, and Bull Moose Run was pure past. It also bothered her that Torrance hadn't said anything about being away from her and the kids. She had spent six years raising Debra and Neil on her own and didn't want to be alone again, even for a week. Torrance went away on business trips, but that was different.

They went back to talking about tattoos.

— Remember all the crazy things you did as a teenager.

— The point is, I wish I hadn't done some of them.

— You say that now, but imagine if someone had tried to stop you. How would that have twisted your psyche? Getting a tattoo when you're young is a way to show your independence, and as long as it's not too big a tattoo, or in the wrong spot, I don't think there's anything wrong with it.

Torrance was reminded about his conversation with Kelly later in the week when he noticed the tattoo on the office administrator's shoulder. *I guess when you're older getting a tattoo is a way of making some person or memory permanent. … Or maybe you're just letting everyone know that you're okay flying solo.*

* * * * *

Relationships that start later in life are as different from early romance as three-dimensional chess is from checkers. With each passing year, personalities become more rigid; responsibilities gather, including the need to care for children and/or aging parents; and memories accumulate, lying in wait to challenge whatever follows. In order for the union of two older people to survive, probably more important than knee-weakening attraction is to have learned that most people have strengths to offset their weaknesses.

Although Kelly wished her mother would stop calling Torrance the white knight, which suggested that she benefited more from their relationship than he did, at least there was no doubt her parents supported the two of them. The limited contact Torrance had with his family meant they didn't know for sure what his mother thought. Torrance said that she used to have strong opinions about unmarried people living together, but he hoped her opinions had softened over time.

* * * * *

Torrance was back to running three times a week to get in shape for the hockey season. Because he was going to have to stay late at work, he'd chosen to go on a morning run on his shorter, riverside route

between the bridges. It had rained all night and was still raining, which meant there were huge puddles everywhere. He was drenched by the time he reached the industrial area near the river. *At least the rain has cleared the air around the cement plant.*
— Sorry, pal!

Torrance's running hat had blocked his view of the cyclist coming towards him on the bridge's narrow walkway. The rider, who had to slow down, was so close when he went past that Torrance was able to reach over and touch him apologetically on his side.

Torrance used to imagine he was trying to win a race whenever he ran. Now it was all he could do to keep going once he got started. A younger runner blew past him on the other side of the bridge. Torrance yelled out through the noise of the traffic and the rain, not sure if he would be heard:
— You champion! You might not believe this, but I'm running as fast as I can.

A person who would yell at someone he didn't know as if running was a team sport was who Torrance was on good days.

Even though it was early, there were a dozen or more cars in the 4 Bridges Casino's parking lot. Torrance could only hope the cars were for staff and not for people with nothing better to do than play a game of chance before breakfast. While he didn't call casinos weeping sores like someone else had, he had no illusions about them doing anything positive for the community. As he got closer to the large new building (built with money that gamblers had either already lost or were expected to lose), he thought about how things had changed since the era of the movie *It's A Wonderful Life*. When Jimmy Stewart ran through an imagined, alternate Pottersville in the 1940's the gambling halls, showrooms, and drinking establishments were obvious signs of a moral decline. *I wonder what moviegoers back then would have thought about marijuana dispensaries.*

*　*　*　*　*

On an evening Kelly was at the mall with Debra and Neil, Torrance ventured up into the dusty and spider webbed attic to get his father's beaded deer hide gun case. The case had hardened but it still retained the faintest smell of tanned leather. He felt the gun's weight shift in the case as he carefully backed down the steep, folding stairs. Slipping the gun out of the case when he got to the living room, he considered its wood and steel construction. *It sure is a fire stick, with a heckuva punch.* He worked the lever. Although the oil had gone gummy, the mechanical precision to the sliding steel parts was impressive. He walked to the picture window and sighted the gun in on the troll ornament in the neighbour's flower bed across the street and imagined taking a shot. Somewhere in the back of his mind was the advice that you shouldn't pull the trigger on an unloaded gun. He pulled the trigger anyways. Ping!

After putting the gun back into the case, he typed, ".308 caliber" into the computer and then clicked on a promising website. He smiled with involuntary pride when he read the line, "for most hunters thirty calibers rule". He imagined what the first rudimentary gun would have looked like and how unreliable it would have been. *It wasn't that many years, though, before guns got really good. Not just guns, though, soon there were cannons. ... Probably cannons came first. ... If only people could get along.*

Since the bullets for the gun were at least thirty-five years old he checked online to see if there was a bullet "best before date". The gun owner's blog he clicked on wasn't especially helpful and he scrolled down to the comments. The first commentator discussed the difficulty of keeping track of ammunition during a series of moves after a divorce; and the second talked a little too earnestly about the problem of storing food and munitions for long periods of time. *I didn't realize how close hunting is to the survivalist subculture.* But it didn't matter; his mind was made up. Truth be told, it had been made up the moment Martin brought up the name, Bull Moose Run. Torrance was going to go home like a Steller's Jay in spring. Now all he had to do was get a gun license, a hunting license, and whatever other licenses were out there.

* * * * *

Torrance finally had a reason to go inside the American-sized hunting and fishing store that had opened up not far from Kelly's and his older, detached home. After parking as close as he could to the store's entrance, he walked head down through the steady rain to the front door. There were three more-soiled-than-tough young men smoking under the overhang. Given the dull grey of the urban environment, it didn't make sense that two of the men wore green-brown camouflage pants. *That is, unless they've come in from the deep, dark woods. ... Us locals can only hope they aren't dirty dog outlaws with no regard for innocent lives.*

The first thing Torrance noticed inside the store was how young and fresh-faced the members of the staff were in a place with such serious intent. The greeter, like the rest of the employees, was wearing a blue golf shirt with the store's logo. When Torrance asked where the ammunition was kept he was directed to the back of the store with a bigger smile than anyone deserved on first meeting. Making his way down an aisle, he was surprised to see extra boxes of most items stacked nearly to the industrial height ceiling. *Made in China, no doubt.*

The clerk at the guns and ammunition desk was about Torrance's age. Any hope for a rapport between peers, however, quickly evaporated in the face of the employee's automaton aspect.

— Hi. I need to buy some .308 shells.

— We have Remington and Winchester shells.

— I'm going moose hunting, which I haven't done for a very long time. To be honest, I have no idea what kind of bullets I should get, or if it matters. Maybe you can help me.

The clerk reached into the cabinet below the counter and brought out two boxes of bullets.

— The Winchester bullets are 168 grain with a muzzle velocity, of ... 2,670 feet per second. They've got polycarbonate tips and an oxide coating to reduce barrel fouling. The Remington's are 165 grain and have a similar muzzle velocity. Both of these bullets are well rated for precision and bullet expansion.

Torrance waited in vain for the clerk to break into a grin and say, "Just kiddin."

— I'll take the Winchesters, I guess. Do I pay for them here or at the front?

— You pay for them here. I'll need to see your firearms Possession and Acquisition License.

Driving home, it struck Torrance that the supplies in the store had been almost perfectly divided between goods to make hunters and fishermen comfortable—clothing, footwear, sleeping bags, and tents—and goods for attracting, killing, rendering, and cooking game. He began to wonder how long hunting and fishing stores would be around. *I wouldn't buy shares in those stores, that's for sure. What are there, 5,000,000 people and 75,000 moose? The moose don't stand a chance.*

LOT'S LAND

THE DESIGN, CONSTRUCTION AND ADMINISTRATION of Western cities are among the pinnacles of human achievement. Typically located in beautiful settings—"Come and see how amazing the mountains look behind the skyscrapers!"—cities focus on their residents' life, liberty and happiness. There haven't been food or water shortages for decades; weather isn't a concern because most activities take place indoors; and subways and buses make it easy to get around. Whenever bad things happen, as they must, first responders work quickly to reinstate order.

*　*　*　*　*

Torrance was the first one in his family up during the week and he had often finished his commute into the city by the time Kelly rolled out of bed. This morning, during his solitary breakfast in the quiet kitchen, Torrance checked the list of ingredients on the box of porridge to see if Kelly's sister, a vegan, was right about not trusting packaged food. The only item on the list he thought might be threatening was "defatted" wheat, whatever that meant. *To be fair, there is no mention of GMOs.* He tried to decide if the porridge still tasted the way it used to. *It seems a little blander, but then again I use a lot less brown sugar now.*

Torrance made his first business phone call from his car on the way to work.

— Jay, this is Torrance from Hothouse Produce.

— How's the world's wettest city?

— Not today, Jay. The sun's coming out, and we're all getting younger.

— Younger, now that's what I need.

— You start by skipping birthdays; the difficult part is reversing time. How's business?

— It's fall, so there's no shortage of choices.

— I'm coming down to show the corporate flag next week. Is there a day that would work for me to drop by?

— Actually, I did want to talk to you about delivery times.

*   *   *   *   *

During the trip to the US, Torrance was struck anew by how so much land was overrun by nature-destroying urban sprawl. The other revelation was the number of homeless everywhere he went. *Every city has its own 1st Street now.* Outside of a coffee shop he'd stopped at in Portland a disheveled, raggedly dressed man was sitting on stained cardboard mumbling to himself and begging for money. Other like people who'd long ago given up, and been given up on, beaded the sidewalk all the way to the corner. Torrance happened to leave the coffee shop at the same time as a well-dressed woman. The woman, who was old enough to be uncertain about her footing, cautiously made her way around the homeless man before turning to speak to someone she could identify with, which happened to be Torrance.

— Never in my lifetime did I think it would come to this.

Torrance debriefed himself on what he'd decided was a worthwhile trip while he waited to board his flight home, articulating as best he could the mixture of travel boredom, constant eating out, replicated meetings, periodic feelings of success, and the consuming loneliness at the end of each day. The meetings had followed the usual pattern of introductions or re-introductions, authentic laughter and the mini-confrontations that accompany selling. Torrance thought about what Ma, a salesman based in Sacramento, had said about the trend of customers continuing to negotiate after a deal had been struck. Ma's take was it was just the old boys' network giving way, Torrance didn't agree. *It's bigger than that. There's less community ... and everyone making sure they get what's coming to them. ... Especially the younger generation. I wonder how many people under 35 would walk right over you if they thought they could get away with it. ... Society's coming apart at the seams.* Something new on the trip had been the anonymous letter sent to one of their Sacramento customers alleging high levels of heavy metals in Hothouse Produce peppers. *Competition is one thing, but defamation as a business strategy. That's pretty low.*

His flight home was enlivened by sitting next to a well put together woman named Beth about his age who had been determined to talk. Torrance smiled as he thought back on the flight during the short bus ride from the airport out to the airport parking. While meeting someone eligible of the opposite sex was always a buzz, the thrill lessened more quickly now. Beth's story was a variation of some of the stories Torrance had heard during his dating periods. She'd been in a long term marriage, and after divorcing now had money and time to travel—this evening she'd been coming back from Portland where she'd been to see her only child, a daughter, who was attending university. Although at the outset Torrance's mind had toyed with the possibilities, it wasn't long before he decided that Beth's quirkiness went deeper than personality. *Her losses, or what she's been taking to take the edge off, have actually damaged her thinking processes.*

* * * * *

Torrance woke up from another dream. He had been walking at night towards a house where there was a gun he wanted to get to protect himself. He'd had to be cautious because it was too dark to see if the tiger being kept in a cage near the house had broken out. Even as he tried to recall the details of the dream it faded in a fast-thinning jumble of thoughts.

* * * * *

Thursday morning. Torrance had gotten off to a slow start and traffic was stop and go by the time he got to the highway. When he got close to the exit to Hothouse Produce's combined head office, cold storage, and transportation terminal complex he found himself behind one of the company's trucks. As he waited in the slow-moving line he studied the prominent horn of plenty logo on the back of the truck. *I don't think there've been any changes to the original design. It's funny how the first idea is often the best one.*

When he got to his desk he started off by checking his emails. The first email of note was a reminder of an upcoming lunch meeting. Since the lunch was set for the week he would be away, he deleted the email and continued on through his Inbox. He stopped to read an email from a Seattle grocery store chain following up on an enquiry about organic mushrooms. Since Hothouse Produce's inventory manager, Danny apparently hadn't responded to the first email, which Torrance had forwarded on to him, Torrance forwarded the second email on as well. He stopped by Danny's office on his way back from the coffee room.

Danny was coming to the end of a phone call.

— I'll do my best, but I'm warning you, likely the best we can do by Friday is an extra fifty flats.

Danny hung up the phone after saying goodbye.

— I hope that's a gift tie?

— At least I'm not dressed like I just finished weeding the garden.

— Hold on!

— I sent you another email from a Seattle chain enquiring about organic mushrooms.

— I meant to talk to you about that. Let me pull the email up.

* * * * *

Insatiable America. The earth's maw, for years consuming as many resources as the rest of the world combined, all the while giving emerging countries a place to sell their goods. In time, an economic malaise had set in and the great nation had begun to falter, a key marker being the way "Made in China" replaced "Made in the USA" on so many manufactured items.

Everyone had an opinion about what had gone wrong in the land of the free, the home of the brave and the genesis of all things transistor, microprocessor, nuclear reactor and jet-powered. Those on the left focused on inequality and the lack of a shared vision; and those on the right blamed excessive regulations and taxation, pointing out that communist China had relied on free enterprise, albeit a hybrid form called state capitalism, to turn things around. Both sides gave lip service to bringing developing countries into the community of democracies despite the unspoken consensus that the country had already done more than its share.

Then, just when it seemed like the decline would prove irreversible, American oil producers found a way to squeeze more black gold out of abandoned oil fields (albeit the process forever dirtied ancient aquifers). Once the country was freed up from the cost of imported oil, an unexpected revival of the economy followed. What mattered to Hothouse Produce's managers was the resulting rise in the American dollar, along with the lock-step fall in the value of Canada's currency.

* * * * *

Torrance reflexively grabbed the iPad on his way to bed. As usual he went to his cousin's Facebook page. The big news was his cousin had taken a DNA test and found out that while predominantly of Irish, English and Scottish origin, she had Native American ancestors.

* * * * *

Torrance was part of the endless stream of cars returning to the suburbs at day's end. Although the afternoon sunshine had put most in a good mood, Torrance knew his happiness had as much to do with his upcoming trip north. The plan had been for Martin and him to drive up to Bull Moose Run together; but Martin had ended up leaving early to visit an uncle in Jimcana, a mill town between Centre City and the Alberta border. Torrance was as happy as not with the change since it meant he would have the opportunity to enjoy the reverie that settled on him when he drove long distances alone. In anticipation, he'd even repurchased several CDs of music from his youth.

After stopping to get gas for his Korean made Chevrolet, Torrance switched over to take the narrow, winding, historic road on the final leg of his trip home. He'd started taking this route because, in addition to there being less traffic, the road went past one of the few remaining wetlands in the metropolitan area. Approaching the first pond, he imagined a moose standing in the weedy water and gazing nonplussed at the passing cars. Spotting what appeared to be a low-lying mist in his peripheral vision, he slowed before turning his head to take a better look. Bizarrely, what he had thought was a mist, which didn't make sense given the temperature and the time of day, proved to be a blue-wire construction fence. Parked on the other side of the fence, not far from where he'd recently seen a motionless Sandhill Crane, there was a bright yellow steel construction crane.

The pending development brought to mind a conversation he'd had with Bud Reimer at the townhome complex where Kelly and he used to live. Bud was an outgoing, long retired farmer who formed fast friendships. Bud and his wife, Myrna had sold their farm and moved into a one-level duplex townhome in the complex after Myrna's declining health restricted her to a wheelchair.

One day when Bud and Torrance chanced to meet at the complex's centrally located mailboxes, Bud had pointed to the headline on the stack of local newspapers: "McDermott Farm Out of Agricultural Land Reserve."

— It looks like they're going to let them subdivide the McDermott Farm. That farm used to have the best production of all of the farms in the Valley.

— I recognize the barn. It's the big one near the bridge, isn't it?

— That's it.

— I've never understood why they don't limit new housing to the hills above the valley. I mean, there's only so much agricultural land.

Bud had paused before responding.

— There's a problem with that too. I remember how the number of birds, starlings, sparrows, even hawks, went down to almost nothing when they started knocking down the trees for a new subdivision on the ridge above our old farm.

* * * * *

Torrance was working at his desk when his cell phone rang. It was Kelly.

— Hey, what's up?

— Sue Connaught came by the office today. I told her you were driving up to Centre City next week. She said her uncle, Miller Walters, is planning to take a bus to attend a funeral in Centre City and she wondered if you would consider taking him with you. He was at the wedding of Sue and Tim's son, Billy.

— Was he the old guy with the white hair at the next table?

— Yes, that's the guy.

— I talked to him for a minute when I was getting some coffee. He
seemed okay.

* * * * *

Torrance ran past the new regional theater on his last jog before the
hunting trip. As he made his way along the freshly paved path behind
the architecturally interesting three story building, he thought how
buying a detached house had been one of Kelly's and his best decisions. Although the added commute ground him down a bit, the house
had already gone up $100,000.00 or more in value. He was happy that
Debra and Neil seemed to be fitting in at the local high school. *There's
definitely a different culture out here. Maybe it's because everyone has a
patch of land. Imagine, Kelly and me with our own little garden.*

Halfway around a bend a Norwegian rat darted across the paved
path, nearly running into him before swerving away and disappearing into the bushes on the other side of the path. Shocked, Torrance
slowed nearly to a stop. He'd seen squirrels in the area, but never
vermin. *Nature definitely has a mind of its own, always pushing back—
like the raccoon who tried to dig through the wooden shingles on the house
down the street.*

Torrance found running up the hill harder than he'd expected,
and he was barely moving when he got to the top. All of a sudden he
heard gun shots. Even as he was trying to figure out where the shots
came from he imagined bullets whipping through his loose t-shirt
and smashing into his torso. *It's the shooting range.* Their realtor had
told Kelly and him about the range, which had been built long before
the ever-tightening mix of subdivisions, retail stores, and busy roads.
Despite the gun range's historical claim Torrance found it unfair that
a few gun owners had the right to disturb the peace and quiet of an
entire neighbourhood.

* * * * *

On his final day at the office, Torrance kept telling himself that work
was a type of race; and, as with every race, it was the last kilometer
that mattered most. He heard the other offices empty out as he made

his way through the last of his emails and phone messages. When he was finally finished he picked up his briefcase and headed for the main entrance, yelling out, "Is anyone here?" before turning off the hall lights. He was going to be late picking up Mr. Walters. *But, not to forget, I'm doing the old man a favour.*

Miller Walters lived in an older part of town where detached houses were slowly being replaced with multi-family buildings. A new four-story building was nearing completion on Miller's street. The payment terms touted on the oversized sales sign were too low to make sense, and Torrance did some quick math to see how the numbers had been manipulated.

Miller was waiting, suitcase beside him, on the front step of his house when Torrance pulled up to the curb. Torrance's best guess was Miller was in his late 70s or early 80s, which didn't seem as old as it used to. Torrance got out of the car and made his way up the cracked, concrete walkway dividing Miller's front lawn.

— Hello.

Miller, who on his way down the stairs, responded with a smile.

— Thanks for giving me a ride.

The two men shook hands on the walkway. Torrance picked up Miller's suitcase and carried it to the car.

On their way to the highway they drove past the impossibly large, brand new shopping mall.

— I know there's been a ton of people moving here, but I wouldn't have thought there were enough customers to keep all those stores busy.

— I was thinking the same thing.

After entering the highway and coming up to speed, which seemed dangerously fast at first, Torrance was finally able to give his full attention to the conversation.

— I understand letting the dead bury the dead, but Rostern was there for me all those years. I felt I should go to his funeral, for the sake of his family.

— How long did you know him?

— ... forty-five, maybe fifty years. Although it's been nearly twenty years since I last saw him, and almost that long since I've been in the north.

— What did your friend do for a living?

— He had a service station up on Highway 60 on the way north out of Centre City. People complain that all business people think about is getting more than the piece rate. Nothing could be farther from the truth as far as Rostern was concerned. He was one of the most generous people I ever knew, never holding his money too close.

— What about you? What did you used to do?

— I called myself a local missionary. I delivered Bibles to people working out of town in logging camps, mining sites and oil drilling platforms—even a few road-building crews. It helped that I used to work in the camps as a logger myself.

— I never did any logging, but I worked in a mill during high school and spent a summer working for the Forest Service.

When Torrance brought up Sue Connaught's name, Miller explained she was his youngest niece and an especially caring person.

In what seemed like no time at all they arrived at the last suburb before the hinterland. Torrance exited the highway to top up his gas tank. Although Miller forced the issue of paying for their coffee and snacks with the slightly awkward manner of an older man, Torrance wouldn't accept anything towards the gas since he'd arranged to meet with a customer in Centre City and would be submitting his mileage to Hothouse Produce.

A homeless man with a shopping cart stuffed with the detritus of a consumer society was standing near the exit ramp to the highway.

— There doesn't seem to be an easy fix for those guys, does there? And every year there's more of them.

— We used to worry about booze and mental health. Then came drugs. Now there's worse drugs. One thing I've never been able to reconcile is the role of choice, the idea of enabling, and what it says in *James* about God choosing the poor.

— I read that life expectancies have started going down in parts of the US.

Earlier in the year Torrance had driven through the East end of the city on his way to a meeting. It had been a hot day, and the windows in his car were rolled down. Bam!—just after crossing Mardi Gras Avenue—his senses had been overwhelmed by a mélange of smells that included rotting garbage, smoke, oil and gas, human sweat and worse. Carrying on up 1st Street he'd been confronted by a chaotic gathering of hundreds, possibly thousands, of people crowding both sides of the street. Whatever the number was, it was the largest group of people on the edge that Torrance had ever seen. To avoid trouble, he'd slowed down. Even so he'd had to jam on his brakes to avoid hitting a gaunt, disheveled man with scarecrow hair and random, dirty clothing who'd darted in front of his car. When Torrance got near the end of the gauntlet at Las Vegas Avenue he'd seen a thin, stone-faced woman sitting on the curb, needle in hand, using her teeth to help her cinch up the elastic tubing wrapped around her arm. Behind the woman, on a sheet of plywood sheet covering the window of an abandoned store, someone had spray painted the words, "This isn't the end, but we can see it from here."

THE GOOD
MILLER'S TALE

THE CIRCUSES THAT USED TO entertain people have been replaced by professional sports, concerts, plays, movies, as well as civic holidays celebrated with fireworks, banners, and parades. Those staying home can play video games, watch TV or burrow into the Internet.

* * * * *

Torrance and Miller drove in silence across the long bridge spanning the Sturgeon River at the edge of the valley. Torrance glanced downstream at the water flowing towards the ocean. *It's been what, a decade since the last big salmon run? We're asking way too much of the river. … Not that long ago, Natives would have walked the river delta in peace and quiet. Nowadays, roads and buildings plug up the land beside the river. And on top of that municipalities send their spoiled water into the river … Then there's the oily, smelly air … and constant noise.*

* * * * *

Torrance asked Miller if he'd done much hunting.
— The last time I went hunting was maybe fifteen years ago. I went with Sue Connaught's husband, Tim. He's an accountant. He'd never been hunting before and had only ever seen guns on TV. It took him longer than he thought to get his hunting license, and we had to delay our trip up to Quincy until near the end of the season.

— Is Quincy by that big ranch?

— I think you mean the Trent Ranch.

— Ya. That's it.

— Quincy's a ways north of that. It's west of Gold Cliff, not far from where the last of the Taseko wild horses are holed up.

— Did you shoot anything.

— No, but almost. It took us until the middle of the afternoon to find a place to camp. Though it wasn't camping like I think of camping. Tim had a twenty-five-foot RV with everything you could want and then some, a shower, a satellite TV, and so on.

It was still light when we parked so we walked around to get our bearings. There was a skiff of snow and it was pretty cold. We found a small pond south of where we had set up that we decided to walk back to in the morning.

After breakfast we split up and headed to the pond. I heard a gun go off and when I got to the pond I found Tim walking back and forth.

He said he'd come upon three young bulls and had shot one of them behind the shoulder like I'd told him. Apparently, the bull he'd shot had gone down and the other two had run off. The problem was the bull he'd shot had suddenly gotten back on its feet and run off too.

There was blood in the snow near the pond and so at least I knew he'd hit it. We followed the tracks until almost lunch, but we had to give up when we got to a rocky patch where the snow had blown away. Tim was sick to his stomach about injuring the poor animal. I felt as bad as he did. That was the end of our hunting trip.

Tim told me on the way home how thin the bulls were. I explained to him that it was because the rutting season had just ended and the bulls had been racing around the forest doing what nature told 'em. The only reason they could put up with each other was the cow moose were no longer in heat.

* * * * *

Now and then lights from isolated houses were visible from the highway.

Torrance told Miller about his two stepchildren and the sports teams they played on.

— How about you? Did you play any sports growing up?

— I was best at track and field. At a sports day when I was twelve or so I got first place for the high jump and running, and I think throwing a softball. The kid in each grade with the most ribbons, which for my grade was me, got to go up front at an assembly. The guy in the grade ahead of me who went up front made it to the NHL. His first name was ... it'll come to me. He was decent player too. Though none of us ever imagined he would go all the way like he did.

— You must have played some hockey?

— Not organized hockey. Everyone played pond hockey. If you didn't have skates, you played in goal. Young people don't believe me when I tell them we used to tie newspapers to our legs as shin pads.

Torrance told Miller that he still played in an adult hockey league, but had lost a few steps. Miller nodded knowingly.

— One by one your parts stop working, or at least working like they did.

After a pause, he added,

— I think of people the same age like stalks of wheat in a field. Although some of the stalks fail to develop, or die early, most of the wheat matures at about the same rate. Then it's harvest time. But no one likes to talk about that.

Miller spoke up after they'd driven in silence for a while.

— The name of the hockey player I was telling you about was, Erling Mercer. Do you recognize that name?

— No, I don't think so.

* * * * *

Torrance turned in at the 24-hour gas station and restaurant partway up the canyon that he'd stopped at on his way to Bill's funeral two years earlier. After dropping Miller off at the front of the restaurant, he filled up with gas. When he went in the restaurant he saw the rest of the customers, who looked to be locals, were sitting at two tables pulled together at the back of the restaurant. Most seemed either buzzed or drunk.

The young man who took their order seemed off as well.

— Would you like somfing?

— What do you recommend?

— Our spesalty is pissa.

Torrance and Miller settled back into their conversation after ordering.

— So, how did you end up as a missionary?

— My dad worked as a faller near Macken. I started working in the woods when I was still a teenager. I had only been bucking timber for a few months when I cut my thigh at a loading site up near Tamarind. Chainsaws don't cut clean like a knife, and I was in the hospital for a time.

The hospital chaplain dropped by a couple of times while I was there. I still remember his bad breath and yellow teeth. I was a jacket-full of attitude back then and I only put up with him because I couldn't leave. He said one thing, though, that I've never forgotten, "Gratitude only makes sense if it's directed at someone."

A few years after that, I was spending the last of my pay in a bar in Centre City. I was usually out with the guys, but I'm pretty sure I was by myself when the bar shut down. I was walking, stumbling's probably more accurate, back to the rundown motel I was staying at when I found myself in front of this little old church. The lights were on in the church, and I felt pulled, it was like a magnet, to go to the front door. I've never felt anything like it before or since.

An elderly man was sweeping at the front inside the church. I didn't think much of it at the time but later I wondered why he was working so late. The man stopped sweeping and came over to sit beside me in the pew. I'm not sure if he said anything, but I have this memory of him bowing his head. After a while he got up and left.

Religion. Torrance typically ricocheted away from the unknowable, but tonight for whatever reason he wasn't thrown off. *Maybe it's because Miller reminds me of my father.*

— I went to a Sunday service at that same church a couple of months later. When I asked to speak to the janitor I was introduced to a lady who said she'd cleaned the church for twenty-five years. I told her about my late night visit and she said she had no idea what man would have been cleaning in the middle of the night.

I ended up working in a camp with a faller who was getting close to retirement named Abe. Abe was about as nice a guy as you would ever meet, always whistling gospel songs and singing. One night over supper I told him my story about being pulled into the church. He said I was being called. Right away he gave me his Bible. I read it cover to cover. When the camp shut down in the spring he put me in touch with Headwaters Mission.

— I told you I was raised in the north. I was actually born in Bull Moose Run. You might have known my dad, Ed Maki.

— Ed Maki. You're kidding me? No, I hadn't made that connection. Yes, I knew Pastor Ed. I had a high opinion of him.

— Maybe you came to our house?

— There were lots of logging shows around the Moose, and I visited the Valley Copper Mine a couple of times, but no, I don't think I ever went to Ed's house.

Miller told Torrance that like everyone else he was shocked hearing that Pastor Ed had drowned.

— It changed the lives of everyone in the family, that's for sure. It just seemed senseless to me. I was mad about it for a long time. I'm probably still mad.

— I understand. Is your mom still alive?

— Yes. Mom and both my sisters live in Halifax. I've only seen mom a few times since we left Bull Moose Run, but I phone her every couple of months. She came out to the coast when I got married to my ex, Suzanne.

— How are your sisters doing?

— My sisters and mom all live within a few kilometers of each other. Gwen teaches grade six. She's married and has one daughter. Emily's a stay at home mom. She and her two boys bunked at our house last summer while her husband was attending a conference.

— There's something special about being near family.

— I agree. But there's also an advantage in not living that close, you don't keep comparing. I see lots of that between my wife, Kelly and her siblings.

The noise level was rising at the joined tables at the back.

Torrance figured out the server was also the cook when he brought their meals. Torrance waited to start eating until Miller finished a silent prayer.

— I remember eating in a roadside restaurant with my dad and mom. I would have been about six or seven years old at the time and the twins were babies. Some logging truck drivers at a nearby table were swearing up a storm. My dad walked over and asked them if they could stop swearing because he had his family with him. They stopped right away. Those were different times I guess.

— Pastor Ed was a good man and the truck drivers probably realized that.

* * * * *

Back on the highway, the reflective dividing line on a newly repaved section was as bright as a light itself. Torrance spoke.

— How about you, do you miss the north?

— I miss the open spaces. And I think people are a little different in the north. They're more independent, and yet more willing to help out, if that makes sense. Down south, everyone's so busy. There isn't much time in the city for thinking. People just keep doing and doing.

After a break in the conversation he added,

— I call cities human ant hills. I've never figured out what it is that makes people want to live in such big clumps. Although I guess it comes down to how there's so many people now.

Torrance enjoyed listening to Miller talk and asked him if he was a reader, which it turned out he was. They began to talk about the kinds of books they liked to read. Torrance was a little surprised when Miller said he'd read several novels by Torrance's favourite author, Cormac McCarthy.

— McCarthy writes so lean. He's a literary writer, but he never lets the writing get in the way of the story. If you know what I mean?

— The other thing is, he doesn't tell you too much, you have to figure it out on your own.

— I agree, you have to infer. It's the same with Le Carre. Although they write different.

Torrance asked Miller if he was put off by the violence in the McCarthy's novels.

— I could deal with violence better when I was younger—when you're young you figure you can deal with anything, and you don't think anything will hurt you. The older I got the less I wanted to be around bad people, and people who are suffering. Even fictional bad people and made-up suffering.

They drove a few kilometers in silence.

— Reading McCarthy always reminded me that conflict is part of who we are. I'll bet you don't know who told his friends to sell whatever they had and go and buy swords?

*　*　*　*　*

Miller started to yawn. Torrance told him he might as well get some shuteye since they were still an hour or more out of Gold Cliff. A few minutes later Torrance could see by the glow of the instrument panel that Miller's eyes were closed and his mouth slightly open. Torrance waited a while longer before finding a country music station on satellite radio. He eased the volume up until he could just make out the words: "I'm not looking forward, I'm just looking back. I've become what I started out to be." *A theme song.*

He began to think about women from his past. He'd always been amazed by both the potency of the initial attraction—which rendered him as powerless as if he'd been seized in the jaws of a huge animal— and how quickly the attraction could weaken.

Torrance had lived with Suzanne the longest and had assumed they were married for life. However, her comment about not being able to love or be loved had proven prescient. Although he'd been happy to feed off her manic excitement whenever she got it in her mind to have fun, he couldn't remember her ever being content for a long stretch of time.

He'd always known that his rebound relationship with Robin was temporary since he was never going to be able to bridge the gap between the way she waited for life to come to her and how he kept moving forward, fixing whatever could be fixed the best he could. *Anytime I told her she needed to do her share, she said I cared too much about money.* It was around the time Robin moved back to the Sunshine Coast that he had begun to see life like a collection of short stories rather than a long, drawn out novel.

Hearts may grow fonder when people are apart but the rest of a person prepares for permanent separation. Torrance had only been on the highway for a few hours and already tendrils of doubt about his relationship with Kelly were beginning to form. Trying to fight back, he reminded himself that his heart still jumped when he saw Kelly after they'd been apart for any length of time, whether he came across her in the backyard at the end of a workday or when she picked him up at the airport after he'd been away on business. From somewhere deep within, though, came the rejoinder that he'd always be jealous of the father of her children.

Unable to right himself by reaching over to touch Kelly's thin shoulders, he decided to call her. He turned the radio off and disengaged the Bluetooth system before pressing "home" on the screen of his cell phone and propping it against his ear. Kelly, who usually stayed up late to read, answered on the second ring. Torrance whispered that he had to talk quietly because Miller was asleep beside him.

— How much farther until you stop?

— Maybe forty kilometers. How did it go tonight? Did Neil get his homework done?

— He said he did. When I looked at some of his math I was sure glad he didn't ask me for help. Was grade ten math always this hard?

— You work with formulas all day long, imagine someone like me who just adds and subtracts. How about Debra? Did she hear anything more about the tournament on the island?

— She said the team had gotten in, and she seemed excited about that.

— That's really good news, since the coach was late getting the application in. We should plan to take the ferry over.

They talked for a while longer before Torrance said he should go. Kelly said she loved him and he said he loved her too.

There were very few vehicles on the road and Torrance began to imagine he was travelling in a tunnel being bored out in front of him by laser headlights.

GOLD CLIFF

OUR MELIORISM BOTH AS INDIVIDUALS and a society comes from our past successes. Consider the young professional who excelled at university, was a sought after hire in a high-paying profession and has entered into a relationship with an estimable companion. It might seem that all that's left to do is acquire a luxury penthouse with "great views north to the mountains and west to the ocean, an airy West Coast feel from the natural sunlight filtered through floor-to ceiling windows, window shades with blackout blinds, an entertainment system with built-in cabinets by Joey Rozin, sustainably harvested, Ecuadorian Ipe floors, a forty-inch paneled refrigerator, two Blummel wall-mounted ovens, and a Fuar wine fridge."

* * * * *

Torrance hadn't had a decent sleep for several days, and tiredness hit him full force just before a sign that said fifteen kilometers to Gold Cliff. Without caffeine, he was down to the standard nighttime driving tricks: shaking his head; opening the window to let the cool night air in, although because of Miller he couldn't lower the window as much as he wanted; and reminding himself that a lot of people, including his sleeping passenger, needed him to stay awake. As a last resort, he began pinching his leg.

His judgment began to fail. It didn't seem to him that there was anything wrong with briefly closing his eyes ... *really no more than a delayed blink.* After allowing himself to keep his eyes closed for two seconds at a time, three at the most, he began having random, surreal thoughts. Too tired to react ...

... he jerked his eyes open in a panic. He was on the gravel shoulder on the other side of the highway, heading for the ditch. He cranked the wheel to straighten the car out and return to his lane. Looking over at Miller, he was glad to see the old man was still asleep. *He'll never know how close we came.*

Torrance could still feel flashes of body heat through his cold sweat as he drove across the elevated bridge at the start of the resort town of Gold Cliff. Taking the first left after the town's large welcome sign, he was soon at the start of the tourist zone. Although many of the shops had Spanish arches and dun coloured adobe brick exteriors, the intended illusion that visitors were arriving for a holiday at a southern destination was lost on him.

*   *   *   *   *

Torrance had booked a room in the Riverside Hotel, which was on the inside bank of the winding Islacl River. Miller didn't know it yet but because Torrance's room had two twin beds he was, for the first time ever, getting the opportunity to sleep on the corporate dime.

Gold Cliff was near the edge of the Winnigen Valley, with the eastern shore of Winnigen Lake a scant twenty minutes away at the higher speeds possible on the newly widened road. The valley, famous for its warm summer weather, orchards, and farms, as well as the recreation afforded by its forests and lakes, was inexorably being transformed into a checkerboard of concentrated recreational zones, compact residential lots, and commercial properties choked by service roads. While the valley's citizens had no power to slow the influx, most were happy enough with the increased economic opportunities and rising land values.

Torrance had stayed in the Riverside Hotel when he'd driven up to Gold Cliff to attend Bill Tennant's funeral: like Miller, it had taken the death of a friend to unstick Torrance from the coast. He had first met Bill at a 300 level university course university featuring *Thoughts from Walden Pond* and a *Discourse on Inequality*. That year had ended up being Torrance's last in school. Twenty years later, having long since lost touch, the two former classmates happened to purchase townhomes in the same complex. Bill, who faced a lengthy commute to his job at the university library after the move, had only been able to enter the heated property market because of an inheritance.

Kelly and her kids had moved into the townhouse with Torrance prior to their purchasing a detached home together. While they were still at the townhouse, Kelly and Torrance had attended Bill's 50th birthday party, which he'd organized for himself. It had seemed especially dark on the evening they made their way over to Bill's townhouse in Building E, the short trek taking them through the complex's narrow, paved lanes, past identical, squished townhouses fronted by fast-eroding wooden supports on undersized, open garages, many of which had unwashed, smelly garbage cans ready for pick up. Kelly and Torrance decided to let themselves in Bill's main door when it became obvious no one could hear the doorbell over the sounds of Deep Purple. After climbing the narrow stairs up to the compressed kitchen and living room level they'd done their best to start conversations with party goers they didn't know.

— Hi. I don't think we've met.

— No, I don't think so.

— I'm Torrance and this is Kelly.

— Nice to meet you.

Pointing to herself and her companion,

— Tammy, Adam.

— So how do you guys know Bill?

— I work with him at the university.

...

— I keep asking how did he ever get to be premier? The guy did so many marginal things when he was representing the union. I understand that you might agree with some of his policies, but how could you ever vote for a guy with that kind of character? Doesn't honesty have to be the baseline?

...

— Our issue is whether it's better to be at the top of the B group or the bottom of the A group. They're a lot more serious in A, that's for sure.

— I don't know much about Dragon Boats. Do you race every weekend?

...

— Mine's the same. Except when he's not at the computer he's organizing his running shoes, he calls them sneakers. He won't tell me how many pairs he has, most he doesn't even wear.

When they'd stayed long enough to leave, Torrance went looking for Bill to say goodbye. He found his old friend smoking pot in a huddle on the deck. While they were shaking hands, Bill told Torrance he'd quit his job and was planning on moving upcountry.

— I haven't found work yet but my costs should go way down. For starters, I won't have to pay strata fines for smoking the stuff.

Bill's townhome had sold quickly. On moving day, Bill's older brother Linden and Torrance were the only volunteers to help load Bill's ticky-tacky possessions into a rented moving truck.

The following February, Torrance got a phone call at work that was put straight through. It took Torrance a moment to figure out it was Linden.

— Bill had a heart attack. A neighbor found him lying frozen outside the old farmhouse he was renting. They say he'd been there a long time. It's a wonder some critter hadn't started chewing on him.

Despite work demands and the risks of winter driving, Torrance had driven up alone to Bill's funeral. On the way he'd considered what it said about his own makeup to have had a friend as eccentric as Bill.

Attending the funeral along with Torrance were Linden, Linden's bone-thin, spiteful wife, Hannah, and the Tennant triplets Rennie, Gilbert, and Verne. Listening to the triplets talking loudly in the hallway about a global conspiracy on gasoline prices, Torrance was reminded of a sord of quacking, unthinking waterfowl. When he'd walked over to introduce himself, he'd had to stop himself from taking a step back because of the affronting smell of mothballs, dirt and dust. During the brief exchange that followed he'd been distracted by the triplet's teeth: two of the triplets had unbelievably bad teeth and the third triplet's teeth were too uniform and white to be real.

Linden gave the eulogy. The only time he looked up from his handwritten notes was to make sure his wife still approved.

— Bill was a funny guy, and I'm not just talking about all the pot he smoked. I told him he was crazy to move to Gold Cliff. Not that living up here's what killed him. He died 'cuz of his heart. My doctor tells me that one of my own arteries is more'en half clogged and a couple of other ones aren't much better. Yet I still feel pretty good.

...

Bill kept to himself, but if you got on him, he'd usually give you a hand. He didn't forget us in his will, which is only right because he got all of Aunt Beth's money. So's you know, Bill kept a list of who owed him what—and you know who I'm talking about. I'll be deducting what you owe him from your share of what's left. And you can stop asking me when you're getting your money. It'll be a while.

...

Hannah put Bill's ashes in little baggies for those who want'em.

After the service, Linden went out of his way to tell Torrance that the triplets rented a house together, and that Rennie, who worked in a feed mill, was the only one with a fulltime job.

* * * * *

The dark faux wood paneling and low ceiling in the empty foyer of the Riverside Hotel made it seem even later than it was when Miller and Torrance entered. Torrance had to ring the bell at the front desk twice before the sleepy, middle aged attendant, her frizzy hair gone pure white, emerged from a back room. She was almost fully awake by the time she'd processed his credit card.

While waiting for Miller to finish in the washroom, Torrance flicked through the TV channels looking for business news. His constant concern over the exchange rate heightened as he watched the end of a report on currency speculation and the falling American dollar. His mind went into overdrive as he thought about how fast and how far the dollar might fall. *If it drops more than, say, ten per cent, Hothouse Produce's US business will be wiped out.* Trying to stay positive, he told himself it would be easier to look for a new job now than after he turned 50.

* * * * *

Miller's sleep in the car conspired with the pain from his right shoulder to keep him awake. He'd hurt his shoulder while growing up, the worst time when as a risk-taking teenager he'd jumped out of the box of a moving pickup. The shoulder had started giving him grief in his early 50's and by this point hurt most of the time. *Wanting the pain to be gone is one more reason to look forward to going Home.* While there was no doubt he was only a shadow of what he had once been physically, he found it harder to assess the decline in his mental capacity. The best indicator he could come up with was the difficulty he had remembering people's names and everyday words.

Lately, long-lost memories were beginning to return to him, sometimes in pieces but other times fully intact, like frozen bodies exposed by a retreating glacier. The last couple of evenings before falling asleep he'd found himself anxiously reliving the night he and a group of boys had smashed out the basement windows in an abandoned house. The verisimilitude of the memory was such that he'd found himself overtaken by the same guilt he'd felt running away from the scene all those years ago. Trying to calm down, he'd reminded himself that everyone involved was at least eighty years old by now, assuming they were still alive.

It's funny, how people's eyes glaze over when old people talk, like you're not worth listening to. Fair enough, I have to admit I've lost my sparkle. How long has it been since I've had a lengthy conversation with someone I've just met, like with Tory. Mind you we were stuck in the car ... and it's easy to reminisce. ... Then there was my connection with his dad. ... What was that name of Pastor Ed's minister friend? Richard. Richard ... it'll come to me. ... They've got a new name for affairs now. ... "Moral breaches", that's it. Saying it like that kind of takes the sting out of it.

... Not that I'm any better than Richard. I was happy to tell Tory about all the good I've done but as usual I avoided saying what I did wrong. And still do: pride, about the smallest things, selfishness ... and the way I still think about women—you'd think I'd be past all that by now. "Oh God in heaven, please forgive me and help me to change before I'm done."

... Although Tory has his father's calm, he hasn't found his way yet ... which describes so many. You've got to be in real trouble to look beyond yourself; and everyone has it so good now. ... There's so many clamouring voices, especially in the city. ... It makes sense that he's focused on business. When you're as busy as he is you're fooled into thinking you're making progress. ... And, you don't have any time to think. .... I should have talked to him more about faith; then again, I'm sure he's heard everything he needs to hear. ... Not to say I'm half as effective a witness as I used to be.

He began his evening prayer as he normally did, by petitioning on behalf of people he knew that lived in other countries. But when he got to his old friends the Soronsens in Lebanon he had to give up, conceding that, at least tonight, he was too old to address the world's problems. He fell asleep praying for Torrance and his stitched together family.

Miller had spent as much time considering the meaning of life as anyone. Most challenging was trying to come up with an explanation for pain and suffering and its variant the basic unfairness of people's lives. Above that was trying to reconcile the claims of competing religions. And, at the very top, there were the confounding doctrines of his own faith. Although Miller was reconciled to the fact that certain mysteries wouldn't be resolved here on earth, he felt a surge of joy whenever he was given even a partial answer. He'd recently heard the best explanation yet of the triune nature of God, namely, that God's makeup was like that of an atom, with protons, neutrons and electrons. Thinking about God in that way made sense to him, especially since it explained the cataclysm that had accompanied Christ's separation at the crucifixion.

Miller's faith had been permanently fixed in place when he was convinced God had spoken directly to him. Beyond the church incident, the most memorable of these occasions was when Miller was on a solo, overnight hunting trip. While looking at a waterfall he had distinctly heard God say, "I am". Another time was when he'd had a dream that was more vivid than any other before or since describing the events that would lead up to the death of a minister friend who'd abandoned his calling. The exact details of the dream had later played out with an uncanny precision.

* * * * *

Waking up in the middle of the night, Torrance wondered if his dream had been so weird because he'd eaten late and was sleeping in a strange place. In the dream he'd been with the last group of people on earth, possibly a family, waiting in a house for the final attack by terrible creatures that would come that night. He'd been able to edit the dream as it progressed and had re-imagined the house as having long steel stilts to lift it above the ground. Then, he'd imagined rockets being attached to the outside of the house so it could fly up into the sky before the attack came. Now that he was awake and could think clearly, the plan of shooting off into lifeless space didn't seem nearly as appealing as it had when he was dreaming.

When he woke up again the clock radio read 6:02 a.m. Since Miller was still sleeping, he made his way to the bathroom as quietly as possible and closed the door behind him before turning the light on. He studied his face in the mirror not able to objectively process what he saw. Pawing at his cheeks, he concluded he was aging most under his eyes and below his jaw line where there was no underlying bone structure.

Although Torrance was normally optimistic at the start of the day, he didn't feel great even after he'd showered. Retracing his thoughts, he tried in vain to figure out what had put him in a mild funk. *No, it wasn't just falling asleep on the road and nearly getting killed.* Needing to do something, he decided to go for an early morning walk. Opening the door, he looked back at Miller in the half-light. *If it wasn't for the white hair you'd think you were looking at an infant.*

Torrance had to walk quickly to stay warm when he got outside. On his way through the sleepy residential area he thought about suburban neighbourhoods back home where lights were being turned off and on and cars backing out of driveways to form a funnel of determined commuters headed downtown.

He stopped in front of a midsized grocery store to watch a lone clerk stock shelves. Although the store had the distinguishing characteristics of a locally owned business—a corny name; its central location in the old part of town; an ageing, low-height building, complete with a rusty pedestal sign out front; a friendly, handwriting font used on the sales posters in the windows; and the casual piling of boxes at the end of store's aisles—Torrance knew from being in the food business that the store had been bought out by a retail chain long ago.

* * * * *

Miller woke up while Torrance was out. He wanted to get out of bed, but was frozen by the pain in his shoulder that had spread to most of his joints. There was also the pressure in his chest he'd felt off and on for several days that felt like a cold iron bar pressing down. *If each day of life is like arriving at a new train station, there can't be that many stops left.*

Slipping back into a near sleep, he found himself trying to remember the name of the red-headed girl he'd been smitten with in grade eight. For whatever reason he was convinced he would die if he couldn't remember her name. Fantastically, he imagined watching row upon row of neon names in alphabetical order moving in stacked unison through his mind. Suddenly, there in the front row was the girl's name: Dorothy.

Miller was perched on the edge of his bed trying to generate the will to stand when Torrance returned to the room.

— Good sleep?

— I must have been tired. I hope I haven't kept you.

— Not at all, we're ahead of schedule.

Miller looked at the faded face of his old watch before subconsciously winding it.

— Do I have time to shave?

— You've got lots of time. I don't have to be in Centre City until 4:00.

The restaurant in the hotel is decent and so we may as well eat here.

Miller left the door of the washroom open while he lathered up with bar soap.

— Do you want to use my shaving cream?

— No thanks. You get used to things.

*   *   *   *   *

The name on their waitress's name tag, "Resa" suited her high energy personality. After flitting to and from their table with coffee and to take and deliver their orders, she stopped to talk for a moment when they were finished eating. In the briefest of conversations she managed to inform them that she and her husband were first generation Filipino Canadians, her husband worked as a mechanic at a car dealership in town, and they had three children, the oldest of whom was in second year at university in Calona. In response to Miller's query, she said, yes, her full name was Resurrection.

Miller and Torrance had divided up the copy of yesterday's edition of the newspaper Miller had purchased at the front desk when an older couple walking past stopped at their table.

— You wouldn't be Miller Gauthier, would you?

— I am indeed. And you are …?

— Joel Hidey.

— Joel. I didn't recognize you. How long has it been?

— Let's see … the last time we saw each other was … I think it was when we were up in oil rig country in northern Alberta … when was that … '78 or '79?

— It was after the Williston camp disaster. Do you remember that place?

— How could I forget? You only get to break up so many fights during a prayer meeting.

Torrance responded in kind to Joel's firm handshake, but instantly adjusted to only lightly touch the arthritic clump of fingers extended by Joel's sister, Tina. Joel turned his head to quietly confide to Miller and Torrance that Tina had several health problems, including the loss of most of her hearing.

Although Joel and Tina had already eaten, they joined the out-of-town visitors. Joel and Miller took turns describing what they'd been up to in the intervening decades. When Joel got to his move to Gold Cliff he explained that Tina and he were an ideal match as roommates, and that they had come to the restaurant that morning as a special treat before going to help out with preparations for an African AIDS orphanage fundraiser at their church. He added under his breath that it wasn't until he'd begun sharing an apartment with Tina that he'd found out what a prayer warrior she was.

When it was time to go, Joel helped quiet, bowed-over Tina get to her feet. She stopped before she was fully up. Miller quickly asked:

— Does your arthritis make it difficult for you to stand?

Tina stood a little straighter before turning to look directly at Miller.

— No. It's not that. It's you. You have a deep faith.

— Yes, I do.

— I can feel it. The Holy Spirit is with you.

* * * * *

Torrance drove back to the highway, turning left at the light to go north. After a while they passed a highway hauler and trailer with "HHP" markings going the other way.

— That's one of our company's trucks. It carries compost from our plant up here down to mushroom farms near the big city.

— You make compost all the way up here?

— Yeah, there are too many regulations—for smell and waste water—to produce it down south. Even after factoring in the cost of transportation, it makes sense to truck the ingredients ... primarily straw and chicken manure ... up here for composting before sending the finished substrate back down to the farms.

— I knew they sent the city's garbage up here, but I didn't know about compost.

— Actually, our composting site is right next to the metropolitan dump. We're the perfect neighbours, since neither of us can complain about the other.

Torrance spoke up again when a German sports car blasted past them in the passing lane a few kilometers from town.

— I used to dream about having a fancy car, but I've started to see them as big chunks of metal that nobody's going to want to own soon.

THE DEAD FOREST

CITIES CROW ABOUT BECOMING SELF-SUSTAINING. This, even though they source their electricity, oil and gas, and construction materials from far away; their food, from industrial farms with huge, single crop fields and block-long barns full of chickens and turkeys; their drinking water, from streams with distant headwaters; and the air their citizens breathe, from oceans, fields and forests. Not to forget that the items for sale in a city's stores are imported; and that cities don't have their own garbage dumps.

* * * * *

Miller and Torrance entered a forest of dead pine trees acting as sentinels to ecological reversal.
— I had no idea the pine beetle kill was this bad so far south.
— Me neither.
— I wonder what will happen to all the dead trees.
— They'll either decompose or burn up in a horrendous fire. Nature finds a way when it's left to itself.
Their conversation circled back to family.
— I agree, being around young people reenergizes you. Two weeks ago Kelly and I went across the line for a weekend getaway. Our heads were a bit down on our way home because we knew we were about to get back on the treadmill. When we were near the border we got a text from Kelly's son, Neil, asking what was for dinner. Kelly and I hadn't thought about dinner, but Neil's text galvanized us into action. We made a point of stopping off at a country store

to get some food, and had a lot of fun buying the food and cooking the meal.

How about you? Did you ever want to have kids?

— Sure. But I never got married.

— Was that because of your work?

— I suppose. I came close once. The lady's name was Linda Seedorf. She was a high school teacher who attended the church I went to whenever I was in Centre City.

Talking helped Miller take his mind off the pain in his chest.

* * * * *

The boat dealership was still up on the flats above the forestry town of Billy's Lake. *Why would anyone want to buy a boat, or have a boat worked on, way up here?* The profusion of billboards nearer town made Torrance wonder if a local Native band had regained control of the area.

Several of the billboards looked like they were no longer being maintained. Seeing a faded and peeling billboard that advertised metal truck grills, he wondered if the protective grills were still being manufactured given the decimation of the moose population. *Like when steam trains no longer needed cow catchers.*

There were several large box stores just outside the municipal limits of town. *The mom and pop stores downtown don't stand a chance. … Some trends are so big they simply sweep you out of the way, no questions asked.*

The highway converted into Billy's Lake's main street in town. Slowed down, Torrance had time to consider the make-up of the hardy little community. Most of the buildings were from the sixties or earlier, and it seemed like everyone on the street was his age or older, which he hoped had to do with the time of day rather than demographics. Spotting the name "Rodeo Drive" on a cross street he kept an eye out for other copycat names. In short order there were signs for Amarillo Street and Steveston Avenue. Not far past the city park there was a large, weathered billboard with a map showing the way to lots for sale at the "New Oxford Place Community".

Torrance was waiting for the light at an intersection to change when a pickup truck shot out from the back of the stopped line of oncoming cars and headed straight for them. Luckily, the cross traffic had passed through by the time the pickup got to the intersection and the driver was able to slalom back into his own lane, narrowly missing the left front corner of Torrance's car. Torrance had a freeze frame view of the inside the pickup's cab as it whipped past. The driver was a man about thirty with a hard face and a confronting beard. A young woman who looked to still be a teenager was in the passenger seat.

Torrance hadn't quite collected himself when he realized the light was green. Before he could get going he heard a police siren. He put his foot back on the brake and waited as a police cruiser raced into view to his left. The cruiser's tires howled as it turned onto the highway, sliding dangerously close to Torrance's Chevrolet before screaming off. Torrance turned to watch the cruiser pursue the pickup through the traffic frozen in place behind them.

Torrance looked across at Miller with wide open eyes after they went through the intersection.

— That was close.

— I was sure the pickup was going to smash into us.

— You don't drive like that to avoid a parking ticket.

Miller asked Torrance if he'd seen the girl.

— She looked young enough to be his daughter.

— If her eyes weren't open already they are now. Most little girls just want to grow up to be princesses—and boys, princes—but it seldom turns out that way. They end up seeing and doing too many things.

They drove in silence before Torrance spoke up.

— I remember when I was in grade twelve I got it in my head that a girl I hadn't paid any attention to before was the girl of my dreams—at that age you just need someone to love. I made a bit of a show of asking her out. She laughed off my offer and told me she already had a boyfriend. I found out the guy she was dating was twenty-four or twenty-five years old. He was part of a rough crowd; and he owned his own tire shop, which was impressive. He also had a hot car and there I was with my VW Bug. A month or two after I asked the girl out the boyfriend was arrested for stealing cars, or possession of stolen goods, something like that. I'm pretty sure he did time in Centre City.

— Do you know what his name was—I visited the Centre City jail as part of my outreach?

— No, I've long since forgotten it.

— What happened to the girl?

— She left town right after graduation. The last I heard she'd gotten married to someone older with money: a dentist or a doctor. She was quite pretty … or at least she made the most of what she had to work with.

* * * * *

Torrance's phone rang. It was Randhawa, Hothouse Produce's head salesperson in Washington State.

— Hi, Torrman. Sorry to bother you while you're out of the office. Are you okay to talk for a minute?

— No problem, Randy. What's up?

— The PW Food Group is really jamming us for a long-term price commitment. They say they can get a 120-day commitment from northern California growers and unless we can match it they're going to switch.

— We've heard that before.

— I know, but I think there's more to it this time. One of their VP's says they're under real pressure to buy American. Apparently a local politician even came to talk to the general manager. Imagine if a politician tried something like that in Canada.

— I told the other managers about the pressure we're under in the US. PW Food's one of our top accounts. The bottom line is we have to do what we have to do. If you think it's going to take a 120-day guarantee, then go for it.

Torrance continued thinking about the call after hanging up. *There could be ramifications from giving PW Food a special deal, and I probably should have talked to Danny before giving Randy the go-ahead.* He suddenly wasn't sure what had been decided at the last management meeting. They'd spent a long time going through the company's options on dealing with price guarantees, but now he couldn't be certain if they'd settled on 90 or 120 days. He momentarily panicked when he remembered the confidentiality provisions in PW Food's contract. *I should have told Randy to remind PW Food about that.*

He phoned Randhawa back right away but the call went straight to voicemail.

On their way up a hill a kilometer or more in length Miller and Torrance passed an old pickup with a beat-up camper. The two guys in the cab looked to be scruffy old hunters. The driver stared back blankly at their car as they went past.

— So when do you hit peak wisdom and stop making mistakes?
— Since I'm still making mistakes, I guess I'm not there yet.

After a pause he added:

— You know where wisdom comes from, don't you?

* * * * *

They finally arrived at healthy stands of spruce and fir at the foot of the coastal mountains. As they gained elevation the trees became smaller and there were more rocky outcrops.

— One thing for certain is if there are any mineral deposits in this area they're subject to a Native land claim.
— Well, we do kind of owe those people.
— I agree the Native Canadian's got the short end of the stick for too long, but how do you reconcile one group having special rights? I mean isn't that why they had the French Revolution?
— No doubt it's a hard problem.

They drove on in silence before Torrance spoke.

— If you think about it we're like a service provider to the PRC now, what with all the resources we sell them; and how they use what they get from us to make the manufactured items they sell us. ... I keep thinking there's something wrong when most of what you buy comes from one country. At some point won't China be able to charge us whatever they want?
— I remember when most goods were made in the US and Britain. After a while I started seeing goods that were manufactured in Japan. Like with China, the first Japanese imports were super cheap. But over time they got better, and more expensive.
— When I was growing up in Bull Moose Run I found a rechargeable flashlight in the snow that was "Made in Japan." The flashlight had a back half and a front half. You plugged the back half of the flashlight, which had a rechargeable battery in it, into an electrical outlet

to charge it; and when the battery was charged up you plugged the back half of the flashlight into the front half. I didn't see anything like it for years.

They talked about advances that had been made in electronics.

— As accessible as music downloads are, I get as much or maybe even more joy listening to old albums on a windup Victrola phonograph I bought at a garage sale. Kelly was worried about my mental health when she found me in the basement listening to White Christmas in the middle of summer.

Torrance's comment on how cell phones had basically replaced home phones and cameras triggered Miller's memory.

— I was helping out at a used book sale outside the mall entrance to raise money for a care home—I tell people I'm happy to help out while I've got the energy since it won't be long until I'm a resident.

There was another volunteer working with me. His name was Mike, I think. He told me his mother lives in the care home. When I asked him what he did for a living he said he was a computer programmer but that he was between jobs. He was an odd guy, for sure. He wouldn't stop talking, even when we had a customer. I thought he might have been on something.

We were set up outside so we had our coats on. Mike was wearing a trench coat. We were coming to the end of our shift when he asked me if I wanted to buy a watch, it was like in that old cartoon.

— You mean where the guy says, "Hey, mister, do you want to buy a cheap watch?"

— That's it. I told him I already had a watch but he opened up his coat anyway. Here's the thing, instead of showing me actual watches, he pulled out his cell phone and showed me pictures of watches he said I could buy.

— Did you buy one?

— No, I figured they were stolen.

Fifty kilometers later, the road was surrounded by mountains that nearly reached the sky. Torrance had forgotten about the shape of Mount Macdonald, which was at an angle and looked like it might topple over.

Near the summit, Torrance craned his neck to up at one of the more impressive peaks. His first thought was that the mountaintop, and not the clouds around it, was moving. He felt small and unimportant.

* * * * *

Halfway down the far side of the mountain pass, they drove past a vertiginous cliff of tumbled rock. There was very little vegetation at the site, which made Torrance wonder how long it had been since the rock face collapsed.

— So, when did you retire?

— We don't talk a lot about retirement in my business, but I've lived at the coast for fifteen years, and it's been ten years or more since cancer really slowed me down.

— How are you doing now?

Miller decided not to tell Torrance about his chest pains.

— My doctor says he can't believe I survived the cancer, let alone the other health issues I've had. I guess there must be something left for me to do.

They came to a place where the highway overlooked a valley that used to support several ranches. All that remained now were dilapidated buildings, unkempt fields pieced up by broken fences, and a scattering of abandoned vehicles that looked from a distance like crumpled beer cans.

* * * * *

Not far after a sign giving the distance in kilometers to several destinations ahead, they came to an unincorporated municipality called 92 Mile House. Next to a row of long-abandoned houses there was an open field plotted by the rusted remains of a green chain, a drying kiln, and the bottom two-thirds of a beehive burner.

— I sometimes wonder what my life would have been like if I had stayed up north and worked in a mill. The repetition of mill jobs is mind numbing, but at least you're done after eight hours. ... I don't suppose there are many of those jobs left; and I'll bet they don't pay what they used to.

— No, I don't think they do. ... Logging had its pluses and minuses too. The good part is you worked outdoors; the bad part is you worked outdoors. Most of the loggers I knew were done in by middle age. Though maybe it's easier now with tree snippers and log processors.

What stands out to me when I look back was how most loggers spent all week talking about getting drunk on the weekend—and I have to admit I used to be one of those guys. The older loggers didn't talk as much about their parties, but drank as much, or more. It was like no one wanted to deal with life straight on. When you're young you don't see the need for change and when you're old you figure you've set your course.

— I have to tell you I have a hard time imagining loggers coming back from a long day in the woods and wanting to talk religion.

— I agree, it isn't easy starting up a conversation with someone who's tired or whose mind has been blunted by booze. Amazingly, though, there was usually someone who had time for me. I could always tell when a guy was coming around, he'd get serious and admit he had problems at home, or he'd become wistful and say he used to attend Sunday school.

One thing I didn't appreciate until later was that I was benefitting as much or more than the guys I talked to. I got to meet the most incredible people in my time up north. One of the guys I looked up to most was Tommy Chung. Now there was someone who loved Jesus. Tommy lost one of his arms in an accident but he kept working—believe it or not I once saw him buck up a tree with one arm using a specially rigged saw. He was always so positive, although he said that losing his arm was about as big a life lesson as he thought he could deal with. Tommy wound up in charge of Western Timber's woods operations for the whole province.

Miller stopped talking and thought back in time.

— Another guy who really inspired me was Pastor Chuck Keaggy. He had this little church in Watamax. He was long past retirement age when he finally shut down. The church offered to let him stay on in the parsonage but he said the new minister's family needed it more than he did. One of the church members told me that when Pastor Chuck went looking for a place all he could afford to buy was a used mobile home; and since he'd given all his money away he had to finance most of it. I'm humbled every time I think about him, since I live so well.

My faith was so strong back then I expected an answer every time I prayed. I can't tell you how many times I needed direction, or was in real trouble, and I was given exactly what I needed. Interestingly, I seldom got more than I needed.

One winter I was miles down a snowy logging road headed to a logging camp that I wasn't sure was still running. I hit some ice and slid into the ditch. I tried to dig myself out but eventually gave up. Even though it was cold and dark, and I hadn't seen another vehicle since leaving town, I had this incredible peace.

All of a sudden, I saw headlights coming my way. The driver of what turned out to be a pickup truck, a young man with a big gap between his front teeth, stopped to give me a hand. We tried to push my car out and when that didn't work we decided to go into town to get a tow rope. As soon as I climbed into the cab of the pickup I sensed the young man was suffering. I told him right then and there that he needed to know God was real.

He started to cry and said his brother had recently committed suicide, and that he had been thinking of giving up himself. I saw him at a church service years later. He came up to me after the service to introduce himself. Even though he was a lot older I recognized him right away because of his gap-toothed smile. He told me he had gotten married to a wonderful woman and they had three beautiful girls.

*   *   *   *   *

They entered an area of fields and wetlands. A V of geese came into Torrance's ken. Looking up and off to his left, he saw five or six larger wedges. When the main group was high overhead he felt like he'd been caught up in a net of moving lines.

He kept watching for as long as he could as the geese traversed against the palette of white, grey and black clouds.

CENTRE CITY

URBAN PLANNERS SAY DETACHED HOMES on large lots are unsustainable because of their low density. But what about the role of lawns, gardens and trees in cleaning the air and cooling the city down in summer, to say nothing of the importance of undeveloped areas to the lives of insects, birds and animals?

*   *   *   *   *

Centre City, which only qualified as a big city because it was so far north, was the hub of the province's mining, lumber, and pulp and paper industries. Approaching its outskirts, Miller and Torrance drove past a combination greenhouse/food market whose meticulous upkeep was more impressive because of its location. A few kilometers on, a new gas bar was getting ready to open. The asphalt extruding beyond the edge of the freshly poured parking lot looked thinner than it should and Torrance wondered if the building contractor was aware of the ferocity of northern winters. *Then again, I guess winters weren't as cold as they used to be.*

Torrance looked down from a railway overpass at a blur of lumber yards, parked rail cars on spur lines, trucks driving over oiled gravel roads, metal fabrication shops, many of whose sliding doors were open, and an organized auto wrecking yard. The only empty lot he noticed had a construction fence bound tightly around it.

Miller and Torrance smelled the pulp at the same time.

— I haven't smelled that for a long time. I remember a businessman telling me I should be happy when the smell from the pulp mills

155

was so bad my eyes watered and I could hardly breathe because it meant everyone was working.

Torrance took the first exit into the city across the old iron bridge. The birch forest that used to act as a buffer on the far side of the river had given way to an oppressive maze of roads, parking lots and retail outlets.

An abrupt change in the age of the buildings announced their arrival at the start of the city's historical centre. Torrance was surprised the row of sagging, wooden storage sheds was still there alongside the abandoned rail lines; and he recognized the series of strip malls, now more than 50 years old, that came next. The once futuristic features of the malls—including sloped metal pillars supporting the roof extension over the walkway of one mall and stylistic tiled diamond shapes on the end wall of another—made them look even older than they were. As part of the urban molt, the malls' former tenants, drugstores, shoe stores, and hardware stores had been replaced by tattoo and piercing parlours, pawn shops, and nail salons.

Downtown, there wasn't a single "For Lease" sign, and it seemed like everyone was in a hurry. Most impressive was the new city hall and court complex confirming the government's claim to the long-settled territory.

*　*　*　*　*

Although Miller couldn't find the piece of paper that had the address of the house he was staying at, he said he thought he would recognize it if they got close. Sure enough, he spotted the house on the second street they went down in an older residential section.

Torrance got Miller's suitcase out of the trunk and placed it on the sidewalk. The two men shook hands.

— I enjoyed your company.

— And I enjoyed yours. Are you sure I don't owe you anything?

— Yes.

— May the Lord God bless you and keep you.

*　*　*　*　*

Torrance continued on to the grocery store. Although he'd had an excellent working relationship with Vern, the store's previous produce manager, there was an awkward dynamic between him and Vern's replacement, Brett. He hoped meeting in person would help.

Since he had a few minutes after he'd parked, he tried calling Randhawa's number again. The call went straight to voicemail again. With nothing more he could do he began to relax. His final thought on the matter was PW Food were big boys who'd know it was in their interest to keep the terms of their deal to themselves.

When it was nearly 4:00 he walked to the service door at the back of the store. Finding the door unlocked, he went in. An older clerk—*no doubt looked after by the better half of the union's two-tier contract*—was unwrapping some recently delivered pallets. In response to Torrance's query, the clerk said he'd seen Brett go up to the office.

Torrance climbed the wood stairs up to the unpainted, plywood-walled office on the mezzanine floor. Looking though the side window from the landing at the top he saw a man about thirty-five years old sitting at a desk. The man looked up and gestured for Torrance to come in when he heard the knock.

— Hi, I'm Torrance Maki from Hothouse Produce.
— Brett Norwood.

Brett stood up to greet him. Although Brett moved well enough, he had started to collect the extra weight of a former athlete who had stopped playing sports. Torrance noticed Brett's eyes were bloodshot.

Torrance's attempt at small talk didn't take and so he got down to business. When he was finished going over the upcoming seasonal price and supply changes, he asked if Brett would mind showing him through the store.

Torrance complemented Brett on the immaculately maintained produce section. Brett, who was clearly pleased, joked that he didn't want Torrence to say anything to the store manager because his staff hours might be cut. Torrance was about to leave when Brett offered to buy him a beer after work. Torrance passed on the beer but agreed to meet for dinner.

* * * * *

The chain restaurant Brett chose was within walking distance of Torrance's hotel. There were several people waiting in the restaurant's reception area when Torrance arrived. His cell phone rang as he was giving his name to the thin, young lady attendant. Despite the background noise on both sides of the call, Torrance was able to make out that Brett wanted a table for five.

Brett still hadn't showed when Torrance's name was called. A second, equally thin, young server who reminded Torrance of Kelly's daughter, Debra, led him to the table. They walked past a booth where three young toughs were sitting with their dates. The men had uniformly short hair; two wore stylized t-shirts and the other, a dress shirt open at the neck. All three had prominent tattoos. The women were dressed in dark colours and also had tattoos. The talking was loud enough to challenge anyone sitting nearby to say something. Torrance remembered the rumor that the restaurant chain had been funded by gang money.

Minutes after Torrance sat down, Brett and three other men, two about Brett's age and the third quite a bit older, who had to be at least six feet four, made their boisterous arrival. Brett pointed to one of the younger men, Calin, and the tall, older man, Kurt.

— They're lawyers so watch what you say.

Kurt sat down across from Torrance.

Brett introduced his friend Duartine, who managed a local RV dealership. Duartine was high energy and he got the dinner off to a running start.

— Is it just me, or was that hostess one good looking woman?

From there the freedom of Friday night, combined with the frisson of adding someone in from out of town, produced a steady fire of opinions, insults, and edged replies. Torrance noticed the others stopped to listen whenever Kurt spoke. Income taxes must have been on the older lawyer's mind, because he became serious and said that anyone who didn't think the deficit would lead to higher taxes was in for a surprise. With his editorial out of the way, Kurt proceeded to tell a story about a couple who had made the regrettable decision to confront their noisy, motorcycle gang neighbours. Kurt's relaxed description of the resulting criminal behavior made Torrance wonder if lawyers had to have a serious twist themselves in order to defend bad people.

Taking advantage of a break in the banter, Brett described his recent online dating adventure. He said it was obvious when he met his date that she was a lot older than stated. He'd asked about her age when she'd let the year of her graduation slip, and she'd responded without missing a beat by saying that the dating agency had made a mistake on her bio. Brett was getting to the grittier parts of the story when the waitress brought another round of drinks.

Calin didn't wait for Brett to start up again when the waitress left.
— A while back I had a file involving three old sisters, the youngest of whom was in her mid-eighties. The sisters were in a dispute over an unregistered easement at the back of their side-by-side lots they'd inherited from their mother. The only reason the dispute was headed to court was one of the sisters' husbands, who was as self-interested and heartless of an old bugger as you'll ever meet, wanted to sell the lot owned by his wife.

My client, I'll call her Mrs. Smith, was the oldest sister. After finding out her age and that her son had to drive her to my office I wondered if she would be able to give me instructions. I became even more worried when I saw her in person. She wore this blonde wig meant for a woman sixty years younger; and she was so frail she could hardly walk. On top of that she was almost blind as a result of macular degeneration—to see me, she had to turn her head and look through the corner of her good eye. I kept thinking there was someone else in the room because of the way she was always looking off to the side.

It turned out Mrs. Smith was totally with it. At the end of her appointment I said, "Mrs. Smith, you are amazing. I've just spent an hour going through complex legal concepts, and you've under-stood everything; and on top of that you've got a fantastic memory. I'm telling you, Mrs. Smith, you're the best." She looked at me side-ways, as usual, and said, "What a nice thing to say. Perhaps you'd like to come by and see me socially."

Torrance laughed and Kurt smiled. Brett and Duartine had stopped listening early on in Calin's story and were talking between themselves.

Table-wide comments gave way to private conversations when the food arrived. Torrance made an effort to engage Kurt, asking him about the latest from Centre City. Kurt cryptically said the news was always the same: the airport needed to be expanded and there would never be enough doctors. Torrance waited a while before trying again, this time commenting on how busy the downtown had seemed that afternoon. This time Kurt looked up before answering.

— The mills are running three shifts but it won't be long before the pine beetle wood is all gone, and then what? Maybe the new problem with spruce beetles is going to be a good thing, at least until all the spruce trees are cut down too.

While finishing his Spanish coffee Kurt asked Torrance how long he was going to be in Centre City.

— Until tomorrow. I'm driving to Bull Moose Run in the morning to meet a friend. We're flying up to a place called Alces Lake to go hunting.

— I've got a three-day jury trial starting in the Moose on Monday.

— I don't remember there being a courthouse in the Moose.

— It's been there for a while.

— Must have been built after I left. I was born in Bull Moose Run.

— Really.

Kurt was suddenly interested in what Torrance had to say and asked him about his memories of Bull Moose Run, especially the dynamic between Native Canadian and white students in high school. Torrance did his best to give comprehensive answers.

When Kurt had the information he was after he announced to the table that he was done for the night. Putting cash down for his share of the bill, but not much more, he said:

— If you fellows run out of things to do, you can always drive up to my house for a late-night snoot.

He smiled conspiratorially as if the invitation was real, although they all knew it wasn't.

It wasn't long after that when Brett, in a voice made husky by booze and cigarettes, said to no one in particular that he was going to go over to the Crazy Palomino to watch the ladies. Although Duartine said he was in, Calin and Torrance stayed silent. Brett got the message and gruffly asked for the bill when the server returned. Brett reached for his wallet when the bill showed up but Torrance waved him off, saying Hothouse Produce would be happy to pick up the tab. Brett managed a cursory, "thanks" before lurching off with Duartine in tow.

After Brett and Duartine had left, Torrance asked Calin to tell him more about their dinner companions. Calin explained that Kurt had helped him out as co-counsel on a case when he was a young lawyer, and that they'd arranged to have a drink when they met in court earlier in the day. Brett and Duartine were former clients of Kurt they'd run into at the bar.

— Kurt is a cheap bugger, isn't he? What can you say, I guess like the rest of us, he is who he is. In his case that includes being "ag'in it", whatever it is. He's willing to take on anyone and anything, whether it's an out of town lawyer or a lost cause, as long as he gets paid. While some of his confidence comes from past successes, I think a lot comes from being a big guy who's used to getting his own way. To be fair, he takes on more than just criminal cases, where all you have to do is raise a doubt—Kurt's theory on running criminal trials is you create enough confusion, he calls it laying down rabbit trails, so that in the end no one's quite sure what happened. There's been more than a few big name lawyers who came to Centre City thinking they had a clear winner and ended up losing. Of course, there's a bit of a home court advantage.

The server circled back with more coffee.

— Kurt is so far out on the edge sometimes that he can be scary hard to figure out. To celebrate that first court case we did together he invited me to go fishing with him and two of his firm's articling students up at Moose Lake. I thought it would be a relaxing weekend. Wrong. If you think being a passenger in a car that's going too fast is dangerous, imagine riding with an angry guy hell bent for leather in a truck that's pulling a boat that's way bigger than the truck. Even though there were some serious waves on the lake, Kurt was the same full on throttle after we launched the boat. And he was well into the booze by then.

When we got to where we were going, Kurt handed out the fishing rods and we began to troll. It couldn't have been ten minutes before there was a strike on the rod in the rod holder beside me. Before I knew what was happening Kurt had grabbed the rod and begun reeling the fish in. You should have seen him yelling at the poor Chinese Canadian articling student who he'd put in charge of the fish net. I don't think that poor bugger had ever been fishing before. Thank goodness they landed the fish—I swear Kurt would have thrown the student overboard if the fish had gotten away. It was a twelve-pound rainbow, the biggest I've ever seen. Kurt never apologized for yelling at the student or for taking my rod.

They talked about how Bull Moose Run used to be a throwback to the Wild West, where life was cheap. Torrance recalled some of his antics as a kid.

— We used to ride our snowmobiles on Moose Lake well into spring. You had to make your own decision when it was no longer safe to go out on the ice. I remember looking behind me once and seeing that my trail was just slushy water. I gunned it straight to shore. There must have been a second layer of ice because I made it back without sinking.

As the evening wound down they talked about things that had changed.

— Centre City used to be this self-contained place where young lawyers came to do their articles and stayed to raise their families. Not anymore. Now everyone wants now is to get back to the bright lights of the big city as soon as they can. It's not just lawyers. Someone was telling me that most of the employees at the new cobalt mine near North Falls live down south and only fly into town on the weeks they're on shift.

*　*　*　*　*

Calin and Torrance shook hands outside the restaurant and walked off in opposite directions. Two blocks from his hotel, Torrance spotted a group of guys coming his way. From a caution he'd acquired as a youth in Bull Moose Run, he crossed over to the other side of the street. When the group was closer he saw it was just a bunch of skinny teenagers hurrying to get somewhere. *Probably to play video games.*

Torrance was staying in the city's Victorian era, railroad hotel that was still Centre City's flagship. The four story solid masonry building had cost a lot to build, with features including oak-walled hallways, granite flooring, and plastered ceilings with medallions. That afternoon in his room, Torrance had taken the time to admire the old metal pulley system for the window that was still in good working condition. He'd surmised that the English or German made pulleys had been built at a time both countries had empires.

It was late and Torrance, who'd had a glass or two too many, was glad to make it back safely to the warm, well-lit lobby of the storied building. It struck him that he would have really been thrown off if he'd arrived to find the staff at the front desk dressed in period piece attire from when the hotel first opened.

He turned on the TV when he got to his room; however, a travelogue about Venice didn't hold his attention. An infant down the hall began to cry when he was climbing into bed. While he blessed every parent and child in the whole wide world, he needed it to be quiet now. The crying soon stopped, and he drifted off thinking about the desires of his heart.

HOME

WE CAN ONLY HOLD ONE or, at most, two thoughts at a time and we screen the others out: a bronze plaque at a local park describes the deceased, honoured donor as a "conservationist, industrialist" without further explanation; the newspaper's lead story is about an increased subsidy for electric cars, and a few pages later there is a picture of an old hydroelectric dam that is being broken up to promote a devastated fish run.

* * * * *

It was the start of a new day. Torrance looked up from his hotel bed at the famous print of a cowboy on a horse chasing a calf. He remembered those details he couldn't make out in the weak light. The power of the picture came from the intensity of each of the three separate but connected stories. The cowboy, his eyes on the calf, was leaning forward as far as possible, a lariat in his mouth, its loop in his right hand, and the horse reins in his left. The horse, which had forgotten the rider, was turning in taut unison with the calf. And the calf was running for its life.

The fresh-faced young woman server in the hotel café was happy to get another customer. On his way to his table, Torrance imagined back to when long-deceased timber barons had entered this same café looking forward to a similar greasy meal of bacon, eggs and hash browns. *When you're in the wheelhouse you think life will go on forever. But then it stops.* A woman about his age was eating alone. Studying her profile, he decided she was one of those people who are attractive

165

at every stage in life. *We think people look so different and yet, like with other types of animals, we probably all look about the same.* The woman's sixth sense told her that someone was looking at her and Torrance shifted his gaze when she turned towards him.

With nothing to read except the menu, Torrance went over his time with Miller. He'd begun to think about their talks like confessions, with he, the confessor, trying to use the exact right words to describe an even truer truth. What was amazing to him was that Miller, the confessor figure, had made it seem like he was benefitting as much or more from their discussions. *Maybe that's how confessions are supposed to work.*

Miller talked about the importance of faith, to individuals and to society, with the same level of moral certainty as my dad. ... How did he put it? ... "A person only feels real significance if they believe there is a design."... His other line was something like, "You can't be greater than yourself." I guess I basically know what he meant. ... Miller was bent on saving my soul ... but maybe he was on to something.

*   *   *   *   *

On the way to his car, Torrance walked past a man in his sixties, cigarette in hand, coughing up phlegm. Keeping a wide birth, he congratulated himself on having stopped smoking when he did.

This was a big day, and after settling into the driver's seat he took the cellophane off one of his new CDs and pushed the disc into the player. After skipping forward to what used to be the third song on the second side of the album, he put the transmission into drive.

He was so focused on the atmospheric sounds of a rhythmic bass and synthesizer he missed his turn and had to wait for another major intersection to go left. On his way up and out of the river valley there were several odd-shaped, pieces of road-building equipment parked on a newly cut terrace that he thought might look like dinosaurs under the right light.

Torrance had started the day feeling pretty good, but after a while began to lose interest in the old music. Even the features of the landscape had started to blur. Suddenly, he wanted nothing more than to talk to someone. But, after going through the short list of his real friends, he had to admit that Kelly was the only person he could call up for no particular reason; and even she wouldn't fully understand why he'd called.

He remembered back to when, as a young boy, he had been walked through the sinner's prayer by a camp counselor. *I would have been nine or ten. Yes it was me, but a much younger me. Almost not the same person.*

* * * * *

He was playing a new CD when he arrived at the farmland surrounding the town of Footing. One of the first homes he came to was so impressive he doubted it was lived in by real farmers.

Just past the "Welcome to Footing" sign, the letters for the sign having been cut out of a large log that lay lengthwise on the slope of a small hill, there was a billboard for a used auto parts business that cheekily advertised "private parts." A little farther on he drove past an old, nondescript building with two smaller windows up front. Although the building didn't look like a restaurant and there wasn't an obvious parking lot, a yellowing marquee sign propped up on the ground in the front yard read: "Ice cream breakfast pizza." *Presumably that's a reference to three, rather than four, or two, food options.* When he drove through downtown Footing he decided that, with the exception of a few new stores, it looked the same as ever.

There were more farmers' fields north of town. Soon, though, the edge of the boreal forest came into sight, the front row of trees as fixed as an international boundary. Entering the spruce tree corridor it dawned on him that the area wasn't called big sky country because trees and changes in elevation were always blocking your view.

Torrance felt an unexpected chug of emotion when the road descended chute-like down to Ringer Creek. It was at the top of the steep hill on the far side of the creek that the father of his friend, Jerry, who had half the team of peewee hockey players in his car, had fortuitously slowed down just before one of the car's rear wheels fell off.

He came to the long hill where the two youngest Johnson brothers and he had given up on their plan to bike to Footing and back in one day. Not bothering to tell anyone, the three youths ... *we couldn't have been more than twelve* ... had set out early on a summer day. Their calculations had proven to be wildly optimistic and they'd had to turn back, exhausted, far short of their goal. The last thing he'd heard about the Johnsons was the old man had been killed in a hunting accident after the family moved to Fort Matthews.

Memories kept tumbling in. He knew he was nearly home when he came to the infamous straight stretch where two testosterone-soaked teenagers had shared victory in a doubly fatal game of chicken, neither driver having blinked. At the turnoff to Sandy Beach, images from the all-night beach party, including the fight between the Timmett brothers, ghosted through his mind. *That was when I met Simone.* Not until years later did he realize just how dumb he'd been rendered by his newfound, worldly wise female friend. Simone had come north to spend the summer with her rich, widowed great aunt who lived alone in a house above the lake. The great aunt's late husband had started off as a bush pilot and finished his career running a national airline. The couple had moved back north to retire, but the pioneering pilot had died before their custom home was finished being built. Simone's great aunt had ended up living alone in the house for years.

Driving across Moose River Bridge, Torrance looked down at the rushing water that forever held the same patterns. He thought back to when Dave and he had raced out to the bridge on their bikes to see the 700 pound sturgeon landed by a Native fisherman.

He arrived at the Moose Lake Reserve ... *assuming they're still called reserves.* There was a row of newly constructed houses on one side of the road, and on the other, a large log building with a sign out front that said, "So'endzin Friendship Centre."

A small green sign said, "Bull Moose Run – Pop. 4,000". Soon he was driving through an area of small, dilapidated houses, interspersed with a handful of commercial properties. The vehicles were a mix of cars and pickups, most of which hadn't been washed for some time. *It's familiar to me, even welcoming. Yet, someone who's arriving for the first time would wonder what kind of people lived and worked in a town like this. ... The fact is it takes a while to figure out that people are people, no matter where you are.*

Torrance came to a four way stop, which he was pretty sure didn't used to be there. With no other vehicles near, he turned right without stopping. In two more blocks he was at the front of his old high school. Icon red false shutters had been installed on the light brown building that he didn't remember being that colour. There was a lone car in the parking lot. *Probably a janitor, or a young teacher trying to make his or her mark.*

Torrance parked in front of the school and looked across the street at the smoke pit.

* * * * *

Torrance had made a single visit out to the unfinished house on North Beach Road where Preston Mahoney lived with his thieving brother, his mom and his dad who was always off working in the woods—try as he might, Torrance couldn't remember what Preston's dad looked like. Torrance's most vivid memory from the visit was watching with a child's misgiving as Preston's mom sprinkled sugar over the raspberry jam on the slices of unbuttered white bread she gave them for lunch.

Few visitors would have appreciated the view of Moose lake from the Mahoneys' because of the property's condition: the sloped dirt driveway was barely navigable because of the deep ruts; an array of abandoned building supplies, a fridge that no longer worked, and plain old litter covered the dirt yard; there were hundreds of empty beer and wine bottles in an unpainted shed that didn't have a door; and wooden scaffolds, unused for years, were propped against the blackened particle board sheeting on the house. Now that he was older, Torrance recoiled at the memory of what he now knew was a classic hoarder house inside, with mounds of dirty clothing on unfinished plywood floors, grimy household goods (some still in boxes), bundles of old newspapers, and bags of garbage. The colour that had stood out in Preston's room was the pink of the exposed insulation.

Torrance couldn't remember how he'd made it out to the Mahoney's for the visit. He biked to most places when he was a kid, but it didn't make sense that a boy in grade two or three would make such a long trip on his own. The other thing that didn't process was that Preston and he must have been reasonably good friends for him to go over to Preston's house in the first place. Regardless, their friendship had ended when Preston was moved to the vocational class in grade four.

It takes a while before a teenage boy figures out that he has become as tough as the men he looks up to. Although Torrance was steel-cord strong from doing vacation relief work at the mill in the summer between grade eleven and grade twelve, as far as he was concerned the student who'd undergone the biggest transformation was Preston. A couple of weeks into September, Preston came to school with a black eye, a gash on his forehead, and a pronounced swagger. Soon everyone knew that Preston had held his own in a fight with Teddy Trimore. The students could hardly believe that someone still in school could survive a fight with Teddy, a feared hockey enforcer in his mid-twenties.

A few weeks before the snow came, the P.E. teacher, Mr. Tolvin took the two grade twelve classes outside to play a game of softball. To save time, Mr. Tolvin pitted the academic and vocational classes against each other instead of picking teams. Although the students in the vocational class were on average older and bigger, the academics had three experienced ball players, including a bona fide windmill pitcher in Trina Edmonds, who had accepted a softball scholarship to a Division II NCAA school in the US. The academics took the lead in the second inning and added to it in every inning after, except the fourth when Preston and his teammate with the nickname "Moose" hit back-to-back home runs. Torrance was the leadoff batter in the top of the sixth inning. His single became a little league home run when the ball skipped past Adrian, the friendly giant in centerfield who regularly fell asleep in class because he cooked nights in his father's Greek restaurant. Rounding second Torrance saw Preston was blocking the baseline. Knowing he couldn't back down, Torrance leaped into the air just before the inevitable collision. Preston instinctively moved to protect himself and Torrance as able to carry on to third before heading home.

Mr. Tolvin called the game right away. As the students walked back to the gym, Preston, who was visibly charged, said to Torrance in a voice loud enough for everyone but Mr. Tolvin to hear, "I'll see you after school." Torrance knew what lay ahead. He'd seen his share of fights at the smoke pit. While onlookers broke up fights between younger students as soon as the winner became apparent, older students fought on until someone was hurt, often badly. Torrance remembered as clearly as if it had happened yesterday when Jim Bob, a serious young man who pumped gas on the weekend, jumped on the extended leg of Timmy Whitman, the loudmouthed son of the local surveyor. Timmy still walked with a pronounced limp even though the fight had taken place two years earlier.

When the buzzer rang to end the school day, Torrance methodically put his books in his packsack before leaving the classroom and making his way solemnly down the hall. He knew he had no choice but to take his normal route home, walking down the side of the bus lane, crossing the street at the school's main gate, and skirting the front of the smoke pit. Outwardly calm, his thoughts were blurred. Word of the upcoming fight had spread and more than the usual number of students were milling about outside the school yard. Preston was in a group standing at the edge of the smoke pit. When he saw Torrance, he threw his cigarette down and came over to stand in the middle of the sidewalk. Torrance didn't say anything and veered onto the road. Preston moved back in front of him; and so Torrance returned to the sidewalk. Preston did the same. They were now standing within a foot of each other. Preston pushed Torrance hard on his chest. Torrance didn't react. Without further warning, Preston punched him full in the face.

Surprised that the pain wasn't worse, Torrance threw himself at Preston. They struggled upright for a few seconds before toppling to the trampled, weedy ground. Twisting and turning, they began rolling over cigarette butts, pop and beer bottle tops, and scattered paper and plastic. Torrance worked his right arm free and got in a couple of quick punches. Strength goes back a long way, and Torrance's short punches carried the stubborn force of his mother's rock-quarrying ancestors.

Torrance's thoughts swung wildly between fear of losing and relief that Preston wasn't stronger. Torrance got in another punch while they were still on the ground, this time with his stronger left hand. Since his hand hurt despite the punch landing square, he knew Preston must have felt it. Torrance panicked when he felt the smokers' log behind his back, and a surge of adrenalin gave him the strength he needed to push Preston off and get to his feet.

The combatants breathed heavily as they circled each other. Although the faces in the crowd didn't register with Torrance, he noticed that his lip was swollen and that one of his front teeth was loose.

Preston, who was bleeding above his left eye, kicked and wildly swung at Torrance a few times. When Torrance heard someone say teachers were coming, he charged, hitting Preston with his left hand before grabbing on.

Torrance tightened his stout arms around Preston's head and, twisting with all his might, pulled him to the ground. Preston tried to free himself from the headlock, but his face soon went red and his reactions began to slow. As if from far away Torrance heard, "Let go, Tory. Let go now." One of the teachers stood over him and pulled on his arm to loosen his grip; but he held on, deaf, dumb, and blind with anger. It took the combined efforts of Mr. Tolvin and vice-principal Stevens to take him off Preston, who stayed on the ground. The vice-principal walked Torrance through the buzz of onlookers and back to the school.

Torrance was crouched over on the heavy wooden chair outside the vice-principal's office staring at his bleeding knuckles when Mr. Tolvin walked by and entered the office. Through the closed door he heard Mr. Tolvin tell the vice-principal that Preston was going to be okay but had refused to come to the school. After a while Torrance heard what sounded like nervous laughter.

* * * * *

A pickup truck drove past, re-awakening Torrance to the present.

Putting his car back into gear, he drove the route to his old house he'd walked so many times. He was shocked with how close his house was to school. *I could have sworn we lived farther away.*

The former parsonage was in rough shape. Large chunks of the diluted beige stucco at the front of the house had been repaired in an amateurish manner with unpainted, now-stained white plaster; part of the metal roof gutter was hanging down over a corner of the picture window; and the edges of the moss-covered tiles on the roof were turned up. *The church must have sold the house a long time ago.* The two maple saplings his parents had planted in the front yard were now awkward, mid-growth trees, their roots ribbing an unkempt lawn. He made a U-turn at the end of the block so he could drive past the house again. This time he noticed the open garage behind the house was jammed full, leaving no room to park a car.

Guessing that the airline's office was near the public beach, he headed west at the first cross street. About where he'd expected on

Beach Avenue there was a circular white and blue sign with the words, "North of 55 Airways" above the image of a floatplane. The first person he saw upon entering the parking lot was Martin, who was closing the back door of his SUV. Torrance pulled into the next stall and got out of his car.

— You beat me. How long have you been here?

— About an hour, I got here early. I was about to call you. Not much to see between Footing and here is there?

— Lots of trees.

Martin said their plane wasn't back from an earlier flight.

— The lady at the front desk said she's still hopeful we can fly out this afternoon.

Martin went back into Airways' office to get directions to a place to eat. On their way by foot to the café down the street they went past a low, abandoned building with several small windows. It took Torrance a second to recognize the pool hall he'd spent so much time in against his father's wishes.

The café was almost empty.

— I've always wondered how businesses like this can survive. Sure, it's the weekend, but you can't tell me four customers pays for the cost of opening up.

— No wonder people in the small towns fought so hard against the tax on restaurant meals.

The attendant was on the phone when they arrived back at Airways. Looking at a smaller version of the company's insignia behind the front desk, Torrance noticed there was a howling wolf below the float-plane. When the attendant got off the phone she apologized, saying it looked like they were going to be delayed until morning. Martin turned to Torrance.

— So, what do people do for fun in Bull Moose Run?

— We used to play a lot of street hockey.

When Torrance asked for a hotel recommendation the attendant suggested they try the newly renovated Bull Moose Hotel.

— You get a great view of the lake from the rooms.

— If it's the hotel I'm thinking of the only thing it used to be known for were bar fights that carried out into the parking lot.

— I don't know about that. I have heard, though, that the owner, Stoney Duke spent more than three million dollars on renovations.

Martin followed Torrance in his own vehicle up the hill to the town's centre. At the far end of main street there was an impressive timber and stonework hotel fronted by a pedestal sign that read, "Bull Moose Hotel". The hotel's parking lot was paved and there were brick flowerbeds, now empty because of the season, at the base of evenly spaced, black-iron light standards.

Torrance spoke over his car's roof at Martin while they were unloading.

— This hotel used to be a real dump on the bad side of town.

— Not anymore. Hey, I guess we should leave our guns in the cars.

— Ya.

They made their way down the pergola covered walkway to the hotel's entrance.

— I remember when I was in grade eight or nine, I saw one of my classmates walking down main street with a rifle he'd just bought. No one thought twice about someone carrying a rifle back then. Nowadays they'd think you were going to shoot someone.

The hotel's oversized doors opened onto an impressive lobby. The walls were lightly stained fir, there was a heavy tile floor, and several rows of pendant lights hung from the high ceiling. An old grizzly bear hide with a taxidermy head and what looked like a brand new shiny red mouth with white teeth was mounted behind the granite check-in counter. Torrance went over to the window at the far end of the lobby wall that overlooked the lake.

— The lake looks huge from up here.

The two men stood in silence for a minute.

— A funny place for a church.

— That's St. Timothy's. It was only used for a few years before they built a new church in town.

— What's the building just down from the church? It looks like a house, but it's as big as an apartment.

— It was built after I left.

The clerk behind the check-in counter wore a Native Canadian sterling silver necklace. Martin asked about the cost of two single rooms and was given a surprisingly reasonable, off-season rate.

— Would you happen to know what the building is beside St. Timothy's church?

— That's Kenny Sloan's house. Kenny had it built when he was playing in Detroit. One of his brothers lives there now. It's been for sale for years.

Torrance had followed Kenny's progress after Bull Moose Run's favourite son made it to the moneyed NHL. A curly-headed scrapper with real talent, he'd been killed in a single vehicle crash in his early twenties. Alcohol was involved.

HUNTER WONDERER

FEW RESTAURANT PATRONS COMPLAINED WHEN lean, wild salmon was replaced by the fatty, farmed Atlantic variety. Expect a similar resigned acceptance when the only fish available has a bland, white flesh, but grows quickly and can survive high stocking densities.

* * * * *

Martin went to his room to take a nap to make up for a poor sleep at a noisy roadside motel the previous night.

Torrance thought about calling up his old friend, Dave; but decided to wait until he was back from Alces Lake. That left him free to take in what he could of his old hometown. He changed and went for a jog, setting off in the direction of the hockey arena. When he got to the arena it was obvious from the number of cars that a tournament was underway.

The sight of the building's main doors cast Torrance back in time to the cold, snowy night when, as a ten-year old boy, he'd walked alone on dark streets through falling snow to attend a senior men's hockey game. The ticket booth inside the main door was empty when he'd arrived. Confused, he'd waited for a minute before hesitantly entering the arena. There was a crowd of people at the bottom of the stairs going up to the main seating area. Making his way to the front, he'd seen an unconscious man lying on his back the cold cement. The man was covered with a blanket and a pool of blood had formed around his head. Apparently the man had been drinking and had fallen backwards off the stairs. Torrance heard later the man had died.

* * * * *

Torrance ended his run at the town's rebuilt fort that was now a National Historic Site. The historical information sign said Bull Moose Run was one of the oldest settlements in the province, having been founded in 1806. *That's not that long after the American Revolution ... and well before the New York Times started publishing.* A second sign stated the fort would re-open to the public on April 1.

Sitting on one of the wood and wrought iron benches at the edge of the collection of replicated buildings, Torrance thought about how the forests and streams must have teemed with wildlife to justify building the outpost so far from anywhere. Directly in front of where he sat there was an empty field and beyond that the lake. To his left, there was a new elementary school whose colourful murals and proximity to the reserve identified it as a Native Canadian school. The classrooms all had doors opening onto individual, fenced-in garden areas. *Smart.*

An elderly Native Canadian man walked across the field in his direction. The man slowed down when he got to the sloped ground leading up to the fort, and he was breathing heavily when he sat down one bench over. Torrance waited a while before speaking.

— Nice day, eh?

— It's going to snow soon.

Torrance wondered if the man knew this because he'd lived so long in the area or if he'd heard the weather report.

A large German Shepherd that could have been a wolfdog ran past them towards the lake. The old man's comment on the size of the dog led to a conversation. Torrance got around to saying that he used to live in town and that his father had been a minister. The old man, whose name was Daniel Rivard, thought for a bit before saying he was pretty sure he remembered the name Maki.

Torrance asked about the new houses on the reserve.

— Ya, they are impressive. The problem is there's getting to be two kinds of people, the chiefs and the rest of us. One of the hereditary chiefs just bought a place in Hawaii.

Torrance asked about the elementary school.

— We're real proud of it. The kids all learn how to read and write Carrier now.

— My stepson's taking a course on Aboriginal history. He really enjoys it.

Torrance was surprised at the level of kinship he felt with the old man.

*　*　*　*　*

After taking a shower, Torrance went up to Martin's room on the second floor and knocked on the door. Since Martin didn't answer, Torrance went back to his room to watch the first period of the hockey game. He tried Martin's door again during the intermission. Martin answered this time but asked if he had a few minutes to call his wife before they went for dinner.

— Of course. I'll go on ahead and get us a table at the steakhouse.

Torrance opened the restaurant door to the welcoming smells of garlic, butter, toasted bread and cooking meat. Almost immediately someone called his name. Looking around, he saw a man waving at him from the lounge. It took him a moment to place Kurt, the lawyer from Centre City, who looked older and less imposing without a suit on. Torrance didn't recognize the man sitting across from Kurt.

Torrance walked over, making his way around the wooden balustrade that separated off the lounge. When he got closer he saw that Kurt's cheeks were red from drinking.

— I guess this town's not big enough for the both of us.

— I thought you were flying out today?

Torrance was surprised that Kurt remembered who he was let alone his itinerary. *Mind you, lawyers are paid to trade in small details.* The other man, who looked to be in his 40's, had a round, vulnerable face and seemed nervous. Torrance assumed he was involved in Kurt's court case.

— Have a seat. This is Andrew. Andrew, Tory.

Andrew and Torrance shook hands before Andrew slid down the bench seat to give Torrance room.

— Tory's from the big city. He's hired a float plane to fly him north to go hunting. Must be nice, eh?

Kurt could see that Torrance was bugged by the comment and moved to make amends.

— Tory used to live in Bull Moose Run. How many years has it been since you were here?

— A long time.

Torrance purposely looked away from Kurt and over at Andrew.

— Do you live in the Moose, Andrew?

— Yes, I've been in town for almost twelve years.

— What do you do?

— I'm an art teacher, but I'm off right now.

Kurt ordered a double whiskey when the server came by and Torrance asked for a beer. Andrew said he was fine. The meeting between Kurt and Andrew must have been finished because it wasn't long before the troubled teacher said he should go. Kurt told him to read through his statement a few more times and to be at the courthouse at 9:00 a.m. sharp on Monday. Torrance got up to let Andrew out before sitting down again.

Kurt curled his big hand around the stubby glass and downed what was left of his drink. Talking as much to himself as to Torrance, he said:

— The damage to my liver is just another cost of doing business.

Torrance kept his eye on the door and stood up as soon as he saw Martin. Doing his best to work up a smile, he waved off Kurt's invitation to join him.

*　*　*　*　*

Martin reported on a walk he'd taken through town that afternoon.

— I had a long talk with the owner of the sporting goods store about the decline in the moose population. He says the Natives blame the out of town hunters, and the whites blame the Natives. Apparently a couple of years ago a young man from the reserve came into the store bragging about shooting three moose, including two cows, in one week.

— How do you take sides on that one? I mean the moose were doing okay when there weren't any Europeans; yet we're all Canadians now.

— The other thing the owner told me was that one of the local bands has set up a toll booth on a road out of town and has been charging hunters a fee. He said it won't be long before someone gets shot.

While they were eating Martin described the scene outside the local pharmacy.

— There was a group of mainly older people standing around in the parking lot trading bottles of prescription drugs if you can believe it.

* * * * *

Early the next morning, Martin and Torrance parked their vehicles at the edge of the Airways parking lot. Finding the front door locked, they walked around the building. A tall, slender man was climbing down from a floatplane tied up to the dock. The man smiled broadly when he saw Martin and Torrance and walked over to greet them.

— Yar right?

Neither Martin nor Torrance could make out much of what the man said next in his heavy accent that was likely English or South African with something else mixed in. The man slowed down when he realized he hadn't been understood.

— "Mu nomes, Late'n Bahry."

Before Martin and Torrance had finished introducing themselves, Leighton was off talking too quickly again. The only thing Torrance caught from the next pulse of words was, "Th'engine was raydoon a phwew 'undred hours ago." Leighton continued to speak with what sounded like a mouth full of marbles as he followed Martin and Torrance to their cars to help with their gear.

They were about to board the loaded plane when Leighton turned on his heel and headed down the dock at a brisk pace, yelling back:

— Las' chance p'for the bog, mate.

Martin followed the gangly pilot, but Torrance waited on the dock. He tried the plane's door again, not quite believing how flimsy it was.

* * * * *

An hour and a half later the plane had begun its descent to Alces Lake. Torrance, who was seated up front beside Leighton, studied the lay of the forested land. There was a sizeable rocky butte to the north, and off to the northeast, a large logging cut block. They were almost on the water before he saw the broken down, old cabin he assumed they would be using.

181

Leighton overshot the little bay the cabin was in and had to work to turn the plane around in the choppy water before taxiing towards shore. Realizing that Torrance was watching him fight the control wheel he spoke through the headset. Torrance was able to make out the words, "the 'eavy wind" in amongst the garble, and smiled back as if in full acknowledgement.

After the plane was beached, the men got out and walked single file up the narrow path to the cabin. There were all-terrain vehicle tracks along the way and a tangle of tracks in the cleared area in front of the cabin. Empty shotgun shell casings were scattered all around, and a soggy, collapsed beer case, half-filled with empty cans, had been left beside the cabin door. Clearly, venatores modernus had come, seen, and had more than a few beers. The matted feathers against the cabin wall were proof that they had shot at least one grouse.

— They must have driven their ATV's in from the cut block. It wasn't there last year.

— So much for hunting in the unspoiled wilderness.

— I's a bit smaarting, ain' it?

The cabin reminded Torrance of the hermit cabins he'd seen as a youth. Pulling open the patched-up door dangling from its hinges, he was confronted by the smell of mildew and rotting wood. A section of stovepipe was hanging from the cabin's ceiling, although there was no stove. The wooden floor in the centre of the cabin had been torn away, exposing dark, pungent dirt. He wondered if the boards had been used as fuel by someone who didn't want to go outside in the cold to get firewood.

Torrance went and stood beside Leighton and Martin in front of the blackened fire pit in front of the cabin. Martin took his thermos out of his ultra-lite pack and offered it around before taking a swig of coffee.

— Leighton, how far do you figure it is to that cut block?

— I donnow, cou' be fi'e kilometers.

— Maybe there's another lake we could fly to?

— Ah'll get the map.

Leighton returned from the plane with the oversized map and spread it out over an upended block of wood. The only lake of any size near them was Chum Lake, which according to the map was in the middle of a web of active logging roads.

— H'is a bit dodgy 'ere now, 'half to say. Sure somefin could be sort-ered out.

After talking it through, Martin and Torrance decided they didn't have much choice but to stay. Leighton was about to leave when he remembered the "attel-height phone" Martin and Torrance were to use if they shot something or in case of an emergency.

* * * * *

They hunted near the lake that afternoon, seeing only birds, squirrels, and a solitary beaver swimming at the mouth of a creek. Torrance beat himself up early on in the walk for not taking his gun to the shooting range to try it out. *Well, it's too late now. I don't want to scare anything off.*

Black humour about their "excellent hunting trip" prevailed during supper. As night fell, the fire grew in importance and the conversation became more serious.

— One thing I meant to look into was whether Lyme disease has gotten this far north.

— I hope not. Though someone said there've been several cases of that tree fungus that gets in people's lungs. It used to only be found on in the coastal forests down south, but it's starting to show up here now because of the warmer weather.

* * * * *

Torrance woke up once to take a whizz and a second time when he heard something scampering under what was left of the cabin's floor. It was getting light when he got up for good. While he was rolling up his sleeping bag Martin mumbled at him from across the gap in the floor:
— What time is it?
— It's early.

Martin turned over and went back to sleep.

Since it wasn't fully light, Torrance took his time going down to the lake to wash up. He stood for a minute on the sloped gravel beach staring into the mist over the bay before stretching out like the Vitruvian Man. Feeling more alive, he bent down and mitted cold lake water up to his face. He found himself thinking about the con-veniences back home—*Wouldn't it be great to grab a coffee and a fresh muffin?*—as he itemized his aches and pains. And yet, for whatever reason, he was happy.

Somehow both Martin and Torrance had managed to forget fire starter. Luckily, they'd found a couple of stained and torn western novels with broken spines, as well as a coverless Bible that was only half there, in the cabin. Torrance had no qualms about ripping up the westerns, which he knew from having read so many as a teenager would contain three fight scenes each. He wasn't sure, though, if he had it in him to finish off the Bible. *Unless we're desperate of course.*

Once the fire was going good he went back down to the lake to fill Martin's dented coffee pot. It was almost fully light now, and the low white clouds above the southern shore looked like puffs of innocent steam.

Torrance was finishing his first cup of coffee when Martin emerged from the cabin. After making a quick trip behind a tree Martin came over and stood beside Torrance in front of the fire.

— Today is going to be a great day.

— It's funny you say that, because that's what I say too.

The bacon and eggs tasted great despite all the burnt bits. While eating, they finalized their plan of splitting up and rendezvousing at the base of the rocky butte.

— Let's agree not to shoot anybody wearing red.

— Right. By the way, are there any predators we need to worry about?

— A few years ago I saw a black bear a couple of kilometers east of here, towards the cut block. Conrad told me there haven't been any wolves for decades.

— No wolves here, and yet they've been introduced back into Yellowstone. Go figure.

* * * * *

Torrance's opinion was that in addition to an across the board ban on hunting, some roads should be closed and towns shut down to give the moose population a chance to recover; however, he conceded that despite the fix being obvious it was unapproachable. Notwithstanding his views on the matter, Torrance got caught up in the excitement of the hunt the moment Martin and he set out from the cabin in different directions. *Say what you will, hunting is part of who I am.*

Save for the sounds he made walking across the forest floor, the scratching movement of squirrels, and the odd bird call, silence prevailed. The Whiskey Jack he'd seen near the cabin led him through the woods for a while before flying off. Not long after, he spooked a grouse that shot explosively to new cover. *Thank goodness there are still a few birds left.*

He was surprised at how much effort it took to walk in a straight line through the woods. The undergrowth was often so thick it could have been intentionally woven to impede. At regular intervals, he was blocked by ponds, where the nearby footing was spongy and wet, and he had to ford small creeks, where the ground was uneven and slippery. Equally difficult were the spots where dried out lower branches of tightly spaced smaller trees acted like piercing turnstiles.

Whenever he wasn't focusing on where to step, or trying to imagine where an animal might be hiding, ready to charge, he was caught up in nature's beauty. An ever-changing variety of plants competed for space among the conifers and poplars— the wispy, dull strands of lichen bearding spruce tree branches were striking examples of how varied the forms of life were. Noticing clumps of untouched, low lying berries, he wondered which of nature's purposes was fulfilled by having berries that weren't easy to digest. *It's like the world's largest terrarium. A place for learning ... better yet, a place to pull back from and leave untouched ... and unexplained.*

When he became hungry, he waited for the advantage of higher ground before he put his gun down and took an energy bar out of his backpack: *oatmeal, nuts, and chocolate—my favourite.* The shining, metallic wrapper looked like it would never biodegrade so he put it in his pocket.

Although he checked his compass every few minutes at first, he soon began to rely on his innate sense of direction. His inner mechanisms proved unreliable and towards noon he found himself at the edge of the logging cut block they'd seen from the air. *Well, at least I know where I am.*

He stood for a moment staring at the roughed up clearing before making a controlled slide down into a skidder track at the edge of the cut block. Although Torrance wasn't against logging per se, viewing it as more defensible than permanently clearing the land around cities, he found it unsettling to walk through an area with so few standing trees and where the majority of saplings had been knocked over, crushed or horribly scraped, the uncovered swaths of their inner bark now rusted. The dominant smells were of exposed soil and sawdust, with the falsely sweet smell of spilled diesel mixing in at the first landing he came to. There were several empty oil cannisters, random pieces of metal, and plastic bags snagged in bushes in and around the landing. *You'd think the logging company would have been obligated to clean up after itself before shutting down.*

He remembered hearing that logging benefitted the moose population because it provided new areas for grass to grow. *If that was once true, the advantage has long since been lost because of the access logging roads give hunters.*

While crossing a small creek in a preserved area where a few mature trees had been left standing, Torrance temporarily lost sight of the forest surrounding the cut block. *I can't see the forest for the trees.*

Turning east to head back to the forest he saw a dark object about the size of a bear. The object didn't move as he approached it, and it ended up being the upturned roots of a blow-down.

He hadn't gone very far back into the forest when he came upon a squirrel's spruce cone cache. The cache, more than a foot high in places, covered the ground between two large spruce trees. The size of the cache would have amazed him if he hadn't seen others like it when he was collecting spruce cones for the Forest Service as a teenager. *Back then all we focused on the $15.00 a burlap bag we were getting paid. We didn't care about the poor squirrels.*

There was no sign of Martin when Torrance got to the base of the butte. Not sure what to do at first, he eventually decided to start hiking up the rocky slope. It wasn't long before he was breathing heavily and had to stop to catch his breath. After stopping and going a few more times he stopped for good. To make sure that Martin saw him he set up a triangle of visuals with his orange packsack, the red vest he had been wearing, and himself as corners. He positioned himself beside a large rock that protected him from the wind and fell asleep the moment he lay back on the hard ground.

He awoke to see Martin making his way up the hill towards him. After closing his eyes for what seemed like only a few seconds, he opened them again to see Martin patiently sitting on a nearby boulder.
— How long have you been there?

— Maybe ten minutes. I was just happy to sit.

— Did you shoot anything? It was quiet over my way.

— I could have shot a grouse. It was weird. I was standing there and it came out from behind a bush and sauntered by me.

— Grouse aren't the smartest animals. We used to say you could hunt them with a fishing rod.

— I didn't see any moose, or tracks for that matter.

— Me neither. Let's dwell on the positive, at least we don't have to carry any moose meat back with us.

— Oh, I got lost and ended up in the cut block we saw from the plane. You should have seen all the garbage that was left behind.

They were on their feet after taking a lunch break, about to head back to the cabin, when they were buffeted by a stream of incredibly warm air. Confused, they stood together without talking until the wind turned cold again.

— That was weird. It was like a vent blowing warm air.

— Maybe it was that El Nino thing.

— Or just the standard, end of the world, global warming.

— This summer was really bizarre. I never thought I'd see yellow leaves falling off trees in the middle of July. It was like we were living in Arizona.

— You wonder how much of the change people are responsible for, most I'm guessing.

They decided to split up on their return journey and had begun to walk off in different directions when Martin whistled softly to get Torrance's attention. Torrance went over to where Martin was standing, pointing down the slope of the butte, away from Alces Lake.

— Do you see that clearing?

— I'm not sure.

— It's to the left of the big tree. There's an opening in the branches. About ten feet from the top.

— Okay.

— Do you see the clearing?

— I think so.

— Do you see that brown spot in the middle?

— If I'm looking at the right spot there's something there but I'm not sure what it is.

— Too bad we don't have a scope on one of our guns.

Energized by slight hope, they raced down the hill. They came to a sharp drop-off almost right away and lost time crossing over to a manageable gradient. When they finally got to the clearing they were disappointed to see that what Martin had thought might be a moose was only a tree stump, the rest of the fallen tree having been long overlain by ground cover.

Martin checked his watch.

— We're going to have to pick up the pace if we're going to make it back before dark.

They were almost at the cabin when Torrance slipped on a moss covered rock beside a small creek. As he fell, he instinctively grabbed at the branch of a blown down tree for support. The branch snapped and the sharp edge effortlessly skinned a large chunk of skin from the back of his left hand. Martin looked back when he heard Torrance swear, but Torrance waved him on.

That evening, Torrance's hand bandaged up, the men took pleasure from sitting in front of the fire and talking about the day. Inevitably, they got to the bigger issues.

— Plastics, aerosol spray, gasoline. Asbestos. Pesticides. … Not to forget the atom bomb. Those advances all looked good at the time, but not anymore.

— Yet, I've heard the argument that this is the best time ever, for the most people. The guy at that dinner that I was telling you about stressed how more people than ever are being freed from poverty. The other thing he said was the world has now gone past "peak child", in other words the rate of population increases is beginning to fall.

— It better fall quickly.

DAVE AND ALTHEA

WHEN ASKED, AN ELDERLY POLISH woman said she had never considered moving back to Europe, "Because it isn't healthy to live in a place with so many people."

* * * * *

Despite having splashed a quarter bottle of antiseptic on his hand the night before, Torrance's injured hand looked far worse the next morning. Hoping this was the normal progression of a skin injury, he told Martin that he was up for a hunt in the heavy rain that had arrived overnight.

They were soaked and cold, with nothing to show for it, when they returned to the cabin for lunch. Torrance showed Martin his hand while he was replacing the water-logged gauze.

— That's a nasty red streak going up to your wrist. It can't be a good thing. How painful is it?

— Not that bad, but it's definitely getting worse. I wonder if you can get that flesh-eating thing in the woods?

They decided to call Airways for a pick up.

Martin read the satellite phone instruction sheet before dialing the number Leighton had written down. He got through on the second attempt. The woman who answered said he'd have to talk to the general manager, Clint, who was out but was expected back anytime.

Even though they were expecting the return call, the phone's ring startled them. Martin picked up the phone. The man on the other end of the line introduced himself as Clint Kerchuk. Clint was a no nonsense guy, but his tone softened when Martin described Torrance's injury. Clint went on hold for a while before coming back to say that, regrettably, the only plane he had available was an Italian trainer that could only carry one passenger. Martin told Clint to go ahead and send the plane for Torrance as he was okay staying overnight in the cabin by himself.

Martin looked towards the lake when he was off the call.

— I wonder if the wind and rain are going to be a problem for the plane.

*   *   *   *   *

Martin and Torrance were eating warmed up pork and beans under the blue tarpaulin tarp they'd put up beside the campfire, rain gushing all around, when they heard the plane. Foregoing the tarp's protection, they went down to the lake for a better view. It was obvious from the approach of the little red and white floatplane that the pilot intended to land crossways on the lake, directly into the bay in front of the cabin.

— I guess he can do that because of the size of the plane.

The floatplane was almost on the water when it suddenly twisted sideways and turned sharply upwards, the landing aborted. Torrance could hardly believe the plane was able to change directions as quickly as it did, and how steeply it began to rise. Just when it looked like it would clear the trees, one of the floats caught the crown of a tall spruce. The plane stalled mid-air before tipping forward and falling straight down. Martin and Torrance caught glimpses of red and white as it plummeted through the trees. The sound of snapping branches and crunching metal was followed by silence against the background noise of the rain. Martin and Torrance stood transfixed for a moment before racing to the crash site. They barely noticed the wet willows that crowded the narrow beach slapping at them, or the dripping, resistant bushes and slippery, cross-hatched maze of fallen trees inland.

They were within a dozen meters of the plane before they saw its red and white form. Caught up in tree branches, it was hanging straight down, its twisted propeller almost touching the ground. The wing on the pilot's side was bent upwards and the float beneath the wing, which had been ripped free from the back strut, was nearly level with the door. There were scratches and indentations all down the side of the plane and a huge dent at the bottom of the fuselage. The engine had been pushed partway out of the cowling. Dripping blood was collecting on the cracked front window below the belted in, motionless pilot.

Torrance got to the plane's door first. He wrenched the door open with his good hand and let it flop towards the ground. Despite the blood on the unconscious pilot's face Torrance recognized Leighton.

Torrance used his left shoulder to push the Leighton back into his seat while he fought to undo the seatbelt.

— Are you okay? Leighton, can you hear me?

Leighton shifted.

— Are you okay?

Leighton still didn't answer.

— Can you hear me?

The plane was hot and smelled of oil and gas. Despite having only one good hand, Torrance managed to unbuckle the seatbelt and direct Leighton out of the narrow door opening and onto his shoulder. Martin did what he could to help carry Leighton, who was heavier than he looked, over to beneath a tree to get protection from the rain. Martin took off his jacket and then his t-shirt, which he used to staunch the cut on Leighton's forehead.

— We're going to need that first aid kit, and the phone too.

Leighton tried to speak, but Torrance, who was leaning over Martin's shoulder, told him to save his breath. Torrance walked around the plane to make sure nothing was on fire before heading back to the cabin through the sodden underbrush.

Leighton regained consciousness while Torrance was away.

— Ee by gum. Wha' happened?

— The plane crashed, but we think you're okay. Can you move your arms and legs?

— Ma righ' leg hur's like crazy.

Martin asked Leighton if he could take his pants off so they could look at the injured area. Leighton said he couldn't and so Martin took out his hunting knife and, inch by inch, cut the pant leg open. Just above Leighton's knee there was a huge circling bruise.

By the time Torrance returned with the first aid kit and the satellite phone, Leighton was holding onto the top of his injured leg, quietly rocking back and forth. Martin pulled Torrance off to the side.

— I think his right leg's broken. He can't move it, and you can see the bruise. Hopefully yanking him out of the plane didn't make things worse.

After putting a bandage on the pilot's head, Martin dialed Airways on the satellite phone. He got through right away. The attendant conferenced in the Flight Service Station in Centre City when Martin told her the plane had crashed. Martin put the phone on speaker when the Flight Service Station representative asked him something odd.

— Could you repeat that?

— How many souls were on board?

Unexpectedly, Leighton spoke up.

— One. Jes' one.

Clint had taken over the Airways' phone. He told Martin he'd send a medic in the company's Beaver first thing in the morning but they'd have to tough it out overnight.

When the phone call ended, Leighton said to no one in particular:

— They ask about soul's when there's a problem. I's an ol' expression. They want to know whos' on t'e plane, passengers and crew boff."

*   *   *   *   *

Torrance suggested they make a stretcher out of limbed trees and a sleeping bag, assuring Martin he could carry his end of the stretcher, bad hand or not.

It took longer than expected to make the stretcher, but they finally got underway. Perversely, Torrance couldn't help smiling at the sight of the pilot in the stretcher who reminded him of a juvenile kangaroo he'd seen on TV that was too big for his mother's pouch.

Leighton was back to his regular, high octane, talkative self after the pain killers kicked in.

— I knew t'ere was't a risk come'n strayt at t'e bay, but t'e wind was okay, an da Steebra's so nimbull.

Bloody 'eck. Everything looked right good until when I'as 'bout fi' feet off the wa'er. I was just starten' ta open up t'e throttle a bit to tilt'er up and set'er down when I seese a gust of wind comin'. I' 'appened so fast, I'as pumping at t'e rudder ta turn but it's too late, and t'e wind pushed me to t'e side.

T'en I'm thirty feet off the wa'er and at an angle, an I'm about t'e stall. I had to t'ink quickly. I jumped on the throttle, crankin' as hard as I 'ould. I was coming up to t'e trees. T'e plane was off 'entre, but I t'ought I'd 'av a go.

T'e trees was getting closer and closer, but I was still going up. Jammy get, then's I hear 'dis thump. T'ers the lass t'ing I 'member.

Torrance gave up his spot in the cabin to the injured pilot and slept under the sagging tarp. Listening to the rattle of the rain and watching the fire slowly die, he thought back on the day. *"Souls on board," I wonder how old that expression is. … If people did have souls it would explain why it seems like more has been lost when you see a dead person than when you see a dead animal.*

* * * * *

It stopped raining during the night.

Martin and Torrance went down to the lake when they heard the Beaver arriver shortly before 8:30 a.m. After landing like a large, graceful bird out in the middle of the becalmed lake, it taxied into the bay. Torrance's confidence rose as he watched two men of retirement age emerge from the cockpit. *A couple of seasoned old pro's, no doubt.*

The pilot introduced himself as James and his companion as Airways' former safety manager, Don. The safety manager stayed behind when James went to tie the plane to a tree.

— How's Leighton doing?

— He's hanging in there. I don't know what we would've done without pain killers.

— We were planning on bringing a paramedic with us, but he had to go to an accident on the road to Footing early this morning. Not to worry, the two of us have handled some tricky situations.

Torrance showed Don his injured hand as they walked up to the cabin. Don agreed it didn't look good but thought a dose of antibiotics would clear it up.

Martin and Torrance carried Leighton out to beside the campfire so his injured leg could be checked out in better light.

— I don't need to see an X-ray to tell you your femur's broken. At least it isn't a compound fracture. You may need some metal, and so we might as well fly you straight on to Centre City.

* * * * *

Airways' general manager, Clint, who was almost as wide as he was tall, had huge forearms, and hair everywhere but on the top of his head, was waiting on Airways' dock when the Beaver pulled in to drop off Martin and Lawrence before carrying on to Centre City. After helping the hunters down, Clint climbed, squat like a bear, up into the plane to see his injured pilot.

Martin and Lawrence put their gear in their vehicles before going into Airways office. Clint had gotten there before them. After listening to a shortened version of events, he told them there'd be paperwork to sign the next day.

* * * * *

Martin stopped by the Airways Office on his way to the hospital in the morning. Clint led him down the narrow, poorly lit hallway to a dated, musty office with worn wood flooring. The bay window in the room was clouded over because of a broken seal. From where Martin sat, the bottom of the window looked to be almost level with the smooth lake beyond.

— Did you get any news about Leighton?

— His surgery was scheduled for this morning. It might already be over.

— Great. Torrance is on antibiotics. The doctor is hopeful he'll be able to travel by the weekend.

Clint handed Martin some papers to fill out. Clint's voice unexpectedly cracked after telling him the Transportation Safety Board might want to interview him.

— I started this airline almost forty years ago. There's not a day that's gone by since that I haven't been worried about a crash. Well, my worrying has finally paid off. I suppose it could have been a lot worse.

* * * * *

Torrance was hooked up to an intravenous drip reading a copy of the local paper when Martin got to the hospital.

— The doctor came by early. He said I should be able to leave Saturday.

— Great, I'll stay overnight and we'll drive back together.

— I thought you'd say that. There's no way, what if there's a delay? You get going. Don't forget, this is my town.

* * * * *

Torrance called the municipal hall towards noon and was patched through to Superintendent Meakins' office. A recorded message said Dave Meakins was out and would be returning calls the following day. Torrance decided to wait and try again on Friday rather than leave a message.

He shuffled through the roughed up pages of the King James version of the Bible back to *Hebrews* to reconsider the stilted language in the 3rd verse in the previous chapter, which seemed to be especially important. *He's talking about where the world came from, which is what we all want to know.*

Later, when a nurse stopped by to see if he wanted to rent a TV, Torrance asked about getting something to read. The nurse said there was a small gift shop in the hospital that would open shortly, and the hospital also had a decent collection of donated books. Torrance said he might as well check the hospital's books out first.

After getting the key, the nurse led Torrance, his mobile stand trailing behind him, to a door marked, "Utility Room". Inside, back behind several rows of shelves holding dry goods, including light bulbs, ballasts and other electrical supplies, and a variety of tools, there were two bookcases separated by a wooden chair and a floor lamp. The nurse asked Torrance to make sure and close the door behind him when he left.

Propped open on the top of the bookcase for children's books there was a well-used, hardcover copy of *Wilderness Champion*, Joseph Wharton Lippincott's adventure story about a dog called Reddy and his wolf step-parent, King. That book, along with *Call of the Wild* and biographies of Crazy Horse and George Washington Carver, had been among the most important books of Torrance's youth. He picked the book up and opened it after studying the cover for a minute. A label on the flyleaf read, "My Book: Howard Ness". The book, a second edition, had been copyrighted in 1944. *Maybe writing a novel about animals took Lippincott away from the horrors of war.*

Torrance began to read. Because it was a children's book he self-consciously started off like an editor, focusing on the author's word choices—*a couple of more edits and he would have gotten rid of the word duplication*—sentence construction and character development. Soon, though, he was caught up in the story and began to feel echoes of the same emotions he'd felt so many years earlier. *I can see why I liked this book so much, there are likeable people, a courageous young dog, and the almost human way King cares for Reddy.* He read the entire book in one sitting. When he was leaving the room he thought about how lonely King was at the start of the book from losing his mate. *I should check to see when Lippincott's wife died.*

*   *   *   *   *

Dave Meakins answered when Torrance's call was put through the next morning. The superintendent's businesslike approach fell away the moment he realized it was Torrance. He could hardly believe his friend was in town.

— I'll come up to the hospital right after our lunch meeting. Oh shoot. Adrian's volleyball tournament in Footing starts this afternoon. But that won't be a problem. I can call the coach.

Torrance refused to let Dave abandon the team, and they settled on Torrance joining the Meakins family for dinner on Saturday.

Dave and Torrance had started their lifelong friendship in grade five when Dave's family moved to town. Dave, who was the best math student in the class, had received the biggest scholarship on graduation and started university in the fall. He'd done well enough in first year sciences to be accepted into the competitive engineering program.

Dave had returned to Bull Moose Run every summer to work in the mill where his dad was a millwright. In between second and third year, he'd had a brief romance with Althea, a popular student who was going into grade twelve. Althea, or Tea as Dave affectionately called her, had unexpectedly broken off their relationship shortly before he was to go back to university.

On the day before Remembrance Day, there was a message from Althea on the telephone answering machine in the basement suite

Dave shared with two other students. His pulse quickened, he'd called back right away. Althea had answered and in a flat voice said that she was pregnant, that she had decided to have the baby, and that she thought he should know. Dave, who had always had the inwit of a much older person, made the fourteen-hour drive back to Bull Moose Run on the civic holiday. Mid-morning the next day the young parents-to-be had the most important conversation of their lives staring out at the pilings in front of the abandoned, waterfront mill at the edge of town. Dave had done a lot of thinking on the long trip home, and had made up his mind on what he wanted to do.

— We need to look at this the right way and celebrate life, especially new life. For now at least, university is going to have to wait.

Dave and Althea were married two weeks before Christmas, and Dave started work with the town's maintenance department in January.

Torrance had only seen Dave twice, both times at the coast, since his friend had moved back to Bull Moose Run—on one of those occasions, Dave had said that marrying Althea had been the best decision he'd ever made. Finally, Torrance was going to meet Dave's wife.

* * * * *

Despite the shortage of streetlights on Sandy Beach Road, Torrance had no difficulty finding the treed property with a split rail fence. The long driveway into the rancher was paved even though the side street was still gravel. *Isn't that just like Dave.* Torrance pulled in behind a pickup with Town of Bull Moose Run markings and next to a beaten up Honda Civic. A new, candy red Camaro was parked in front of the Honda.

Dave came around the corner of the house while Torrance was getting out of his car. Torrance's immediate thought was that, except for graying hair, Dave looked the same as ever. When Dave got nearer, though, Torrance saw the age lines on his friend's face.

— It's been a while!

— Too long. Nice house.

— We had it built, twelve, thirteen years. When was the last time you were in the Moose?

— Almost thirty years. Not much has changed. I see you bought another Camaro. I hope this one gets better gas mileage. Remember watching the gas gauge move on the old one when you matted it?

— Actually, this one doesn't get bad gas mileage.

— Old men and the cars from their youth.

— I told Tea that since everything else about me is falling apart I should at least have a cool car.

Torrance followed Dave to the front door. Entering the house he smelled food cooking. Dave pointed at his volley ball playing son, Adrian who was sprawled out on the couch in the living room.

Althea was taking a casserole out of the oven in the kitchen. She was a classic beauty of medium build, with lustrous dark skin and an exuberant personality. Her bright white teeth and the pink of her gums showed whenever she smiled or laughed, which was often. After learning about her Greek heritage, Torrance imagined her as the welcoming wife of an important public official in historic Athens.

Adrian was recharged and ready to go when he joined the adults for dinner. With the breathless energy of youth, he provided a point by point description of the final game of the tournament. Dave sat back and listened, only interrupting once to remind his son about an exchange between the two groups of fans towards the end of the game.

— The kids from our school started singing our school song. Someone from Footing yelled out, "Your song sucks." Jimmy shouted back, "At least we've got a song."

After bolting his dessert, Adrian jumped up and said he had to be at Bodo's in ten minutes. Althea barely had time to remind him to be back by midnight before he was out the door.

Althea declined Torrance's offer to help with the cleanup.

— Thanks but no thanks. You're our honoured guest. And, you need to look after that hand.

— Come on, Tea, Tory was raised in the north where guys don't care about the little things. Now, if he'd lost his hand.

After the men cleared the table, Dave gave updates on the people in town Torrance remembered. Torrance was struck by how everyone he'd known had suffered one or more of the usual losses, a list that now included the life-destroying grip of drugs on family members.

Torrance got around to asking about Preston.

— Preston left town after his marriage broke down. He had one child, a girl who lives with her mother here in the Moose. A few years ago a cousin of mine working at the oil sands told me about a guy on his crew that was from the Moose. It turned out to be Preston. He's remarried and has a couple of kids with his new wife. Those guys at the oil sands make more money than you can imagine—my cousin says first aide attendants make a couple of hundred grand a year, easy.

When Althea was finished in the kitchen she sat down beside Dave, placing her arm comfortably over his. The men were on to talking about the reserve.

— Not that long ago, the town used to have to deal with Ottawa whenever an infrastructure issue came up. Now the first person we contact is the reserve manager. There's even a plan to set up a separate First Nation's police force. It was the only choice left after a series of arson attempts on the R.C.M.P. station at Likem.

The visit had come to a comfortable end. Althea embraced Torrance goodbye at the door. Inspired by his wife, Dave initiated what might have been his first hug with Torrance ever.

The Meakins stood side by side as Torrance backed out of the driveway. Torrance waved even though he wasn't sure he could be seen inside his car.

Torrance began missing the Meakins as soon as he turned up Sandy Beach Road. *Dave is probably my best friend. And Althea is special … she's this attractive life force. Dave's lucky to have her.*

A PADDED PEW

ONLINE DICTIONARIES RELY ON THE expression, "a stubbornly insular farming people" to show the use of the word, "insular". The reason why farmers, ranchers and woodsmen join in more slowly than others is they have, lifelong, faced hardships and had to make difficult decisions on their own. Imagine getting up in the middle of the night to stand helplessly by as a favourite mare attempts to nudge life into a stillborn colt; having to decide whether or not to seed a field a third time after two summers of drought; and being given but a split second to free a stuck chainsaw from a falling tree.

*   *   *   *   *

Sunday. Torrance awoke to the sound of geese flying south. He knew from the amount of light coming through the window that he'd slept in. His mind had continued to spin long after he'd arrived back in his hotel room. Towards 2:00 a.m., he'd rummaged through his pack for his ear buds, hoping that listening to familiar music would slow his thoughts, which it had.

He flexed his hand still warm with infection as he thought about his life. *If I'd have stayed in town, I probably would have married someone local and had kids, like Dave and Althea. ... I might have even married Kim.* Dave had told him that Kim, Torrance's first girlfriend, from a time of adolescent innocence, had gotten married in her early 20's into one of the region's most successful logging families. The couple had divorced, childless, before Kim turned 30. Dave didn't know where she was now.

A long term relationship with Simone was never in the cards. I'll bet she never came back to town after nabbing her inheritance.

Perhaps prompted by the Native Canadian Artwork on the wall opposite the bed he remembered Alicia, a part Native girl with refined features he hadn't thought about for decades. Elegantly thin, with long, raven black hair, she'd had the comportment of a princess when she was introduced to the grade ten class. In addition to being an excellent student—she'd beaten Torrance out for the best mark in English—Alicia had handwriting that was so perfect it didn't seem real. Her family had moved away at the end of the school year and were never seen in Bull Moose Run again.

Torrance got out of bed and stood by the window looking down at Moose Lake. *It's too bad we don't have a view like this at our house.* He went back to the window when he was ready to leave. There was what looked like an orb of light out near Poplar Island. The light was so bright and well defined that he assumed it was a reflection on the inside of the hotel window. However, it didn't move when he shifted positions. *It must be sunlight hitting the surface of the water.*

He was in no rush to leave town and ordered a full breakfast in the hotel restaurant. He was almost finished when he heard a church bell ringing. He reflexively checked his watch. *10:00.* The bells of the Catholic church at 10:00 a.m. used to also mark the start of Sunday school in his dad's church, with the main service starting a half hour later. When the server came by with his bill, Torrance asked if there was a church on the north side of town. The server said there was but that she didn't know its name. Torrance decided on the spur of the moment to go to church. *To honour the old man, if nothing else.*

Driving through downtown he saw that several of the stores were already open for business. *Which they never used to be on Sundays.* Checking his watch and seeing he was early, he turned in at the entrance to, "Trickle Creek Park", which was new to him. *We used to pick wild Saskatoon berries around here.*

After parking, Torrance walked over to stand on the crown of a narrow, arched, wooden pedestrian bridge over the creek. He visually traced the water pathway to the first bend downstream that was bordered by willows before imagining that he was holding a fishing rod, the line pulled taut by a sixteen-inch rainbow trout. *No one knows a creek like a young boy.*

He wondered what had happened to Leonard, a rawhide tough youth from the Moose Reserve he'd befriended. *Leonard taught me how to make a notched willow whistle ... and how to snare rabbits. I wonder how many rabbits we snared? Ten? It was probably more than that. We were planning to cure the skins, but never did.*

Torrance returned to his car and drove the rest of the way to the church. It felt like he was at the finish line when he got to the top of the hill and saw the recognizable white building that seemed substantial despite its small size. The sign at the edge of the paved parking lot announced today's sermon: "Looking At Life From Both Sides."

Torrance parked at the far end of the parking lot, next to an open ditch. When he got to the church's front door the two elderly ladies who were acting as greeters were about ready to leave their posts. The lady on his right shook his hand, introducing herself as Mrs. Kuyt. Torrance's mind raced as he responded by giving her his first name only. Thirty-five years ago, Mrs. Kuyt had worked full time as a school secretary and yet still managed to raise two football player-sized boys with little or no help from her truck-driving husband. Torrance doubted whether this Mrs. Kuyt, a pensioner with thin hair and vivid blue veins under translucent skin, could complete the easiest of tasks.

— Are you visiting?

— I'm just passing through.

— It's the best place to be on Sunday morning, isn't it?

Torrance edged past a young couple who were sitting by the aisle in the back pew. Although his smile was honest he kept the conversation short.

Torrance recognized the exposed beams that ran the length of the ceiling, the tall, narrow side windows, and the slatted, wooden song selection board, which looked like it hadn't been used in years. The dark vinyl flooring, the padding on the pews, the steel and glass pulpit, the shiny black baby grand piano, and the musical instruments up front were new to him.

A man who could have been the twin of his father's friend, Richard Redmond went to the front to start the service. Torrance checked the bulletin Mrs. Kuyt had given him. *I can't believe it! Matthew Redmond!* Matt began by welcoming the congregation, "especially the guests". Torrance was grateful the guests weren't asked to stand and introduce themselves.

A band took the stage. The drummer was a greyhound-thin, tattooed twenty-year old, with the word "Blam" emblazoned in orange letters on the front of his stretched and faded yellow T-shirt; the bass player, was a stocky, middle-aged man wearing a bleached out and wrinkled, short sleeved dress shirt that had been washed so many times it had lost its shape; and the lead singer/guitarist, was a casually dressed man in his late fifties with shoulder length, grey hair. A big-boned woman in a three-quarter length cut ruby evening dress that didn't fit the occasion sat down at the piano. After the first two songs the lead singer/guitarist smiled at the piano player

— I'd like to thank Joy Compton for standing in. Joy's in town visiting her cousins, the Walkers. Joy happens to be an old musician friend of Billy and mine. She was telling us this morning that she'd attended a Bible camp at the church when she was a young girl. She won't tell us how many years ago that was though.

Torrance could tell from the way she moved that Joy had played some rhythm and blues in a far different setting.

When the singing ended, the lady sitting in the front pew beside Matt, who Torrance assumed was Matt's wife, got up to make the announcements. If Torrance hadn't spent so much time in church when he was young, he would have been surprised at all the things the congregation was involved in: raising money for an orphanage in Central America, organizing a dinner for single mothers, collecting supplies for—*had she said 30?*—Christmas hampers, and on the list went. *No matter what you say, at least churches try to make things better.* After the final announcement about an upcoming joint evening service with their sister church outside the Likem Reserve, the announcer read out the names of people who needed prayer for health reasons. She then closed her eyes to pray, addressing God as directly as if He were in the room, before handing the offering plates to a husband and wife team. Torrance was happy to put a $20 bill in the plate when it went past.

Matt returned to the podium and said a brief prayer before beginning his sermon.

— My mother didn't care for popular music. The only time I remember her saying anything about a pop song was after hearing Joni Mitchell's song "Both Sides Now" on the radio. Mom said she doubted the singer had actually looked at life from both sides.

Torrance became distracted as he thought about the visit his family had made to see Mrs. Redmond and the Redmond boys in North Falls after the parents' divorce. Matt's bedroom had been packed with animal pictures and outdoor supplies, as well as a taxidermied squirrel that looked more like a mini-Frankenstein than the replica of a wild animal. Luke's bedroom held the biggest collection of model cars and planes Torrance had ever seen up to that point.

From that or another visit to North Falls, Torrance had a memory of standing in the snow beside a large backyard rink and watching Matt and Luke play in a game of pickup hockey. He couldn't believe how well the Redmond brothers could skate or how hard they could shoot the puck. For years afterwards he thought he would never be as big and tough—as independent—as they were.

Matt was picking up speed at the front.

— ... Understanding Christ's role in human history changes everything. The good news, the gospel, is nothing less than the story of how the son of God swooped down into human history to cover off all the wrong we've ever done or will do. Imagine how believing in a God like this would have changed the attitude of the educated young man who told me he just wanted to "live and let live" and for that reason had as little to do with others as possible. Or, how it would have changed the lady architect who lived alone and said her motto was to do what she wanted for as long as she could; or the middle aged hockey player who bragged to the guys in the change room about having had an affair with a complete stranger without his wife finding out.

Being aware that there is a caring God would have given the couple I met who were just out of rehab a chance. I'll never forget the young man aggressively asserting that he and his girlfriend didn't need anyone's help. As convincing as he was—and no one commits more to a lie than someone addicted to drugs—I happened to know both the man and his girlfriend had relapsed and that the young woman had two children from a former relationship who were in the care of social services.

... So much happens when you understand how much God loves you. When things go wrong, instead of asking, "Why me?", you pray for the peace that comes from knowing all things are working together for good.

Torrance had finally figured out that the hesitant old man who'd helped out with the offering was his former principal, Frank Wells. He didn't see Mrs. Wells.

He was surprised at the affection he felt towards the other people in church, young and old alike. Wondering why he felt this way he considered the aspect of a sincere, young Chinese Canadian man sitting alone towards the front. *I could be wrong but he looks so ... dependable ... selfless. His faith plays a key role, no doubt. Imagine an entire country made up of young men and women like that.*

When Matt was finished, the worship band led the congregation through a modern take of an old hymn. Tears unexpectedly welled up in Torrance's eyes and slid down his face as he listened to the long forgotten melody. He waited until the song was over before surreptitiously wiping away the watery traces.

He had to wait to for the couple beside him to get up before moving towards the exit with the rest of the congregation.

Matt, who was shaking hands at the door, broke away from the older gentleman he was talking to and intercepted Torrance.

— Something tells me I should know you.

— I'm Torrance Maki.

Matt continued to grip Torrance's hand while he processed the information. His smile changing ever so slightly, he directed Torrance off to the side.

Matt asked where Anne and the girls had ended up, and about Torrance's life since he'd left town. The men also talked about the early years of Ed and Anne Maki's ministry, and the history of the church. When there were only a few people left in the foyer the lady announcer came over and stood beside Matt.

— Tory, this is my wife, Martha. Martha, this is Tory Maki. Tory's father was Ed Maki, the former minister.

Martha invited Torrance for lunch, but he explained that while he'd love to accept he was way behind schedule. A few minutes later Martha said she had to leave to take lunch out of the oven. She asked Matt if he was coming with her. Matt asked if it would be okay if he followed in a few minutes. Martha made an effort to smile but was clearly disappointed

— Of course. But don't forget we have to be at the Toews' by 2:30.

The men resumed their conversation when Martha left.

— Enough about me, how old were you when you left North Falls?

— I was twenty, no, twenty-one when I moved to Calgary. I got a job right away in construction.

— I always thought you and Luke might end up going pro.

— A couple of our coaches thought that too. I probably had more talent, but Luke had more drive. We both played Junior A in Centre City, but neither of us was drafted. In Luke's case it probably came down to his size.

— When did you decide to become a minister?

— I was in my early 30's. After I got to Calgary it wasn't too long before I was running my own company, making more money than I could have ever imagined. Martha and I got the big house, two cars, a boat and even a summer place in Winnigen Valley. Mind you, everything we owned was mortgaged.

Then the country went into a recession—I don't know what you were doing in '81, but business froze up in a way you can't imagine unless you lived through it. I went from selling houses before the foundations were poured to where I almost couldn't give one away. Interest rates were sky high, and being as extended as much as I was—I had just taken out a big loan to buy development property—I was bankrupt within a year.

Having figured out early on that Torrance wasn't comfortable talking about spiritual matters, Matt made an effort to say something of lasting value.

— I'll never forget sitting totally gutted at our kitchen table staring at a stack of demand letters, knowing there was nothing I could do to dig myself out. Martha is this serious—sometimes maybe a little too serious—hardworking farm girl who'd never been perfectly comfortable with our success. She kept saying I needed to start listening to what God was saying to me.

I finally broke down and went to church with her. I hadn't been in a church in years, except for weddings and a couple of funerals. Something gave way inside of me during the service and I found myself walking to the front in tears. My biggest problem after that was trying to love a God who I thought had hurt me, or at least let me be hurt, what with my dad, my mom being alone and my failed business. It took a long time before I began to feel the kind of love I hoped was out there. The change came when I began to understand the importance of taking time to ask God each morning to direct my steps—I tell people the best way to check on their progress is to figure out how much you've replaced His will for your own.

Martha and I went to seminary together. I did maintenance work at the school to cover the tuition, and she worked part time in a bakery. Our first ministerial call was to a small church in southern Alberta. Our second church was in a little farming community called Denton, a couple of hours east of Edmonton. Frank Wells contacted us while we were in Denton to ask if we'd be interested in candidating at Bull Moose Run.

— I didn't see Mrs. Wells in church.

— She died well before Martha and I arrived.

— Sorry to hear. By the way, what happened to Luke?

— He's a pilot with North Pacific Airlines. He and his wife, Sarah, live in Seattle. They have three kids, who aren't kids anymore. Luke and Sarah spent a week with us this summer.

— How about you and Martha, do you have any children?

— No, we weren't able to. To be fair, that was one of our disappointments. Hopefully not having our own children makes us more loving towards the children in church.

— Is your mom still alive?

— Yes, but she's getting old and showing signs of dementia. She moved to Calgary not long after I did and still lives there in her own apartment. She's going to have to go into a care home soon. We're looking for a place for her either here or in Centre City. Moving to the US isn't an option.

— I heard your dad died.

— Yes, from lung cancer, although he'd only smoked as a teenager. It'll be, let's see, five years this February. Luke and I had very little to do with him after he left mom, but he did reach out to us after he was diagnosed. He was alone by then and didn't talk much about his time in the ministry. I wasn't even sure if he still believed in God—although I don't think you can ever leave God's hand. On one of my visits I got up out of my chair and I guess he thought I was leaving. He asked me to say a prayer before I left. Him asking me that meant more than you'll ever know.

Later, while Matt was locking the front door of the church behind them, Torrance asked about the big man who'd sat in the front row during the service.

— I think you mean Grant Williams. I'm told he's the spitting image of his dad, Darwin Williams.

— Darwin the bootlegger?

— I've only heard about Darwin from Grant and some of the oldtimers, but yes, the guy who used to run liquor and drugs.

— Really?

— I should tell you, Grant still talks about your dad's influence in the community. Not only do Grant and his wife come to church, their daughter and son-in-law, Sheila and Doug Peterson attend as well, although they're away this weekend.

— Wasn't there another Williams boy?

— There were three brothers. The oldest brother was shot and killed when he was still a teenager. Grant's younger brother died from a drug overdose not long after Martha and I started our ministry here.

On their way out to Torrance's car, Torrance asked Matt about the church building where his father and mother had started their ministry.

— It's still there. If you want to see it, turn right at 4th Street and go down a block. It's the last building on the south side, just before the corner. I'll save you the confusion, it's been converted into a tavern.

*　*　*　*　*

Torrance drove the speed limit on his way out of town, but had to pull partly over near the bridge to let the determined driver of a black pickup blast past him on a solid line.

Near the Sandy Beach turnoff he noticed a small cloud that appeared to be moving faster than the other clouds. He slowed down to have a better look, wanting to make sure there wasn't anything mysterious about the cloud. It turned out that it was just closer to the ground than the rest of the clouds.

THE OTHERNATURAL

WE ARE FILLED WITH THE wonder of life when we drive through the towering Rockies of a nearly infinite size, look down from a coastal hill at the empty, rolling dark blue Pacific Ocean (its plummeting depth forever hidden), or stand in a barren field staring up at the night sky until the weight of the pinned and distant stars settles on our shoulders.

* * * * *

Torrance lay awake in bed looking up at the darkened ceiling. In his state of heightened awareness the spots and fizzles in his eyes made it seem like the ceiling was in motion. His heart was filled with love and his mind whirring as he thought about Kelly and their newborn son who had stayed on in the hospital. Becoming a father wasn't something he'd ever thought about, and then it had happened. *Even Kelly calls it the miracle baby.* He'd been in a state of confusion from the start, culminating with the intense emotion he'd felt when the doctor dangled the little guy upside down. *For sure that was the biggest moment of my life.*

When Kelly and he talked about names, the only one that had stood out was Matthew. *Amazing that Matthew Redmond is still in my life. Going on that hunting trip, seeing Matt ... and talking to Miller ... definitely jostled me around.*

Although he often prayed blankly when he was in real trouble, tonight he felt drawn to say a different kind of prayer. *A prayer to God of ... thanks ... and protection of course for the little guy and for Kelly.* He tried to adopt the appropriate attitude but each time he was almost ready something distracted him. He finally marshaled an unspoken, *"Thank you God that it all went well, and for Kelly and my son ... please keep them safe, and alive, tonight."*

Even though he didn't expect an audible response he was disappointed when none came.

*   *   *   *   *

It was late on Saturday night. Torrance was tired but grinning as he trudged back to the dressing room with rest of the hockey team. He already knew that for the next few nights he would fall asleep thinking about what had been for him a brilliant cross-ice pass.

The transcendent part of hockey was skating. *There are few things in life that bring more pure joy than stepping out onto new ice and gliding forward before spinning around and skating backwards.* Torrance knew it shouldn't matter, but getting an assist on the winning goal had made it that much better. Just as important, he hadn't been hurt when he'd slammed into the boards after being tripped.

The players began to kibitz in earnest when they got to the change room.

— At least we have our own shower this time.

There was raucous laughter as they all thought back to the previous weekend when they'd played a rare day game. Alex, who'd been the first one to the showers after that game, had raced back to the dressing room to announce he'd just flashed a group of hockey moms standing in front of the open door to the adjoining change room.

Torrance was sitting between Kazo, an optometrist, and Mike, a contractor. Kazo suddenly became serious.

— I was worried about Tan. This was his first game back after bypass surgery. I think it was a quadruple. I figured as long as Dr. Ming was out on the ice, we'd be okay. I was worried, though, about what would happen if Tan went down while Ming was on the bench.

Mike leaned forward on the bench and spoke past Torrance at Kazo.

— What about you Kazo? You're almost a doctor, you could step in.

— Optometrists don't get that kind of training. Seriously, I wouldn't know what to do if someone had a heart attack.

Mike leaned forward again.

— You could always ask him, "Is it better, worse, or the same?"

The streets were surprisingly busy on Torrance's drive home from the rink. *You can't tell me house prices are going down when there's this many cars on the road after midnight.*

*   *   *   *   *

One night when Torrance couldn't sleep, rather than reaching for his iPod to quiet himself with old progressive rock tracks, he'd silently recited the Lord's Prayer. Saying the prayer had such a calming effect on him that several nights later he recited it again. It wasn't long before the prayer became part of his bedtime routine.

One night when he was more awake he analyzed the theme's of the prayer: our tiny fears, which are usually far short of not having food to eat, mean something despite the vastness of the universe; God is aware of our unrelenting temptations; we need to seek forgiveness for our own shortcomings as much as we need to forgive others; evil is always nearby, ready to pounce; and because everything is God's, not only don't we understand everything, we have very little control over most things. *And "thy kingdom come", whatever that means.*

*   *   *   *   *

Although Torrance was dead asleep when the alarm went off he still managed to reach over and shut the buzzer off in an instant in order to protect Kelly, who'd been up with Matthew during the night. He was about to drop off again when he remembered it was Sunday. *Shoot, church.* Somehow he forced himself to get up. He felt almost normal after a shower and a bolt of coffee. Earlier in the week he'd gotten it into his head that he should scout out the church near his house with a view to having his son dedicated. *Being dedicated didn't hurt me.*

There were only a few cars in the church's parking lot when he pulled in. An elderly man holding a handful of bulletins was by himself in the hallway beyond the empty church foyer. The man greeted Torrance with a smile and directed him towards an open door down the hall.

— No sense a group our size getting lost in the sanctuary.

Instead of the children's artwork on the poster board in the hallway Torrance expected to see, there were several handbill-sized posters for senior wellness events. *"Wellness", there's a classic Orwellian nonsense word.*

There were a dozen or so retired people in the classroom quietly waiting for the service to start. A couple near the door got out of their chairs to shake Torrance's hand. The flowery dress the woman wore was made from a heavy, durable cloth and looked relatively new; however its shape and floral design was from decades earlier. The man had on a wrinkled beige suit that should have been donated a long time ago. Torrance did his best to respond with like friendliness to the couple's effusive welcome.

A few minutes later, the woman in the flowery dress went to the front to start the service. After welcoming those in attendance she led the group through several songs sung a cappella. Although her voice was still strong, she had no sense of timing and was oblivious to her role as song leader. *She thinks she's a soloist.* The only song that Torrance recognized was "Morning Has Broken."

A man who could have been in his 80's entered the classroom during the last song. Even though his colourful winter sweater hung squarely on his shoulders in a way that might have made him look younger, his dull, craggy face, exaggerated nose and ears and thin grey hair confirmed his true age. After reading through several passages of the Bible that seemed unrelated to Torrance, the man explained in a thin, reedy voice that just as God could be described differently so too a person's concept of God could either serve the purposes of love and light or they could be twisted to justify one's ambitions. Torrance fought to stay awake. When the speaker finished his homily he said anyone who wanted to could stay and meditate. *Not a lot of talk about the supernatural here.*

Driving home, Torrance wondered how long it had been since there had been children in the classroom. *We have to take Matthew to a church with kids.*

* * * * *

Torrance had agreed to meet with a Hothouse Produce customer downtown on a Saturday morning. The traffic was lighter than he'd expected, and he had time to stop at a coffee shop. It was a warm spring day and he sat at an outside table.

One table over, a young couple, their baby asleep in a stroller beside them, was sitting with a single man. Although Torrance was initially interested in the sleeping child, he soon began to follow the adults' conversation. All three were from Eastern Europe, possibly Poland, and by the sound of things they had all worked in the US.

— I have another interrrview.

— You have to get ona good seecurity team.

— I agree, it is the seecurity teem that matters most. It is beeg.

The woman went through a list of potential employers. She explained her concerns about one of the information technology companies.

— Eef you work for them you weel only last for a couple of years. They hire for a certain job and don't let people move up. Eet's a problem with their business model.

Their conversation broadened.

— Eet's too bad this place doesn't join the United States.

— Why do you say that?

— It would be loats better then. There would be less regulation and mor' cash. Mor' creativity, faster moving things.

— You're right.

— And then maybe wee wouldn't be as cold as the rest of country.

Torrance was taken aback by the casual discussion about breaking up the country. The joke about the weather aside, he wondered if the lack of patriotism had to do with moving around so much and working for international corporations. Later, he thought about how being immersed in a virtual world would affect the way a person thought.

* * * * *

Despite problems at the border resulting from the decision of the US Food and Drug Agency to start testing for a pesticide that had been approved for use in Canada for years, Hothouse Produce ended up having a stellar year. On top of their bonuses, the company's eight managers were sent for a weekend of fishing at the world famous Kaan Fishing Lodge.

Early on a clear, summer morning the managers flew in a medium sized jet out of the southern terminal of the city's airport; and an hour later they transferred over to three antiquated Grumman Goose amphibious planes at a much smaller, coastal airport.

Flying high above the shining blue water and matte green forests, Torrance decided that it was probably safer to fly in an old plane with an antiquated instrumentation panel and whose fuselage was held together with visible rivets than flying in a brand new plane with a hidden design flaw.

The three seaplanes splashed down, belly first as they were constructed to do, in regimental order near the fishing lodge's impressively large, new cedar dock. Staff from the lodge was waiting in golf carts at the dock to ferry the managers and their gear up to their cabins.

Torrance was amazed by how luxurious the cabins were.

— So this is how the rich go fishing.

Martin and Torrance were checking out the high end stove in the kitchen when a fresh-faced young lady delivered homemade cinnamon buns and coffee to their door.

There was a general welcome in the restaurant at 2:00 p.m. The lodge's spokesperson, Tony, who acted like he was everyone's friendly cousin even though rumour had it he owned half of the valuable resort, concluded his remarks by saying the guests could order anything on or off the menu anytime between 7:00 a.m. and midnight. The announcement was met with loud cheering.

The managers were split up between two guided boats for the initial foray out to the fishing grounds. The boat Torrance was on spent the day trolling back and forth behind a large island at the mouth of the inlet. Each time the boat turned at the end of the island, Torrance thought about how the powerful, rolling waves were finally getting the chance to break after crossing thousands of kilometers of empty ocean.

The guide in Torrance's boat warned the managers that there had been a lull in the fishing because of the warm weather. Sure enough, they only caught two salmon that afternoon. It almost didn't matter, though, because of the setting: Humpback whales regularly breached nearby; the bottomless, dark blue water was covered by a shimmering, false surface that alluded to magic nearby; innumerable dark green trees on the surrounding hills acted as a still chorus to the vitality of the natural world; and stretched out overhead was the endless blue sky that was a portal to the entire universe. On the following day, after a night of rain, the tops of the tops of the hills were shrouded by clouds that looked as fluffy and artificial as the snow cotton on model buildings in a department store Christmas scene.

After supper back at the lodge, several of the managers arranged to go back out fishing in two-man Boston Whalers. With the hope of winning the salmon derby, Martin and Torrance asked the staff in the supply room to add extra weights to their lines. With the added weights, the two rods were bent over like they already had fish on.

Martin and Lawrence were the first ones down to the dock. The lodge's old marine mechanic who helped them load their sturdy little boat talked freely since there was no one else around.

— They always tell guests it's just a bad stretch for fishing, but it's getting worse every year.

Martin and Torrance were getting ready to leave when a boat returning to the dock tied up behind them.

— How'd you guys do?

— Pretty good for some guys from the city.

One of the fishermen reached into the boat's ice chest and, one by one, lifted up four good-sized Pinks.

— We got them on the south side of Peregrine Island.

It was the inside information Martin and Torrance had been waiting for.

Martin kept the Boston Whaler's throttle open all the way to Peregrine Island despite the pounding the boat took from the waves. Torrance grabbed the wheel when they got near the island.

— You have the first go.

Martin was grinning when he went to lift one of the fishing rods out of a holder above the cockpit. His face suddenly clouded over.

— You're not going to believe this.

— What?

— There's no fishing line.

It took them a minute to figure out that the pounding on the boat must have unhooked the lure from the eye of the fishing rod, and, with the lure free, the added weights had dragged the entire spool of line to the bottom of the ocean. Martin swore when he looked up and saw the second rod standing up pole-straight as well, its lure, weights and line also missing.

On their way back to the resort to get new equipment they met another Boston Whaler piloted by Hothouse Produce managers. Torrance barely noticed the quizzical looks on the managers' faces because he was busy thinking about the damage their sunken fishing lines would do to the aquatic life below.

There was still an hour or more of light when Martin and Torrance got back to Peregrine Island with their replacement rods. With two other boats already working the front of the island they had no choice but to stay farther out. It took them a few minutes to set up. The guide had taught them how to tie a lure on, making sure to lick the line so the knot would tighten. He had also told them about the trick of spraying their lures with a penetrating oil whose ingredients included fish oil. Martin didn't hold back with the penetrating oil, but Torrance barely misted his lure, not wanting to pollute the water. With the lures ready, they let some line out, attached the downriggers, and then loosened the drag on the reels until the downriggers had dropped another 10 or so meters.

Martin said Torrance could have the first shift monitoring the rods:
— Fishing's all about luck, and you know how much of that I have.

Torrance's expectations were low and he was soon distracted, watching, in turn, the waves, the random swells and ripples of the water, the bobbing ends on the fishing rods, and the darting fish birds. Every now and then he looked at the hills and mountains that framed the inlet.

Martin spoke over the burbling engine.
— You can see why they call it sport fishing and not collecting food. It's not like the fish are jumping into the boat.
— How much do you think the gear we lost was worth?
— Had to be hundreds. Thank goodness Hothouse is paying.
— If you do the math, a day of fishing is as expensive as going to the Super Bowl. There's the equipment, the cost of the boat and, a trailer. And a truck to pull the trailer.
— What about a guide? I don't know if I ever told you about the time we hired a guide to take us fishing in Why Sound, which wasn't cheap. There was a lot of wind and so he took us way south, almost to Livingstone Park. We ended up trolling for salmon in between

the huge container ships lined up in the bay waiting to be loaded. That was bizarre.

"ZZZWWWIIIIINNNGGG" the rod on the port side of the boat was bent way over and jerking about frantically, looking like it might break at any moment. Torrance leaped to his feet and grabbed the rod. Martin shut the engine off.

— That's not the bottom, it's a fish! And a big one!

— I'll reel in the other line!

Torrance got his fingers whacked too many times to count trying to grab one of the two handles on the reel to slow it down. *Knuckle-buster!* It was same "smack, smack, smack" when he attempted to reach in between the handles to tighten the drag adjustment knob. He was finally able to slow the outgoing line by cupping his hand over the edge of the spool.

There wasn't much room in the boat for Martin and Torrance to maneuver.

— I'll stay by the engine and you move to the front.

Torrance knocked the tackle box over, splashing hooks into the engine well. Moments later there was a flash of silver in the water thirty feet behind the boat.

— I see it!

The fish made two more extended runs before Torrance was able to reel it in close to the boat.

— I wish the handle on this net was longer!

Martin plunged the net straight down beside the fish before lifting it up out of the water and into the boat. As if on cue, the fish spit the lure out the moment it hit the boat's floor.

— Wow! You got him just in time! Five seconds later and he'd have been gone!

The Chinook was flopping about on the bottom of the boat.

— He's got to be 15 pounds!

— That fire truck Hoochie is the real deal!

Martin grabbed the club.

When they got back to the resort and cleaned the Chinook Torrance was thrilled to find out they hadn't caught a female and wasted roe needed for the next generation of the king of fish.

* * * * *

Although Torrance's salmon was the only fish caught after supper, everyone was in holiday spirits that evening in the bar. Stories from the day, including Martin and Torrance losing their lines, were added in with often retold stories from the office to keep the group up until late.

Torrance woke up at 6:00 as usual. Knowing he wouldn't be able to get back to sleep, he got up, grabbed the novel set in the Midwest he'd brought with him and walked over to the lodge's restaurant. There were two urns of fresh coffee and a plate of fresh pastries just inside the entrance to the seemingly empty building.

After pouring himself a coffee and grabbing a butterhorn, Torrance went and sat down at a window table in the cavernous dining room. *The best hour of the day.* Savouring his first few sips of coffee he reread the book review excerpts on the inside cover of the novel. He'd originally picked the book up because of the Pulitzer prizewinner sticker. The clincher had been finding out the novel was written by someone raised on the prairies. His theory was that if the author was from the country there was a chance they would at least share some views about life.

He looked across the fjord. *If you didn't know better, you'd think there was nothing under all that water.* He had barely gotten started reading when Charlie, an accountant, and the newest member of the Hothouse Produce management team, came into the restaurant. Torrance hadn't said much more than "hi" to Charlie but he waved him over. An easy going exchange between the two early risers ensued and Torrance soon forgot about reading his novel.

Torrance was telling Charlie about what the old mechanic had said about the decline in fish stocks when he remembered an economics article he'd read in university almost thirty years earlier.

— The thesis was something to the effect of that it makes sense for individual countries to keep fishing until all the fish are gone. If that's right, it says more about humanity than you want to know.

* * * * *

Despite bold predictions in the bar, the fishing was no better on Sunday. When it got close to suppertime the guide had a proposal:

— If you want, we can up the inlet and try for ling cod and rock cod. At least then we'll have something when we show up back at the lodge.

Everyone thought it was a great idea.

In no time at all their boat was anchored high up one of the inlet's narrow channels. Torrance, who hadn't had anything to drink, got his line in the water first. Almost immediately he felt an almost imperceptible tug. Although he knew the fish was tiny, he had no choice but to reel it in. In a handful of turns of the heavy stainless steel reel a baby rock cod that looked more like bait than a caught-fish broke free of the water. It flipped helplessly back and forth until Torrance got a hold of the swaying line. By the time he had taken the hook out of the fish's mouth and had released the fish back into the water it had stopped moving.

Torrance was overtaken by sadness as he watched the motionless fish float away on its side. *What a waste.* Suddenly, an eagle with wings as wide as a man is tall swooped down from a tree to talon up the fish before flying off in a buffeting show of power. Torrance's heartache lifted in tandem with the rising bird of prey.

Thank you … .

Printed in Canada